A DANGER TO HIMSELF AND OTHERS

ALSO BY J.E. FISHMAN

FICTION

Primacy: A Thriller
The Dead Field (short story)
Cadaver Blues: A Phuoc Goldberg Fiasco
The Dark Pool: A Thriller

AS CONTRIBUTOR

The Beautiful Anthology

NON-FICTION

Dynamite: A Concise History of the NYPD Bomb Squad
All I Need to Know I Learned from My Horse (co-author)
Life Is a Series of Presentations (co-author)

To Vicky,

BOMB SQUAD NYC INCIDENT 1

Thanks for your support,

A DANGER TO HIMSELF AND OTHERS

J.E. FISHMAN

VERBITRAGE
More Than Words

This is an advance reading copy made from uncorrected proofs. Please check any quotes against the final edition before publishing.

Published in the United States of America and throughout the world in English by Verbitrage, LLC.

Edited by Patrick LoBrutto.
Book design and composition by 52 Novels.
Cover design by Cory Clubb, Go Bold Designs.

E-Book ISBN: 978-0-9898461-0-3
Paperback ISBN: 978-0-9898461-1-0

Dedicated to Paul "Buddy" Bucha,
whom I am honored to call friend

SERIES TECHNICAL ADVISOR

Mark Torre
Lieutenant, New York Police Department
and Commander of the NYPD Bomb Squad

AUTHOR'S NOTE

Members of the NYPD Bomb Squad respond to more than 1500 calls a year. Most of these are precautionary sweeps or false alarms. When they find unexploded bombs or dangerous explosives, Bomb Squad technicians remotely disarm them or remove them ninety-nine percent of the time with minimal risk to themselves and others.

Naturally, storytellers—and readers—aren't so interested in the ninety-nine percent. It's the unusual cases that call to us—the possibilities, the what-ifs, the dangers of tomorrow.

With the help of Mark Torre, who currently commands the NYPD Bomb Squad, Kevin Miles, who retired in 2013 as the FBI's leading bomb technician, and other sources, I have made every effort to achieve technical accuracy in this book without compromising the safety of law enforcement personnel or the public. In the interests of storytelling, I have taken some liberties with regard to police procedures. I hope readers will make appropriate allowances for this. After all, no one wants to spend his leisure time watching cops fill out forms.

The real NYPD Bomb Squad, as many know, consists of fewer than forty individuals annexed to a police precinct in lower Manhattan. To avoid any confusion between the world in my head and the world "out there," I have moved the Bomb Squad to an imaginary precinct on a different street.

This is indeed a work of fiction. Names, characters, businesses, organizations, events, and incidents are either a product of my imagination or are used fictitiously. Any resemblance to actual persons, living or dead, or actual events is entirely coincidental. Like any novelist, I am ultimately not hunting facts here but the greater truths of the human condition.

The real-life heroes of the NYPD, the FBI and other members of the Joint Terrorism Task Force do their best to protect all of us from harm. At some point, if not all of the time, even real heroes must face their own troubles and demons. The difference between them and the rest of us is that they set aside those troubles every day to pursue the greater good.

In sum, this book isn't factual. But you may find it true.

A DANGER TO HIMSELF AND OTHERS

TICK, TICK, TICK, TICK, TICK, TICK, TICK,
TICK, TICK, TICK, TICK, TICK, TICK, TICK

1.

DAY ONE: LIGHT

MANNY DIAZ HAD THIS DEAL WHERE sometimes he'd play the voiceover to his own life in the back of his head.

"Here's Manny, down the sidelines—thirty, twenty, ten!" Or...

"As Supercop walked along the dark alley, demons and serpents fled from his path." Or, more poignantly...

"Manuel Diaz occasionally wondered whether he was the hero of his own life or if someone else had landed the part."

In Iraq, when he was part of an EOD team, Manny would run a voiceover while looking for tripwires: "Lieutenant Diaz, fifth call of the day and not even two in the afternoon. One-twenty in the shade. Dust thicker than paint from a spray can. He approaches the target with caution, knowing that one false step could mean the end."

Kind of cute, right? But it wasn't a joke exactly, more like comic relief, a means of keeping your heart light under pressure, of banishing distractions from the task at hand. Because, as everyone in this game knew, sometimes you looked away on purpose. Sometimes the booby trap was harder to see head-on and easier to see from the corner of a man's eye.

Today was nothing like that, more a way to keep the boredom at arm's length. Manny was the junior detective on their third bomb sweep of the morning, tasked with the role of sweeper in half the hallway of the VIP floor at the Waldorf-Astoria while one of the dogs, Sheba, and her handler, Detective Third Grade Cam Fowler, went about their business sniffing for trouble in each room of his segment. A few other guys, including the sergeant, were playing sweeper behind another EDC or doing visual checks of their own.

The US Secretary of State, someone said, would be staying here tonight in preparation for a speech at the UN. In another suite, some Arab potentate planned to sleep with his harem on satin sheets. Before all that, the Secret Service would take up their posts when the NYPD gave the all-clear. They already had the lobby secure.

And Manny's voiceover silently intoned: "In the shadows, danger lurks." Except that it didn't. Not here. Both Labrador retrievers came back without once alerting. The sergeant reappeared and began filling out his report. All as routine as could be.

After raising the Secret Service guys on the radio, the Bomb Squad team waited to be relieved from covering the elevator and the emergency exits. The USSS agents showed up quick enough, chests out like someone held the tip of a knife to their spines. Showy. More full of crap than a week-old latrine, so far as Diaz was concerned.

The cops left together via two elevators. Down on the street, Diaz ended up in one of the response trucks with Fowler, the dog resting inside the built-in cage in back, still licking his chops from the Milk-Bone reward.

"You're quiet today," Fowler said. "Something on your mind?"

"Nah. Just bored. I was thinking about that expression: danger lurks. Why does it lurk? Where does it lurk?"

Fowler bit his lip. He had a long face and a sharp jawline. His blue eyes looked past the expansive white hood of the vehicle. "I don't know. Is this some kind of brain puzzle?"

"The thing is," Diaz said, "for the infantry, the marines, you know, danger don't lurk. It smacks you in the face, dares you to confront it. This stuff here, what we do—"

"It lurks."

"Yeah."

"And you miss it, the other kind, facing it head-on."

Diaz's defenses went up. "I didn't say that. It's just a different feeling. That's all."

The Bomb Squad occupied the rear garage and a handful of cluttered upstairs rooms of the Third Precinct building on Commerce Street in the West Village. Most of the crew from the Waldorf had stopped along the way for coffee, but Diaz and Fowler came straight back because Fowler was eager to uncrate his dog. When they walked in, there were only a few warm bodies upstairs.

Diaz heard Patti Morris, the squad secretary, fielding a call. The head of the squad, Lieutenant Joseph Capobianco, to whom she usually fed important decisions, had called in sick that afternoon, available only by phone or radio in an emergency.

Morris placed the receiver in its cradle and turned to Sander Kahn, a sergeant supervisor who was the highest-ranking person in the room at the moment. When you reached that rank you got a higher pay grade, so colleagues sometimes affectionately called you, "Money." Sometimes not so affectionately. She said, "Hey, Money, report from the Seventeenth of a suspicious package at Saint Pat's."

"We have anyone in the vicinity?"

She consulted a sheet. "Not really."

"I'll take it myself. Diaz!"

"On it." Diaz turned right back around, checking reflexively for the Glock in a hip holster under his pullover.

"Some kind of luggage by the Fifth Avenue steps," Morris said, "south side."

"Great." Kahn shook his head as he removed a key from the metal box on the wall. "Right by Saks. Should be nice and zooish this time of day."

The key belonged to one of the response trucks. In the garage Kahn opened the back doors and they peered inside to make sure they had all necessary equipment. Everything looked in order. Diaz climbed behind the wheel and Kahn slid in next to him. He was a large man, stocky with thick forearms and a broad chest. His hair and his eyebrows were fully gray, a shade or two lighter than the color of his suit, and the contrast made his dark eyes all the more penetrating. He carried himself like a person of formidable strength, but while Diaz didn't doubt the man's toughness, he suspected that Kahn had gone soft in the midsection like anyone middle-aged.

Diaz had had a lot of opportunity to study the sergeant over the past six months. Nobody said anything specific, but they rode together a lot and Diaz thought he knew why. Although a detective third grade with six years on the force, Diaz had only joined the Bomb Squad eleven months ago. He figured that his rides with Kahn were supposed to season him. In the army, eleven months in theater burned you out. But in civilian law enforcement things moved slower. Even the Bomb Squad didn't match the intensity of a combat environment.

"Squad room's like a damned ghost town today," Diaz said as they drove up Hudson Street, heading for Eighth Avenue.

Kahn kept his eyes on his phone, where he was thumbing out a text. "Eight guys down with the flu—eight! Plus two sergeants and the lieutenant. Never seen anything like it. Cap, I'm told, is totally on his ass, can't even get out of bed."

"They say it started with some chickens in China. All these crazy diseases always seem to come from Africa or Asia."

"Maybe those Chinese cooked it up in an effort to reduce the local population. Wouldn't put it past 'em." Kahn lifted his eyes to see rain falling and traffic building around Twenty-Third Street. He pocketed the phone and took hold of the squawk box mouthpiece. "Better hit the lights. Take it easy at the intersections though."

The voiceover in the back of Diaz's head kicked in again. It said: "After two hundred rides together, SDS Sander Kahn still didn't trust the new guy behind the wheel."

Lewis Salinowsky needed a fix. He was also hungry for food, but that could wait. With great effort he pushed and pulled himself up to a standing position, bent over and picked up the cup that had lain at his feet. The soggy cardboard sign he left behind. He had a fresh Sharpie in his pocket and could always make another one.

After hours sitting on the cold concrete, Salinowsky's body felt like one of those frozen fish he always saw on the street tables of Chinatown. If a giant hand came down from heaven and lifted him off the ground and smacked him against the side of a building, he felt like he just might break in two. It would be so easy because other forces had already cracked him.

He fished around in the paper cup with his stiff fingers, uncrumpling bills, refolding them, and slipping them into his pocket. Twenty-three dollars there plus the fourteen he already had—that made thirty-seven. He tilted the cup and dumped the change into his palm and counted. Looked like another seven bucks plus. Forty-four. He could buy half a bundle—carry him through the meat of the week if he was careful—and still have a few dollars left over for pizza. The pizza would hold him until the soup kitchen opened for dinner. Sounded like a plan.

Rain began falling, small drops but tightly spaced. Salinowsky had to get from midtown, where he'd been testing new panhandling territory, to the Lower East Side, but he didn't want to waste money on the subway. He thought about jumping the turnstile, but couldn't risk that, had seen plenty of guys get caught lately with that stunt. Going to jail, even for a night, would bring on the super flu—withdrawal sickness. Not worth the risk. He decided to walk the sixty-some-odd blocks down to his neighborhood.

Beginning near Columbus Circle, he went mostly east at first, then down Madison Avenue where, near the back of St. Patrick's Cathedral he got diverted by some police action. After that it was smooth sailing except for the general wetness and the gimpiness that had begun forming in his bad leg. By the time Salinowsky reached Avenue C, he had a blister on his stump. But knowledge of what awaited kept him going.

At East Second Street, he turned the corner, opened the door to an old tenement house, and hobbled up four flights of stairs. The door was unlocked, several people inside. Dripping on the stained rug, Salinowsky held out his forty dollars and watched the dealer count it with excruciating slowness. He got his half-load and went into the next room, where nearly a dozen people sat on the floor or on an old bed with a soiled macramé blanket bunched in one corner of the mattress.

He leaned against a wall and collapsed to the floor.

His hands shook. He'd cut this trip close.

Some girl took pity on him and did the cooking with her blackened spoon and a Bic lighter. She didn't even ask for anything in return, just handed him the loaded syringe and went to work on her own fix. From there Salinowsky managed to do himself up, finding a vein near his groin. He leaned his head against the wall and his mind floated off on angel wings.

It didn't take long for him to forget about the pizza.

Working the radio, Kahn learned that the police had set up a perimeter by closing off East Fifty-First and East Fifty-Second to cars and pedestrians and taking two lanes out of action on the east side of Fifth Avenue.

"The book says a thousand feet," Kahn sniffed. "Never managed close to that in midtown except for a car bomb. Turn here."

Diaz didn't need any reminders on what the book said, but he followed the instructions.

"Probably they closed the north-side doors to Saks," Kahn went on. "No doubt Fiftieth is already packed with people getting in the way of traffic. Let's go north past it up Sixth and wrap around."

They had the siren on, as well as the light bar.

"We'll go down Lex and through the barriers they got set up on Fifty-Second," Kahn said. "Fifty-Second runs east but they'll have it cleared, so we can go against traffic. Turn here for—"

"Where you from originally, Sandy?" Diaz was starting to seethe.

"Long Island. Merrick. Why?"

"I grew up in Brooklyn myself. I know my way around Manhattan pretty well."

"And how much of that in a police car going to a bomb call? Turn it here, please, Detective."

They were making okay time. Diaz felt strongly that micromanagement from the guy in the passenger seat was unnecessary. Fortunately, Kahn cut off his own turn-by-turn directions to work the radio, checking in with the midtown precinct and with their precinct downtown. Nobody, so far, had called in any bomb threats against Saint Patrick's or the Catholic Church in general.

By the time Kahn started paying attention to the street again, Diaz had navigated them to Lexington and Fifty-Fourth. But from there complete gridlock ensued, even with the siren going and with Kahn over the squawk box telling cars to move aside.

"Sometimes this city reminds me of Baghdad," Diaz said. "One second we'd be doing eighty on the Highway of Death and then we'd hit town and it's just a free-for-all, no lane markers, cars inching along at the speed of a donkey cart. Difference being that there you felt like a sitting duck. Here it's only a pain in the balls."

"Yeah." Kahn reached for his door handle. "Well, half the drivers look the same, too."

He jumped out and rapped on the window of the cab that blocked them, flashed his badge at the turbaned driver, and started barking words of one syllable. He moved onto a delivery van and two more cabs, giving them the same treatment.

That cleared the worst of it. Kahn jumped back into the truck and Diaz started moving before the door closed. Out of habit, Kahn re-buckled his seatbelt. Then he brushed the water from the lapels of his raincoat.

They nodded to the uniformed cops at Lexington and Fifty-Second, chirped through the intersection at Madison, and nodded again to the uniforms at the blue sawhorses, obtaining immediate admittance. Along Fifth Avenue by the cathedral, eight police vehicles stood in a line, functioning as a steel curtain.

Kahn rolled down his window and talked to a uniformed sergeant. Over his shoulder, a family of duded-up Hispanics, held back by police along with the rest of the crowd, shouted in hysteria, the woman alternating between wails and the dabbing of her tears. The guy looked so agitated that steam rose into the cold February air from his shoulders and slicked-back hair. From what Diaz could glean, they were missing a funeral.

"It's on the other corner," the uniformed sergeant said. "What took you?"

"We're shorthanded this week. Friggin' bird flu. We'll jump the curb here and take the sidewalk."

"Roger that." The uniformed sergeant instructed his men to move the barricade. Diaz took it slow and the response truck rode high, but its suspension groaned and the equipment in back rattled as they clambered over the curb.

Diaz had been on a hundred bomb calls in New York City, but this one involved more craziness than usual: rain coming down in a fine mist, honking cars and wailing mourners pressing to get inside, cops shouting at everyone, cameras flashing in the hands of rubberneckers, sirens still converging on the scene. Kahn had predicted right, Diaz admitted to himself. The place was a zoo.

But, over the din, when they stepped outside he thought he perceived organ music coming through the closed doors of the cathedral.

"You hear that?"

Kahn half nodded. "Guess the funeral started without us."

The uniformed sergeant pointed out the suspicious package and retreated. It rested against the bottom step, an overstuffed black messenger bag with unnatural bulges, partly held together with brown packing tape.

"Whoever made that," Kahn said, "had no appreciation for aesthetics." He took the key from Diaz and opened the truck's rear doors. The Wolverine robot inside looked like a folded stainless steel crane. They checked for obstructions and unlocked the black nylon straps that held fast the gleaming machine. Kahn powered it up, watching closely as it rolled down the aluminum ramp and onto the sidewalk. Then Kahn twisted the joystick on the controller. The robot began to turn, juddered and appeared to die.

While Kahn fiddled with the control panel, Diaz used a pair of khaki green Celestron Cavalry binoculars to peer over the hood of their truck at the suspect IED. Given the constraints of midtown geography, they were closer to the device than they'd like to be, no more than forty feet. If a blast went off, it would reach them in a fraction of a second. But at least that proximity afforded him a pretty good look.

The messenger bag was frayed at the corners, like someone had carried it around for a good long time before repurposing it as a means of terror. The tape had been applied hastily but not recently. It appeared to hold together a tear where the fabric met the piping, and it also showed signs of wear. From the top of the bag, the corner of what looked like a manila folder protruded. Between that folder and the half-open zipper, a pair of white wires looped out of the bag and back inside.

Kahn was cursing at the robot, which rested right where it had frozen two minutes ago, hadn't made a sound or moved an inch. He crouched over it, checking the inner workings and looking back and forth to the control panel, which lay on the floor of the truck bay like a prop in a *Batman* movie, Diaz thought. Kahn worked the joystick some more and turned a couple of knobs. The thing didn't respond. From what Diaz could see, no image feed from the camera appeared on the controller screen.

Fifty feet behind Kahn, the Hispanic woman with the handkerchief broke past the police barrier wailing like her hair was on fire. She made a run for the front door to the cathedral in her patent leather high heels, big bosoms flopping like water balloons under an open coat. A police officer gave chase in his long yellow slicker, and it proved to be an unequal match. She collapsed on her ass as he caught up to her. Didn't even make it to the first step.

"Fucking thing!" Kahn said. He'd attached the orange backup cable and resumed working the robot's controls, but he continued to stare in astonishment as nothing happened.

"The definition of insanity…" began the voice in Diaz's head. Kahn looked up at him. Had he said it aloud?

"It worked yesterday morning and I know the battery's good," Kahn said. "Couple more things I can try."

Diaz went back to analyzing the bag. The wires looked like the kind that attach earbuds to an iPod. Beyond the actual explosives—for which in practicality there were only a few options—the materials that went into a bomb were as limitless as the human imagination. Yet Diaz thought someone's imagination had run wild on this one, and it wasn't the bomb maker's.

He might take a ScanX x-ray kit and get a shot inside the messenger bag, but instead Diaz went around the truck and approached the thing with what he considered to be appropriate caution. That tape...unless someone built this bomb months ago and carried it around ever since, it didn't add up. The tape was there to fix the old tear, not to help hold together a bomb package. And without the tape the bag looked a lot less suspicious.

When he got within fifteen feet, he felt pretty confident that his judgment had been correct. He lifted his right pant leg and reached into the scabbard on his calf, extracting his Leatherman folding knife. Again he thought maybe he should go get the bomb suit and initiate an x-ray procedure, but he knew x-rays and personal protection would be a waste of time.

Diaz looked over his shoulder just once. Kahn was still messing with the robot, paying him no mind. The hysterical funeral people had been hustled away. The rest of the crowd and the traffic had fallen silent—not in real life, but their constant murmur had receded beyond the periphery of the bomb tech's concentration.

Using one hand, held up at the level of his ribs, Diaz flicked the blade launcher to open the knife. He kept it as sharp as any folding knife could be and the straight-edge/serrated blade combination gave him maximum flexibility. With even strides he closed the rest of the distance to the bag and dropped to one knee in the rain.

Now a sound did come from behind him. It was Kahn, calling over the noise of the crowd. Diaz couldn't hear the words exactly, just his own name, delivered with an attitude. Screw it—today forced patience felt nearly as suffocating to him as the bomb suit could be. And he'd already drawn his conclusions about the bag. Crouched on top of it now, Diaz ignored the sergeant. Steadying the messenger bag gently with his left hand, he used the straight edge of his knife to slice with even pressure through the middle of the fabric.

For two seconds blade through nylon sounded vaguely like fingernails on a chalkboard. When he'd finished, the insides lay exposed.

This was no IED. It contained only a sheaf of legal papers, a navel orange, a paperback book, a tin of Altoids, and, as Diaz had suspected, an iPod Nano with earbuds attached.

"You! Don't! Do! That!" Kahn was still red in the face halfway back to the station house.

"I could see it was nothing," Diaz repeated for the third time.

"You could see—how could you see? Did you x-ray it?"

Diaz shook his head. "The time it took—what? I was gonna climb into the bomb suit while you messed with the robot? Or we were gonna send back to the garage for another robot? Stand out there getting wet? Block Fifth Avenue for half the day for a bag of papers? It was nothing. I could feel it and I could see it."

"First of all, the rain isn't an excuse for anything. Second, how did you do the RSP?"

"There was nothing dangerous, therefore nothing to render safe."

"How did you open it?"

"With my knife. You saw."

"Why not pull the zipper?"

"Because it could be booby trapped."

"But you said it was nothing. You knew there was no bomb—just knew! So how could it be booby trapped, a bag of papers?"

"Better safe than sorry. If it was a bomb—"

"So you didn't know. If you knew for sure, why not use the zipper? Why cut it open?"

Diaz scratched his forehead with his thumbnail. "Following procedures? Is that what you want me to say?"

Kahn stared out at the street. At least he'd stopped giving driving directions. "You're damn straight that's what I want you to say. You cut it open because you were following procedures, but the procedure starts with the Wolverine, doesn't it? We use the robot to make the assessment, not our hands. Not our guts."

By the book, Diaz thought. Which one is the robot?

He turned the truck onto Seventh Avenue near the boarded-up St. Vincent's Hospital building. Used to be ambulances stacked up there. Now it was too quiet. Diaz waited for some people to cross, turned on the light bar for a second, and ran the stoplight.

Next to him, Kahn had the incident report form on his lap and was writing with vigor. "All those people there... no way around this, Diaz. I gotta tell it straight. I like you, kid, I really do. But I gotta tell it straight for Cap's sake."

Diaz wanted to say he didn't give a rip, but that wouldn't accomplish anything, and besides it was untrue. He said, "The other day I looked up 'procedure' in the dictionary. It comes from the word 'proceed.'"

"Yeah?" Kahn turned to peer at him over his reading glasses.

Diaz nodded, kept his eyes on the road. "And the word 'proceed' comes from the Latin for 'to go forward.' That's all I was doing, Sergeant. Going forward."

Kahn's jaw went slack. "You looked that up—procedure?"

"I sure did." Diaz grinned, smug.

"And you think that's a mark in your favor?"

"I don't know."

"Because to my mind the only reason a person would look up the word 'procedure' in the dictionary would be in preparation for questioning the department's procedures. Do you know how many cops in the NYPD Bomb Squad have fallen in the line of duty?"

Diaz pictured the wall of honor at the precinct. "Six?"

"That's exactly right. Six in more than a hundred years, and one of those at the Twin Towers, which was a whole different thing entirely. Why so few? Because they followed procedures and those procedures constantly improved over time. One of those improvements is the robot for remote threat assessment. That's why we use it—not to get too close—to save lives."

Of course Diaz knew all of that. "It wasn't working."

"You might've worn the suit then."

"The suit? The bag contained no threat!" He pulled into the small parking lot of the station house and cut the engine. Neither man moved for a couple of breaths. Then Kahn pocketed his reading glasses and climbed out.

Diaz followed him to the side entrance. "All I'm saying is that sometimes you just gotta proceed, play it by ear if you have to. It's an imperfect world."

"It sure is, Manny." Kahn stopped in his tracks. "Return this vehicle to the garage and figure out what the hell's wrong with that Wolverine."

Albert Horn worked as a computer programmer in the research department of National Bible Publishers at 1440

Broadway. It had the potential to be a peaceful job and Albert Horn coveted peace. He saw it in the eyes of his coworkers, in their placid manners, in their kind smiles, and he wished he could find it in himself.

Mercifully the seventh floor felt more like a library than a business office. The small programming department huddled in one corner around a bend, the only part of the floor where people didn't speak in hushed tones by default. Miles of bookshelves occupied most of the other areas: volumes upon volumes on subjects so esoteric that Albert Horn couldn't explain them if he had years to prepare. All day long, on that part of the floor, scholars came and went. Editors settled down in carrels and at giant wooden tables, poring over ancient Greek and Hebrew and Aramaic. When Albert Horn once asked a research librarian what those people were looking for after so many years, she replied with one word: "Insights."

Insights. Albert Horn could dig it, looking for insights in books. Why not? He'd tried every other way and it had gotten him nowhere—worse than nowhere. He'd long ago mastered the computer world, once relished the places the Internet could take you, the way it could stimulate your mind. But that was a tease. You couldn't touch and smell those places. On the screen they were just words and pictures.

In late 2002, when he was eighteen years old, Albert Horn had left Jamaica, Queens, for the United States Army. War was afoot and Horn considered himself a patriot, but it was more than that. He wanted to imbibe the world, touch it and taste it. And if he had to risk his life to do that, to his youthful mind that seemed worth the chance. He trained at Fort Jackson in South Carolina—first time he'd set foot below the Mason-Dixon line in his life—and got posted to the Eighth Cavalry Regiment at Fort Hood,

Texas. Before he shipped out, he and some buddies hiked the Blue Ridge Mountains.

Albert Horn used to tell whoever would listen that he never again felt as close to God as he did in the Blue Ridge—not in America or Europe or the Middle East, not in any church, and certainly, sad to say, not on the seventh floor of National Bible Publishers. Not that he didn't try like hell to keep his chin up. In Hollis, Queens, where he lived, he rented a back-room apartment from his sister and her family, who were for the most part kind to him. They often ate together, sometimes went to church together, even hung out watching football and playing video games together. But, for all that, Albert Horn felt a creeping despair that carried him further from God's love every day.

This was no secret. His sister knew there was something wrong with him, something deep in his mind, something beyond his physical disabilities. His boss, Youssef Naftali, also knew. Their team was halfway through a multiyear project but had fallen behind schedule. If this had been Microsoft or Oracle, some geek with a Coke in his hand would be standing over them pounding the table, urging them through all-nighters. Albert Horn couldn't have handled that. He couldn't even handle Naftali standing over him two hours ago, telling him gently that last week's coding turned out to be dog poo. "Dog poo"—those were the words he used. Management allowed no cursing in the building.

Now, as a kind of forced leave, Horn had two tickets from Naftali to a Broadway matinee in his shirt pocket.

"They're for *Spider-Man,*" Naftali had said. "Take them. Turn off the dark! You earned it, guy."

Delivered in an Indiana twang, the cheerleading made Albert Horn sound like a man on the verge of a nervous breakdown. Horn himself had a pronounced New York accent, but he hadn't used it that morning to protest any further. He'd pretended to call his sister and invite his niece to accompany him, although in reality he'd done no such thing.

At exactly 2:30 he called for the elevator. A minute later he rode it down to the lobby. And a minute after that he walked out onto Broadway.

He called his sister, Lydia, from his cell phone as he hit the street. Naftali, he told her, in suggesting that he leave early had implied that Albert Horn's prosthetic legs couldn't carry him as well as another man's, which was true up to a point, but just barely. After years of practice out in the real world, he hardly thought of the legs as a limitation—at least not in his daily routine, which took him on and off the subway, along city sidewalks, in and out of chairs, even up and down steps.

He turned east onto Forty-First Street, away from the theater. He had plenty of time to make the curtain if he decided to go, but he had to think first. All in all, it had been a pretty depressing day—a pretty depressing week or two. Something had triggered within Albert Horn and he'd gone into emotional free fall.

It pertained to his brother-in-law, Kyle Butterworth, who was trying to decide whether to join the marines at the age of thirty-six. Even though they ate dinner together nearly every night, Albert never felt close to Kyle. He didn't hate him or anything, but they didn't connect either. Kyle worked as a plumber and Albert Horn had an office job. Over dinner they might exchange a few words about the weather or the neighbors, but they never shared their inner thoughts with one another. They could sit in front of a baseball game for two hours and never exchange a word between them, just talk to the television if at all.

A few weeks ago, however, the dynamic had changed. All of a sudden, Kyle wanted to talk and talk about joining the marines and wanted to hear stories from his brother-in-law's days in the army. Albert Horn wondered how much Kyle had researched this thing on his own. *Can you even join the marines so late in life?* And where did the desire come from? *Not like Kyle hates Muslims or needs the job.* Horn wondered whether all this talk of the marines was just a way to draw him out, maybe Kyle's curiosity getting the better of him after so many years not hearing a peep from this guy who strapped on his legs every morning in the rear apartment.

Meanwhile the memories that Horn had repressed for nearly a decade began to come back, first in dreams—you couldn't call them nightmares, he told his sister, because they weren't all horrible—and then in waking flashbacks. He might see a young girl in the street and he'd flash to a young girl in Kabul, crouched over her dead grandfather. He might pass a shadow and his mind would flash to a bloodstain on a pockmarked wall. He might be sitting on the subway and see a blemish on someone's face and flash to the first man he ever killed, a black-bearded militant in an open window across a dirt road.

But the worst—and what had turned Horn's code to "dog poo," he was sure—were the memories that came back unbidden from the Battle of Fallujah, where Horn lost his legs not to an IED, as many soldiers lost limbs, but in house-to-house combat. You might call it a freak accident, but it was no *accident* because it involved an enemy RPG and it was not *freak* because nothing in combat was freak. You attempted to do violence to one another and awaited the results. The RPG...since Kyle had started asking all his questions, Albert Horn had begun to see the smoke from its launch when the light caught a window in a certain way. He'd go into a miniature seizure, almost like a trance, he told his sister, see the grenade sail under his outstretched arm, missing him as he dove for cover, then scutter along the splintered wooden floor and embed itself in the wall for a long fraction of a second. Albert Horn knew what happened after that but he couldn't remember it. He knew from the accounts of others that stones went flying and the floor gave way and his unconscious body hung trapped between beams, his legs dangling into the space below as a vicious firefight ensued on the ground floor, eventually reducing his lower legs to shattered bone and bloody pulp. Unsalvageable.

Company C, 3rd Battalion, 8th Cavalry Regiment. For two tours in Afghanistan and three in Iraq, Albert Horn gave as good as he got, but it all caught up to him in Fallujah. That cursed city took away more than Horn's legs, more than his sense of invulnerability, more than his curiosity about the wider world. It stole his patriotism.

Because today, he informed his sister, speaking in tears into his cell phone as he rounded Sixth Avenue and Forty-Third Street, he realized that he'd repressed these horrible visions now floating back to him not to avoid reliving the fear but to avoid unmasking his own hatred. His hatred of God, of man, of country. It had consumed him.

Albert Horn crossed Broadway with the tickets in his pocket and paused in front of the Times Square US Army Recruiting Station. His sister, still on the other end of the phone, noticed that her brother stopped talking in mid-sentence and that the air between them had gone silent, not even a crackle of static.

On the sidewalk, Albert Horn would never hear the explosion that destroyed his eardrums, shredded his internal organs, and severed his left hand at the wrist. The force of the blast lifted his torso eight feet into the air and dropped him on the now-exposed rear of his sacrum and iliac bones. Without another word or voluntary movement, he fell backward from that position. Stone dead.

The Third Precinct garage had been given over entirely to the Bomb Squad long ago. It consisted of two asymmetrical bays with steel shelving at the back and sides, loaded with equipment and supplies, all kept as neat as the contents of any firehouse. With the doors closed, Diaz and Detective First Grade Lakshan Higgins examined the Wolverine on the floor beside the rear workbench. Behind them, the squad's two newest and most sophisticated response trucks gleamed blue and white under fluorescent lights.

In a unit that increasingly attracted gadget lovers and puzzle solvers, Higgins was the most techie. Of both African and Indian extraction, he was thin, slight, and barely tall enough to fulfill the old NYPD height requirement—lucky for him they dropped it when they allowed women onto the force. He had skin the color of a purple potato, pitted cheeks, straight jet-black hair combed into a part, and he wore spectacles with thick clear plastic frames and lenses that always made his eyes appear to goggle.

That was the outside. Inside, he possessed the intuitive flair of a math and physics whiz, having attended the Bronx High School of Science and graduated from RPI with an engineering degree in three years.

All of this intellectual firepower he'd brought to bear on the robot. He tightened the last bolts, tapped a few keys on the laptop he was using, threw the control panel power switch on and off, rested his hands on his hips, and declared, "I give up."

"You really mean that?" Diaz said.

"That thing hasn't jerked one millimeter, hasn't emitted so much as a peep, even though the batteries test fine. Software problem is all I can think. Maybe someone up the chain can call it in to the manufacturer. I'm sure as heck not authorized."

"More rules." Diaz shook his head. "This place has more procedures than the army ever did."

"You can't be serious."

"Well, my last two tours of duty it was a situation involving more slack. Put it that way."

"That was, like, eight years ago. You still have a hard-on for it?"

"I don't know. I'm probably just out of sorts because Kahn's vigilance is testing my limits. The guy hasn't shut up for a year, and I'm tired of having him on me like white on rice, no room to breath. I really lost it today, opened a suspicious package without the robot or the suit."

Higgins let out a whistle. "That was a mistake."

"I know. He's, like, got me jumping into the deep end just to cool off."

"Reprimand?"

Diaz shrugged. "Maybe I'll get off light with the lieutenant out sick."

"You'd better watch your step. Kahn has Capobianco's ear. Neither one likes guys getting restless on them. Why they don't take more than a few EODs at a time in the first place."

Diaz looked at Higgins glumly. "I wish I had your interests, could lose myself in the guts of a machine, but that ain't me."

"You have other assets."

"After all this time I'm still addicted to the adrenaline rush. Useless bomb sweeps don't do it for me no more."

"Sounds like you *want* to find a live bomb." Higgins tapped his fingers on the workbench and studied Diaz from top to bottom. "You'd better keep your head down, Manny."

Diaz frowned. Before he could respond further, the inside door flew open.

"Diaz!"

He took a deep breath and muttered to Higgins, "Here we go."

Kahn appeared, spotted Diaz and began walking fast toward the side door to the parking lot. "Explosion in Times Square," he barked over his shoulder. "You and me!"

An old feeling, one that had almost been lost, awakened inside Diaz's chest. He jogged a few steps across the painted concrete to catch up. "Times Square?"

Kahn nodded. "Casualties."

Until you knew for sure, you assumed the worst. No more complacency. That was the signal impact of 9/11 on attitudes in the law enforcement community. A bomb went off, it could be a lone nut, but you allowed for the possibility of terrorism. A series of bombs or—like this happened—a suicide bomber in front of a US government installation: you presumed terrorism unless and until you confirmed otherwise.

So Don Burbette, one of the supervisors out of the local FBI office, was already there when Kahn and Diaz arrived. They pulled up to a crime scene well under control with blue sawhorses lined up end-to-end blocking the nearest lanes of traffic along Broadway, Forty-Third Street and Seventh Avenue. Dirty whitish canvas that stretched between stanchions shielded the views of gawkers from strategic angles, while police and other emergency service vehicles screened out most of the rest.

Burbette greeted Kahn and Diaz at the curb. As it had begun to drizzle again, he escorted them to a police trailer that had just been locked into place. They went up the few steps and through the door, but they didn't sit.

"What we got?" Kahn asked Burbette.

The FBI agent drew his shoulders back. He presented as your average straight-laced white guy, medium height with good posture and blondish-gray hair cut short. Across the bridge of his nose he had some youthful sun freckles that had decided one day to stay year-round. He had fingers so thick and long that they could only have been developed doing daily chores on some Midwestern farm. Except that he grew up in downtown Dorchester, Massachusetts, son of a fireman.

"The suspect blew himself up in the middle of the sidewalk in front of the recruiting station, but by some miracle no one else got it bad, only some minor flesh wounds and some shock, what looks like temporary hearing loss in a few pedestrians."

Kahn nodded. "Anything known about him?"

"Negative. He's fresh. ME hasn't moved the body yet, CSU still snapping pictures. They should be done in a minute. Take a look?"

"Sure."

They climbed into white Tyvek suits and sterile booties and walked with great care sixty feet up the sidewalk, through a cone of spooky silence. A photographer, a CSU tech, and an assistant medical examiner, all similarly clad, were just throwing a tarp over the body.

"Are we clear?" Kahn asked the ME.

It was a woman they all knew, Sabrina Thompkins, short and chubby, otherwise nondescript. She nodded.

"You can search what's left of him, but try to keep your fingers out of the body cavity."

"Go ahead," Burbette deadpanned, "ruin all of our fun."

Thompkins tucked some hair back into the netting on her head. She said, "Oh. I get it." Stared a mock challenge at Burbette. Added: "Don't get too attached. Your new friend will be gone in a few minutes."

"Watch your step on the way out," Burbette said, as if she didn't already know. Blood and flesh greased the sidewalk. Thompkins playfully shot the detectives the middle finger as she retreated.

"God, she's cool for a geek, isn't she?" Burbette concluded.

He and Diaz elevated one end of the tarp and all three men looked down.

It was a body, all right, African-American and lying on his back, what was left of him. He'd been wearing khaki pants, a patterned sweater, button-down shirt, open winter coat. The face remained relatively unscathed but the rest was a mess. His open eyes had rolled back into his skull.

"Yuck," Diaz said. "Where'd the legs go?"

"Good question," Burbette said.

They looked around the sidewalk. Thompkins had also thrown a small tarp over another object about fifteen feet away. Burbette walked delicately toward it and lifted one corner.

"That's a hand," he said.

"Left hand," Kahn said, still looking at the corpse.

"So where are the legs?" Diaz repeated. "Pulverized?" All he saw were burned and bloody stumps.

"They have to be around here somewhere," Burbette said. "Or most of them." He shook a finger at Kahn.

"Officially, it's my crime scene because of the federal installation, but you know how this works. Too many cooks..."

There was mutual respect among them. Kahn said, "Two more from our squad should be here in a minute, Cai and Hassan."

"All right. Do your thing. I'll be in the trailer with my secret weapon if you need me. The local precinct guys already know to keep everyone away."

Diaz watched Burbette's back. "What's his secret weapon?"

"Telephone," Kahn answered absently, honing in on a bulge in what remained of the corpse's pants. The randomness of an explosion could be amazing. Some things got obliterated and others stayed remarkably intact. He tugged his thin rubber gloves on tighter, knelt down, and with some effort pulled out a fat nylon wallet. He flipped it open and read, "Albert Horn. Two Hundred and Tenth Place, Hollis, Queens. I'll call and we'll scramble a crew to make a sweep there. We'll get this wallet to the A and E guy as soon as he arrives."

"Roger that," Diaz said, producing a plastic bag for the wallet.

Kahn looked around the area. "I figure the perimeter as between the sawhorses east-west, to the building on the south side. You agree?"

Diaz nodded.

"They need to block all of Forty-Third here and across the pedestrian plaza. Hustle over and tell Burbette, give him something to do."

"Okay. I see Cai and Hassan are here suiting up."

"Got 'em. You can lay out the quadrants. Give me a second to make a couple a calls, including Cap. He has to know about this."

Watching his steps, Diaz hurried over to the trailer. Cai Yong and Victor Hassan were standing at the entrance in their Tyvek. Cai had grown up in Flushing and had the accent to prove it. Hassan was a naturalized American citizen, a Palestinian originally from Jordan. "This one's for real," Diaz told them at the entrance.

"No shit," Cai said.

Diaz couldn't tell whether he meant it sarcastically, so he kept his reply even. "Sarge says await instructions." He went inside to give Burbette a fill, and by the time he returned, the corpse had left and Kahn was just wrapping up his call with Capobianco.

Kahn hung up and all four detectives stood silently on the empty sidewalk, getting their bearings.

Improbably, above the noise of traffic, they could hear soft rain pattering on the wrinkled tarp that moments ago had covered Albert Horn. Puddles were forming in the depressions.

In one corner of Lieutenant Joseph Capobianco's bedroom, a police radio sat atop a chest of drawers and crackled quietly. In the other corner, his wife, Jill, sat on a hard chair and read a magazine. The radio didn't bother him. The sound of the snapping magazine pages made him wince.

"What time is it?"

"Late afternoon. Almost time for your medication."

"I'm nauseous."

"Go puke. It'll make you feel better."

"It didn't the first six times."

Jill set down the magazine, *Sports Illustrated*—work reading. Tall, blond and leggy, she'd been a college track and hoops star and now worked in the marketing department of the NBA offices on Fifth Avenue. Sometimes Capobianco got to visit the league's executive skybox at the Garden. Today he could barely lift his head from the pillow. Jill looked concerned. She'd taken the day off to minister to him.

"I'm glad Sam is out all week on that school trip. She doesn't need to catch this."

Samantha was their teenage daughter. Capobianco agreed with his silence. He swallowed a plug of mucus with effort.

"You want some Coke, some ginger ale?"

"Sure, thanks. Either one."

As she went to the kitchen he dragged himself to the bathroom, had an ugly time of it in there, feeling the blood draining from his face, cold sweat stippling his forehead. When he emerged he went over to the police radio and turned up the volume. Jill came back through the door, stormed over and twisted the knob down to zero with emphasis. "You need to rest, Joe."

"Aw, hell. I woke up just three minutes ago."

"What'd you do in the bathroom? Still coming out both ends?"

"TMI! Do we need to talk about this?"

"Only until your fever comes down."

"Yes, nurse."

She set his Coke on the side table and handed him the digital thermometer. "You're welcome."

He held the tip of the contraption in his ear until it beeped. She grabbed it from him before he could press reset. "Damn it. Hundred and four. The doc said it would be high for a while. No school for Joey tomorrow."

Capobianco didn't have the energy to protest. He hadn't kept down a piece of toast in thirty-six hours and he felt dizzy when he sat up.

"I'm running down to the grocery store," Jill said, "for more liquids and Tylenol. Anything else you need?"

"How 'bout my youth back?"

"If I could do that I'd still have my fast break." She brushed back his greasy brown hair and kissed him on the forehead. "You're burning up."

"Thanks for reminding me."

"Keep the radio off or I'll call the doctor and we'll send you to the hospital, really embarrass your ass."

When she left he slid back down into the pillows, feeling useless. He closed his eyes and saw the hard face and sharp chin of Hank Gowen, his predecessor as head of the Bomb Squad. Gowen was a living legend, now working directly with the mayor's office as a consultant. He reputedly hadn't missed a day of work in thirty-eight years on the force. Just Cap's luck to follow a human specimen like that, someone who leapt tall buildings in a single bound. Capobianco himself had made it just nine months in the new job before the bird flu knocked him off the pedestal. Little solace that it had also broadsided a quarter of his squad. In fact, that made him all the more anxious to get back, wondering whether they could handle the action so short-staffed, whether the whole thing would go to hell before he reached his first anniversary in charge. Maybe, he thought, facing the ceiling, eyes closed, he should ask for reinforcements from the precinct regulars. But what the Bomb Squad did was unique. You couldn't just slot in another cop, even an experienced detective. A guy in that position would only get in everyone's way.

Capobianco propped himself up on his elbows and took a couple gulps of Coke, bent over and held the cold can against his forehead. His body had been alternating between chills and hot flushes for hours—covers off, covers on. The blanket still felt damp from sweat. He lay in his boxers atop it, sinuses on fire. Miserable.

The ringing phone startled him alert. As he had all day, he thought he'd let Jill take it, but the damn thing kept ringing. Then he remembered that she'd gone out. He picked it up.

"Cap here."

"You don't sound too good, my friend."

"You got that from two syllables? Thanks, Kahn. What the hell is it?"

"Sorry to bother you, Lieutenant. Just that I didn't want you to be the last to know."

"Spit it out already, Sandy. I only got so much time between bathroom visits."

Kahn told him what they knew so far: African-American male, thirty-three, army veteran, employed by National Bible Publishers nearby—they were sending someone there to check it out. Lives in Hollis—scrambling a crew there, too. JTTF notification sent out by Burbette of the FBI, minor casualties other than the perp, insignificant property damage—just a couple of cracked first-floor windows, not at the recruitment center, which had ballistic glass. AES notified and on the way, four Bomb Squad guys in the hole gathering evidence, some complications due to rain.

Finally Capobianco interrupted. "Blew himself to smithereens and only cracked a couple windows? Sounds like an idiot. News cameras there yet?"

"Yeah, but kept at bay."

"Good boy. I guess I'd better call the inspector. I'll be down to you in half an hour."

Capobianco felt Kahn hesitate, but think better of what he was about to say. "Roger that, Lieutenant. We'll proceed."

"Of course you will."

Capobianco used his department-issue Blackberry to call his chief, who worked out of the Forensic Investigations Division in Jamaica, Queens. The clerk who answered said the inspector, Rex Brennan, was in with the chief of detectives at One Police Plaza and not to be disturbed. "Hold on," the clerk said.

In a minute, the phone rang through without introduction.

"Gowen here." Slick how they'd shunted him off. "How you been, Cap?"

"Just swell."

"I heard you were down for the count with the Spanish flu."

"Bird flu, actually. I'm all right."

"On the job?"

"Sure, in a manner of speaking. Listen, I was calling Brennan because we got a situation in Times Square." He coughed—great moment for that. "I thought the mayor and you other big shots should know before the whisper war gets going."

"I'm on it. Just heard on the radio. The chief and the captain are in with the mayor. Brennan may darken your door if it gets bad. What can you tell them?"

"Seems contained." The lieutenant shared all that he knew. "I'll be on scene myself in half an hour."

"Okay. I'll let you know if anything else is expected of you. Thanks for the heads-up."

"Sure thing." As if Capobianco had called him directly. Or maybe Gowen really thought he had. Monkey in the middle.

The current commander of the Bomb Squad ran to the bathroom and splashed some water on his face, went to the closet and pulled out a gray suit. His shirt was open and the slacks unbuttoned and he had one sock on when Jill walked in.

"Where are you going?"

"Bombing in Times Square."

"Bad?"

"One dead."

"Who called you?"

"Kahn."

"Let him handle it. He's capable."

"It's high profile."

"Tough. You're not going. You're too sick."

"Jill!"

"I mean it, Joe. Don't be stupid."

"They're expecting me."

"He called here? The land line?"

Capobianco blinked.

Jill went to the phone and pressed star-six-nine. "Sandy, it's Jill." Pause. "You, too. Listen, Cap can't make it today. He's running a hundred and four. I stepped out for a sec and I caught him getting dressed, but he looks like death warmed over. Can you handle it without him?" Pause. "That's what I figured. Keep him in the loop so he doesn't drive me crazy, but don't call more than once every couple of hours, 'kay?"

She hung up. "That was easy."

Capobianco bent over to fix his left sock and dizziness overcame him. Feeling a creeping despair, he admitted to himself that he was no Hank Gowen. He collapsed into the nearest chair and let his throbbing head loll off to one side.

With the cloud cover and the rain and the time of year, it turned dark at four o'clock that night in the shadows cast by the high-rises. The crew had set up floodlights, so they kept on working.

Diaz knew he'd have a crick in his neck tomorrow from all the time spent staring down at the ground, but the adrenaline kept him going for now. At Kahn's instruction he'd used string to mark off the quadrants—two strings at right angles crossing where Albert Horn's body had lain.

Soon after they'd removed the wallet, Horn's corpse had been taken away, leaving only some blood and blast stains in the center of the sidewalk and a crater in the concrete no more than an inch deep. But initial fragmentary evidence showed signs of high explosives, so Diaz had used a handheld HEPA evidence vacuum around the seat of the incident, bagging and labeling the cartridge for the CSU lab.

Curiously, the detonation had produced a pretty small initial blast radius, Diaz thought. No wonder collateral damage was so minor. Maybe the guy got nervous and hit the button too soon. Maybe he planned to go through the army's recruitment office door and give the commander a bear hug, but he chickened out or ran into technical difficulties. Or maybe he just didn't know how small a blast zone he'd create. Not, it appeared, a very professional job in any case.

The four men had lined up shoulder-to-shoulder and walked the first two quadrants already. There was trash along the curb and in the plaza, which complicated things. They picked through carefully, going along an inch at a time, turning over everything. CSU would shovel it up later, give it another going over, but the Bomb Squad team wanted to see the pattern in which remnants had been thrown from the blast site. They hit pay dirt right away, what appeared to be the suspect's cell phone, though it may have come from someone who passed close to the explosion. Hassan waved it at them. He pressed the ON button but it wouldn't boot up, so he bagged it.

When they finished the second quadrant, Diaz straightened up, stretched his back, looked around. Cai and Hassan and Kahn and Burbette were all stretching their own backs and limbs in the crinkly white Tyvek suits, each looking worse for the wear of the past couple of hours. They'd placed markers where they'd gathered anything interesting, and they carried plastic bags that they'd labeled with corresponding letters. Nobody had much yet, including Diaz, which was strange because bombs meant for terrorist purposes oftentimes contained large amounts of shrapnel that the bomb maker packed around the explosive charge in order to maximize casualties. Diaz had only found a few ball bearings so far, along with some gnarled pieces of lightweight metal that may or may not have had anything to do with the bomb.

Exchanging glances, they all went back to the blast site and shouldered up at the wedge of Quadrant Three. Diaz bent from the waist and continued searching. Under an empty Doritos bag by the curb he found something interesting, a three-inch chunk of molded white composite, solid with a curve in it. Cai found another and Kahn found a smaller piece. They continued to drop markers as they went, following the trajectory across Forty-Third Street. When they paused, Diaz more carefully examined the few fragments he had, tried to fit them together, but to no avail. He re-bagged them. Then Hassan, who was crouched to Diaz's left, found the first piece of a cell phone under a table in the plaza, right by an aluminum chair leg. That was curious. Could Horn have been carrying two phones? It might indicate a remote detonation. Diaz held it up for others to see.

"Anyone else find cell phone pieces?"

Kahn said, "I got a bunch of them. No SIM card yet."

His phone rang and he walked off, returned a minute later. "That was O'Shea," he told the others.

O'Shea was a leading detective from AES. "Brian?" Diaz said, glad to hear it. "He's working this?"

Kahn nodded. "Turns out our man Horn had a pair of prosthetic legs."

"Interesting." Diaz held up the evidence bags. "That explains this odd substance, I guess. Looked like pieces of a toaster at first."

"You find all kinds of strange shit on the streets of Manhattan."

"How many ball bearings or similar, all together?"

"Only a few."

"Me too. Helluva bomb maker."

"Yeah, well, thank God for that, huh?"

"So you think it was the legs?"

"Could be. It explains where they went, that's for sure."

"What evidence did you gather at the seat of the explosion?"

"Ran the HEPA vac," Diaz reported. "I swabbed for lab tests, too. We'll see."

"Yeah," Burbette jumped in. "I also did an ETK, but... damnedest thing. I can't get a reading on the spot—maybe the rain. You guys need a break?"

Diaz reached up and worked his neck. "I got a couple more hours in me." The others agreed. They went back to their slow walk, finally found the giveaway on the legs: a pair of artificial feet clad in rubber-soled shoes. They also found some more parts to the prostheses, now that they knew what they were.

Half an hour later, Cai cried out. He had the remnants of an electric blasting cap—the crimp and grommet with two partial leg wires protruding. "Man, I almost stepped on the damn thing, blended in with the sidewalk. I'm going blind from staring."

But finding that part encouraged them all. They'd piece this thing together, Diaz thought. They always did eventually.

In the Fourth Quadrant they worked their way from the "seat" to the tables by the plaza. Under an abandoned wool scarf, Diaz found a plastic fragment with a serial number on it. *Hot damn!* He felt a warmth rise in his chest, and his mind went to the first World Trade Center bombing. After that attack, one of the Bomb Squad detectives found the VIN from the van that the terrorists had rented, leading to quick arrests. In this case, of course, they already knew who'd carried the bomb, but a serial number could still be a big deal, lead in all kinds of directions. Still, Diaz tamped himself down, trying not to manifest too much excitement. He decided to wait until they wrapped up to tell Kahn, didn't want to come across as an overeager rookie.

The detectives didn't find much else of note, a few more pieces that looked like they came from the prostheses, some bits of cell phone, a couple inches of wire. It would all get turned over to the lab for analysis.

Kahn gave the signal an hour later and they called it quits, went to the trailer, and stripped off their protective coverings. When Diaz mentioned the serial number, Kahn nodded his approval and said, "We'll prioritize it for O'Shea." Nearly as an afterthought, he added, "Nice work."

Diaz didn't mind the faint praise. They were all tired and damp.

Kahn offered him a lift but he chose to walk alone to the subway just up the block. Away from the cordoned area, Times Square manifested the usual bustle. All around him Diaz caught snatches of conversation about the bombing, saw people shaking their heads, lifting their eyebrows, clasping their coats closed out of self-protective instinct.

He paused at the top of the subway stairs to read the second-floor news crawl across the street. It said: *BOMB IN TIMES SQUARE...ONE DEAD.*

Some days on this job, Diaz thought, were just too surreal.

He turned and trotted down into the subway.

**TICK, TICK, TICK, TICK, TICK, TICK, TICK,
TICK, TICK, TICK, TICK, TICK, TICK**

2.

DAY ONE: DARK

IF YOU MULTIPLIED "PLAIN" TIMES "DULL" and divided by the square root of "nondescript," you'd get the sum of the apartment that Manny Diaz shared with his roommate in Washington Heights. The outside appearance was of an unadorned square box clad in tan brick. Inside was a two-bedroom with galley kitchen and a small living space on the fourth floor. The living room and eating area looked out through the fire escape across Bennett Avenue at similar boxes, and both bedrooms gave on the same perpetually shaded, equipment-stuffed airshaft.

Still, it sported a Manhattan location, only a few blocks from the Number 1 train, and Diaz could jog along the Hudson River Greenway through Fort Washington Park when he felt like it.

Also, his roommate—found through Craig's List—always paid her share of the rent on time. And as a bonus, though light-skinned she was otherwise the spitting image of the singer Jennifer Lopez. Diaz considered J-Lo the most beautiful woman in the world. Although his roommate's last name was Foster, her first name was Jennifer, too, so he sometimes playfully called her J-Fo. The occasional banter aside, they'd never had a thing together and they hardly saw one another for the first six months of her tenure, Jennifer mostly spending time with her boyfriend, who had a nicer pad somewhere farther downtown. Diaz didn't feel too bad about that, as this was primarily a business transaction. And, besides, for a good long time he'd avoided worrying at all about relations with women. Still, there was something gratifying about having her around now and then, and his heart skipped a little tonight when he got home and saw her bedroom lights glowing.

"Hey, Jennifer," he said on the way to his own room. He felt too tired from work to be playful with nicknames.

"What's up, Manny."

He saw through the corner of one eye that she wore a loose-fitting t-shirt and terrycloth shorts. Though it was near forty degrees outside and raining again, in the building dry heat piped up endlessly.

Diaz replaced his damp clothes with an NYPD t-shirt and torn jeans, threw his socks into the laundry pile in his closet, and went to the bathroom. He was standing over the toilet with his joint in his hand when he saw that the bottom drawer to the vanity had been left half open. That was Jennifer's drawer, the bigger one, filled with things only women needed, but now on top of the feminine hygiene products lay a vibrator. Diaz couldn't help but look. The thing was gigantic and pink and had certain other attributes that emphasized sexual pleasure without great subtlety. He finished peeing and slid the drawer closed with his foot, amused, thinking only that after a period of acclimation Jennifer had finally begun making herself more at home. Good. It sure beat bunking with another guy.

In the living room, Diaz threw open the window for fresh air. He needed dinner somehow but felt exhausted from the day. There was beer in the fridge and a couple of takeout containers.

He twisted the top off of a Bud Light. "Hey, J-Fo! Did you eat?"

"Yeah. Chinese. You can have the leftovers if you want."

"How much?"

She appeared in the doorway and leaned one shoulder against the jamb. No lipstick, toenails painted pink, hair a little wild. Still beautiful. "Don't insult me."

"I'm not. But we made a rule—no food raids. What'd they get you for?"

"I don't know…ten, twelve."

Diaz went to his room and fished a five-dollar bill from his dresser.

Jennifer took it from him and folded it in half. "I left my boyfriend."

"Yeah? When was that?"

"Two weeks ago. Why I've been around a bit more after work. I didn't want to talk about it for a while."

"So it's a bad thing?"

"Not really." She ran her fingers through her hair and shook it. "I guess it means maybe the rules will be a little harder for me to follow now that I'm around more. It's easy to follow rules when you're not around, right?"

"Hell, Jen, I've never been big on rules anyway. It just seemed like a good idea when we didn't know each other."

She laughed, tried to hand him back the five, but he wouldn't take it.

"That rule didn't change yet," he said, waving her off. "Like a beer?"

"Sure. Mind if I watch you eat?"

Diaz lifted an eyebrow. "Not if I can watch you back."

After Diaz scarfed the beef chow fun, they popped another couple of beers and played Mario Kart on the Wii with their bare feet splayed against the edge of the chest that they used for a coffee table. She was pretty good with the virtual wheel, outraced him as often as not.

When they grew bored, Diaz went to the fridge again. "Only one Bud left. We can share."

"You take it. It's your beer."

"It *was*." He chuckled. Then he looked down at the bottleneck. "Maybe it'll help me sleep."

She sat up. "I saw on the news about that thing in Times Square. Were you part of that?"

"Yep."

"What did you see?"

"I can't really talk about it. What did the news say?"

"Some guy blew himself up."

"They got that right. So what do you think I saw?"

"A body? In pieces?"

He pebbled his chin and nodded. "Pretty much."

"Is it freaky? Did it disturb you?"

"Not as much as seeing buddies of mine get blown up."

She shuddered. "How can you even look at any of that?"

He pictured Albert Horn lying on his back on the bloody blackened sidewalk. "You look but you don't look. In a way, you deconstruct it."

"What does that mean?" She drew her feet to the couch and hugged her knees.

"You have to see the individual parts sometimes and ignore that it was once a person. There's nothing you can do to help him except try to catch the bad guys."

"But it was a suicide bomber, they said. He was a bad guy himself."

"Maybe. But even so, suicide bombers rarely act alone. Can we talk about something else? How about *your* work?"

"What? Selling insurance? That's just a job. It's not worth re-living."

"Somebody has to do it."

"But we don't have to talk about it."

Diaz washed out his food container and threw it into the recycle. He sat at the table to finish his beer, couldn't get the image of Albert Horn out of his mind, all of a sudden.

Jennifer lay down on her back on the couch, facing him. "Did I make you mad?"

"Nah. Just thinking."

"Can I change the subject?"

"All right."

"So I've been wondering what you meant about the rules. When I came you said it was best to have things a certain way, so we both knew where we stood, respected each other in the apartment. The thing is, my circumstances have changed now, you know?"

"How so?"

"I told you. No more boyfriend."

He gave her a long look. She was lying modestly, had her legs closed. She draped one arm up over her head and flopped her wrist across the armrest behind her. Her body language was insouciant, but her eyes told a different story. She studied his face like she wanted to know an answer before she asked the question.

"I'm kinda tired," Diaz said, pushing unwelcome images of that afternoon from his mind. "Why don't you just spit it out. You planning to move?"

"Nothing like that. I like it here. I'm just wondering—we originally said no visitors—but now that I'm single again, would it be okay if I brought a guy up now and then? I'd feel safer here and I promise to be very respectful."

Diaz picked at the label on the Budweiser. "Respectful of what?"

"Of—I don't know—your rights."

"Hey, it's a free country. But this is my place originally. I don't want to be around, you know—"

"What?" She sat up in one motion, crossed her legs, grabbed a throw pillow, and covered her lap.

Diaz flushed. "I don't want to hear any noise, okay?"

"Noise?"

"You know...when you're in there."

"Sex. You're talking about sex. It's okay to say it." A twist formed in one corner of her mouth. "You think I'm a screamer?"

In his mind's eye, Diaz pictured the vibrator in the bathroom drawer. "I don't think anything."

He felt hotter than ever as she broke into a teasing smile. "You're not embarrassed, are you—embarrassed to think about the things women do?"

"Of course not!" But he did feel something—something uncomfortable. "Just keep the noise down and it'll be fine, okay?" He finished his beer in one gulp and set the bottle back on the table too hard.

Jennifer froze at the sound.

Diaz sensed her gaze on him, but he wouldn't meet it. He felt the redness washing across his face and neck, like a rush of steam rising from a deep dark shaft. If he wasn't careful, he'd fall toward that place.

He touched the back of his neck and felt clammy sweat there. The apartment was a furnace and the pipes were knocking. Without another word he put on some shoes and a coat, stepped out into the hall, and pulled the door closed behind him.

North of 181st Street, a pedestrian bridge connected Riverside Drive to a walking path known as the Hudson River Greenway. Diaz crossed at a brisk clip and headed south, this portion of the path running close to the northbound lanes of the Henry Hudson Parkway. Near the George Washington Bridge, the path meandered through some trees—leafless in the winter cold—and passed through a tunnel under the southbound lanes.

He felt restless. Pent-up energy shot through his legs like an electrical charge and with his hands in his coat pockets a shudder pulled his shoulders toward his ears. It may have appeared to a passer-by as a response to the cold, but Diaz didn't feel cold. He felt like a man on fire.

Twenty feet above him, traffic roared over the road. He went through the concrete underpass and proceeded along the river past the tennis courts, which were dark. The rain had stopped but the air remained damp, bone-biting. There weren't many people about, only the occasional jogger or brave cyclist. In front of him, Diaz could see his breath in clouds like exhaust from a smokestack.

Why had he responded that way to Jennifer? Resistance to change? But if he didn't want her bringing other men back, he could've put the kibosh on it right there and then. It was his apartment, the one place where he had complete latitude, but he caved in and ran like a coward as soon as she challenged him. Did he have feelings for her? He didn't think so, but he'd never considered that before. She was stunning, but that wasn't the same as an emotional attraction.

No, he decided, it wasn't that. What had angered him was the lack of control. Up in the apartment, he didn't want to lash out in response, ruin a good thing. That's why he had to get out of there. That and only that.

Where the path crept close to the parkway, Diaz paused and turned to look at the giant bridge, the George Washington, its suspension cables lit up like a string of beads, the tops of trucks gliding along the roadbed in a straight line like hockey pucks on ice. It would take a lot to blow that bridge, he thought. Still, it was only a matter of time before someone tried.

His mind jumped to the package near the steps of St. Pat's. To succeed as a bomb technician, he'd learned many years ago, it wasn't enough to concentrate on the mechanics of an IED. If that was all he'd done back in the armed forces, he'd have ended up in no better shape than this guy Albert Horn. Maybe worse, if there was such a thing. No, the key was to get inside the head of the bomb maker. If you could think like him, you could anticipate how he might operate.

Maybe, Diaz thought, he had to approach Kahn the same way. Because he felt that the space between him and Kahn had become a minefield, and maybe he wasn't doing such a good job of watching his step anymore. Like that thing with looking up "procedure" in the dictionary. He was trying to win an argument, but that was like trying to win an argument with a drill instructor. The drill instructor didn't want to hear anything but "Yes, sir, yes"—no matter whether they'd gone off for a Sunday stroll or Armageddon had erupted outside the chain-link fence.

Still, that damned package near the steps...Diaz knew for sure it was nothing the second he'd wrapped his mind around it. Just knew it.

Altoids! He scoffed. *Oranges!* The damn thing couldn't have been more harmless. He barely felt threatened when he stooped over it, therefore experienced little relief when he cut into it and saw the contents.

Out on the greenway, Diaz took a deep breath of cold air. Suddenly he felt too calm—like he could fall asleep right there on the path, his eyelids and feet heavy with the stress of the day. He forced himself to walk forward, still heading south, away from the apartment. Soon the path came tight along the parkway again. Diaz felt the whoosh of each car roaring by, the vacuum tugging at him. It raised a familiar sensation in his chest, a sensation that he may or may not like, but to which long ago he'd become accustomed.

Without thinking further, Diaz lifted his left leg and scrambled over the jersey wall. There were only a couple of feet between the curved concrete of the wall and the solid white line of the shoulder. He hewed to the wet, narrow space, absorbed the rush of air from passing cars time and again, ignored their occasional horns.

This was crazy, he knew. *But the feeling!* It made him high—as high as any drug—and as he walked abreast of danger, all of his worries melted in the intensity.

In front of a building in the financial district, the stalker spotted Gavin Littel at last. The time had gotten past nine o'clock. The stalker knew the time as well as anyone, having checked his watch every fifteen minutes for more than two hours. He'd come to the corner of Wall and Hanover Streets at seven o'clock because Littel worked late most nights, no point in freezing one's ass off any longer than necessary. Already the stalker's fingers were stiff and achy, his raincoat wet through. A few degrees colder and it could snow.

Gavin Littel walked out the grand front entrance of his office building and up the sidewalk. The stalker followed thirty paces behind. If he lost his target he'd just come back tomorrow and start again. He was eager to get on with things, but aborting the mission would be better than getting too close here and running the risk of raising suspicions. Littel worked as some kind of vice president in the bowels of Powers Bank. That much the stalker knew, but he didn't know precisely what the man did up in that tower all day. The means of employment didn't figure much into his calculations. He only guessed that Littel worked a job befitting his name. He wasn't an investment banker or a big-money trader. He didn't have the look. Button cuffs wouldn't cut it in that crowd and the tie didn't seem lush enough and the suit just didn't hang the same way as the ones on the guys who rushed in and out of limos all day long.

When Littel went down into the subway, the stalker had to close the gap. Fortunately, there were plenty of people down there, even past rush hour. The stalker hid in the crowd on the Number 3 subway platform and in a few minutes they were on the train heading in the direction of New Lots Avenue.

Littel paid the stalker no mind, stood there leaning against the pole in his raincoat and working the toggle on his Samsung with his good hand. The stalker grabbed the last seat and faded into it, unnoticed. Just another drone. But when Littel exited the station at Utica Avenue in Brooklyn, things got trickier. Many of the people getting out were Hasidic Jewish men dressed in black with black hats and side curls. Most of the rest were

African-Americans. The Hasids mostly headed west. Littel and the stalker headed east, two of only a few white guys in a stream of darker faces.

The stalker hung back again and had to allow Littel to turn off of Eastern Parkway onto Utica before wading after him into the larger crowd by the commercial strip. He spotted him again a quarter-block down, a man of medium height with a head of thick light brown hair cut conservatively. Littel's walk was measured and strong, even athletic, and you would only perceive a slightly unnatural swing in the shoulders if you were looking for it.

The stalker was in fact looking for it. That hitch affirmed that he had the right man.

Littel went into a pub near the corner of Utica and Prospect Place. Through the window, the stalker watched him hang his raincoat on a peg and take one of two open seats at the bar. The rest of the place appeared to be three-quarters full, which was perfect, so the stalker went inside and slid into the banquette by a table for two. Speaking in a pronounced New York accent, Littel ordered tap beer and some food. In more neutral inflections, the stalker did the same, but would nurse his beer, only taking enough sips to keep up appearances. Littel watched the Knicks game on the television over the bar and chatted occasionally with the bartender. The stalker ate a cheeseburger and fries while he watched Littel's back.

After a while, Littel shed his suit jacket. He wore a long-sleeved shirt, but without the jacket the stalker got a better look at Littel's prosthetic right hand. He watched carefully now as Littel employed it almost like a real hand, holding a fork with it, even using it to lift his beer. The fingers moved individually and with great precision, all things considered. This confirmed that Littel still used a myoelectric externally powered prosthesis. It would have a six-volt battery inside and electronics that read muscle signals like a miniature nodule of artificial nerves. When Littel lifted his arm to wave for a third beer, his sleeve rode down, exposing more of the prosthetic arm, and the stalker let out a sigh of relief.

Given the expense and rarity, myoelectric prostheses were no picnic to steal. It had taken the stalker several months to find enough parts to replicate one just like Littel's, and it was a relief that his target hadn't changed equipment in the meantime. The stalker studied the artificial arm from across the room. It was a showy variety, styled more to stand out than to blend in—more cyborg than imitation flesh. Indeed the outer casing consisted of discernible parts rather than unified artificial skin.

The stalker smiled to himself. This construction played in his favor when replicating the prosthesis, as a casing with seams would reveal less tampering. In a short while, just to be sure, the stalker planned to get an even better look at it.

Around 11:15, the Knicks concluded their defeat at the hands of the Jazz and Littel finally got up to go. He'd drunk quite heavily and now appeared unsteady on his feet. He struggled to crawl back inside his jacket and raincoat, declining help from the bartender.

The stalker, whose name was Warren Manis, appeared to look on impassively, but inside he felt delighted. A drunk target made his job much easier. He paid the waitress in cash and followed Littel from the pub.

Littel stumbled along the sidewalk for one block and turned left onto St. Mark's Avenue. His row house had two stories and a basement. Behind a low wrought-iron fence, the empty poured concrete front yard measured six by eight. A red aluminum canopy covered part of the stoop closest to the door, and someone—Littel himself?—had painted the roof cornice red to match. Most important, a row of trash bins hid but did not block the door to the basement, accessible under the stoop. Littel himself used the main front door, and Manis watched him disappear inside.

Manis knew that Littel lived alone, his ex-wife having moved out several years ago. He knew that he slept on the top floor and that he never used the burglar alarm and that a series of night-lights cast a faint blue-green hue over every room in the house. He had been there before when the house was empty, but he needed to visit now when Manis was at home, in order to see the arm in person, touch it, measure it, download the software, get the replica just right. And to do so with the greatest margin of safety he had to make sure that Littel had come home alone. Any visitors—and most especially a light-sleeping date—would create complications that Manis didn't need.

Now he walked around the block, waiting for Littel to settle in. Though puddles remained in the street, the dampness of the evening had lifted, and a crescent moon hung over Brooklyn to the east.

At half past midnight, Manis returned to the row house. With no one about, he stepped over the low wrought-iron fence and went immediately to the basement door. Mechanically inclined, he faced no challenge with the simple lock, using a tool he'd specially crafted to jimmy it. He removed his shoes inside the basement door and proceeded toward the upstairs bedroom, pausing to listen patiently after every few steps.

Manis found Littel passed out in bed, his head at an angle that suggested drunken sleep. He was snoring loudly with his good arm extended across the queen-size bed. The prosthesis was not in the bedroom, so Manis walked gingerly to the bathroom down the hall, where he found the arm lying atop a clean towel on a shelf.

This was perfect—just perfect. He wouldn't even need to risk using a flash.

Manis closed the bathroom door and took a tape measure from his coat pocket. He extended it eighteen inches and laid it parallel to the arm on the table, then snapped a series of pictures, making sure to get all sides and every angle.

By one o'clock he had gone and Littel still lay sleeping, none the wiser.

**TICK, TICK, TICK, TICK, TICK, TICK,
TICK, TICK, TICK, TICK, TICK, TICK**

3.

DAY TWO: LIGHT

ATOP THE PUTTY-COLORED FILING CABINETS IN Lieutenant Capobianco's office stood a collection of framed pictures: his wife, his parents, his daughter at various ages, as well as pictures from his time on the force, the earliest one showing him on the street as a beat cop and the latest at a ceremony in the Chief of Detectives' office when he took the reins of the Bomb Squad. There were piles of paper and manila files everywhere, but the tops of these cabinets seemed to be the boss's one sacred space.

Diaz found it odd, getting called into this office by Kahn instead of Cap. He waited for the sergeant to close the door before taking one of two battered guest chairs. Kahn must've felt funny, too, as he didn't go near the back of the desk. Instead, he pulled the other guest chair sideways and faced Diaz from there.

"The lieutenant asked me to speak with you." Kahn took a deep breath. "About your behavior yesterday in front of the cathedral. I told you I was going to have to put it in the report."

"And the lieutenant read it?"

Kahn shook his head. "He's sick as a dog. I don't think he's reading many reports just now. For the Times Square thing, yes, but not for false alarms."

"So how's he know what went down?"

"I had to tell him."

Diaz crossed his legs. "Thanks. Thanks a lot."

"You knew I'd have to."

"No way. You said you'd have to put it in the report. I got that part."

"Well, you can't act out of turn like that and expect a superior officer not to say something. What if you did it again and weren't so lucky, got yourself blown up? Hell, got someone else blown up?"

Diaz nodded. "I get it. You're covering your ass. Don't expect me to be pleased about it."

"It's got nothing to do with pleasing you, Manny. It's got to do with your behavior. You can't go around doing shit like that. I explained it to you yesterday."

"You explained it yesterday. So why are we here in Cap's office with the door closed?"

"Because you're being issued a reprimand."

Diaz rocked his free foot in silence.

"A letter will be put in your file."

"Great. Who's applying the reprimand—you been deputized?"

"Not exactly. The lieutenant will do it when he gets back, but he wanted you to be aware ASAP so it doesn't happen again."

"To protect yourselves."

"To protect the public!" Kahn tented his fingers. "Look, Diaz, you know what they say about every new bomb tech in the first twenty-four months: a danger to himself and others. It's our own version of a little bit of knowledge can be dangerous."

"I ain't some rube, Kahn. I got more than a little bit of knowledge. I've disarmed more IEDs than..." Diaz caught himself, swallowed.

Kahn dropped his hands to his thighs. "Than I have. That what you were going to say?"

"Than anybody here, probably." Diaz gathered himself. "I don't mean it as disrespect. I know this is a different theater than a war zone. Just saying I'm not all green, Sergeant."

"Then stop acting green!" Kahn had raised his voice. He shook his head and lowered his tone. "I'm still rooting for you, Manny. I'm on your side. I know it doesn't always look that way."

Diaz nodded, chewed the inside of his lower lip, thinking this was a time to keep his mouth shut for once.

Kahn, seeing he had nothing to add, stood up and put a hand on the doorknob. "We done here? We square?"

"Yes, sir."

"Let's go, then. We got a crime to solve."

AES OPERATED OUT OF A couple of rooms on the fourth floor of the PSA 4 building on the corner of Avenue C and East Eighth Street. It was a surprisingly modern structure—much more modern than the Third Precinct building that the Bomb Squad shared. Where the Third had a cramped and dark entrance, PSA 4 headquarters featured an atrium with natural light, and the halls were more antiseptic than at the Third, lacking the character that a patina of decades-old dirt could impart to a place. In addition to all that, the people who worked there were different. The Housing cops—who worked *in* the NYPD but were not *of* it—gave the building downstairs an altogether different vibe.

Diaz himself had entered the building only a few times, always to visit one of the AES detectives. He never failed to feel like a trespasser in there. But Brian O'Shea certainly didn't feel that way. He had his office in the building, of course, but there was more to it than that. O'Shea was the kind of person who seemed at home in whatever space he occupied. He was the kind of guy who walked out of a rumble in an alley with a bloody lip but a smile on his face. The kind of guy who didn't bother asking to pet your dog and in minutes had it doing tricks that you'd never taught it. He was the kind of guy who always had his feet up and always wore a placid expression.

"Like some joe?" he said, working the plastic stirrer around in the Styrofoam cup on his desk.

Diaz and Kahn shook their heads in unison.

"Can't blame you. Why doesn't the powdered milk ever fully melt—floats on top like toxic residue." He sipped it anyway, smiled. "Burbette ain't coming. Says he's got other stuff to do, but I think he just wants to give us some room."

"Generally his style," Kahn said. "At least until they start giving out medals or until you screw it up. Then the FBI rides to the rescue."

"On whose horse?" O'Shea laughed. While Diaz and Kahn settled in, he lowered his feet to the floor, opened a file on his desk, and plucked a pen from the suit jacket that hung over his chair.

He was tall and lanky with red hair cut close, light skin and blond eyebrows that almost disappeared over his blue eyes. Diaz thought a clerical collar would become him, and O'Shea had in fact attended Jesuit seminary in his youth. But in the end he'd opted for the family business, following his father, his grandfather, his uncles, and his older brother and sister onto the police force. No pressure, just couldn't help himself. Old school.

"I've looked at the pictures," he said, "and read the preliminary coroner's report. What'd you guys scrape up yesterday?"

"Pieces of what appeared to be both of the suspect's prosthetic legs. The crimp and two partial leg wires, and possible remnants of what looks like a pretty small device. Not much hardware in the vicinity of the seat."

"They dug a bunch of ball bearings out of the guy's abdomen, though. Really cut him to ribbons inside."

"Maybe the bomb maker didn't want him to survive and testify."

"Overkill, though."

"Or he strapped it on wrong."

"That's possible." O'Shea looked into the middle space. "Not a vest. It must've been low in his pants, to judge by the pattern. It slips down further, he tries to adjust it, maybe it flips sideways when he does so and the direction of charge misses its mark."

"Could've slipped down right in front of the recruiting center," Kahn added. "Explains why maybe he set it off prematurely. Accidental detonation when he grabbed for it."

"Wait a second," Diaz interrupted. Kahn had told him to keep a low profile for this meeting, being the junior detective. But Diaz couldn't help but wonder at this train of thought. "There was some evidence of heat on some of the artificial leg parts that we found. We also found cell phone parts."

"You mean in addition to the intact phone in evidence?" O'Shea said.

Diaz nodded. "This other cell phone took it on the chin—pulverized."

"Maybe the guy carried two, and bigger pieces just flew farther than the perimeter you marked off."

Kahn shrugged. "Could happen."

"Bullshit," Diaz said. "The cell phone was part of the bomb."

"How do you know? We didn't find a SIM card."

"SIM card maybe got reduced to dust with the rest of it. Only happens if it's in close proximity to the main charge."

"Burbette couldn't get an explosive identification reading at the scene," Kahn said. "Rain washed away the residue, it seems."

"Raining that hard?" O'Shea asked.

"It was what your people would call a soft day," said Kahn with a grin. "Gets wetter than it lets on."

"Kinda like most Irish girls." O'Shea laughed.

"Forgot to mention," Kahn said, "we had better luck with the swab. Turned up C4 in the lab, not powder."

"C4?"

Kahn hadn't yet shared this with Diaz, but the junior detective nodded like he knew anyway. "Explains some witness reports of black smoke, though some others had it white."

"And still such a small charge…" Kahn wondered. "Maybe it was homemade stuff."

"Yeah, right," O'Shea said. "Your guys didn't find a lab at his house—clean as a whistle, in fact."

"Maybe he had a secret place."

"That shit's near impossible to make in the kitchen and you know it."

"Just thinking aloud."

"Maybe—damn." O'Shea bit his lip. "Not good if it's C4."

"Was there a taggant?" Diaz asked

"FBI crime lab's running that one down."

"So what do you figure so far?"

O'Shea sat back. "Incompetence possibly exacerbated by panic. Not a major terrorist-type operation. Maybe a gripe."

"Against the army?" Kahn asked.

"Sure. Could be. Or an individual in the recruiting center."

"You interview anyone there yet?"

"Only preliminarily. I'll go back today."

"And?"

"No one knew him there."

"When did he get out?"

O'Shea consulted his file. "Four years ago. Spent nearly two years rehabbing in Texas. Honorable discharge."

"So...a grudge for the lost legs. But the guy's working, holding down a job, getting around. Why do this now?"

"I'll hit the sister and the employer today. Maybe they have some insight into what set him off."

"You think there are others?"

"I doubt it. No evidence of coordinated attacks. No claim of responsibility. Incompetent bomb maker."

Diaz hated where this was going. They couldn't be right about Horn. Angry about losing the legs, how the army treated the guy...maybe he could accept that. But his gut told him this didn't add up. "Not that incompetent," he muttered. "The thing went off, didn't it?"

"Yeah. In his nuts. I don't want to sell it short, but it feels like a lone act to me. I'm guessing depressed, maybe a touch of PTSD. Cry of pain. Albert Horn wanted to go out with a bang."

"He got his wish," Kahn said.

"Aw, that's just stupid," Diaz finally blurted.

O'Shea looked a little startled.

Diaz struggled to tone himself down. "Did the guy leave a note?"

"Not that we know of."

"So what makes it suicide?"

Kahn sat up, red-faced. "Were you out on the street with me last night, Diaz?"

Diaz ignored the sarcasm. "I'm not buying it. What type of unit did this guy serve in?"

O'Shea consulted his folder. "Cavalry regiment."

"Not engineers? Nothing like that?"

O'Shea shook his head.

"So he had no access to C4, probably wasn't even close enough to steal any ever."

"He might've acquired some on the black market."

"The guy's working for—what?—a bible publisher? And he's on the black market for plastic explosives in his spare time?"

"Could be the bible thing was his cover."

"But you said yourself he ain't no terrorist."

"I said he might not be one."

"So, let me get this straight." Diaz knitted his brow. "Probable suicide bomber, acting alone, manufactures a bomb with an apparent directional charge. Even though he wants to make a statement, he doesn't make one, and he limits the damage to himself. Plus, even though he can build a bomb with a directional charge, he's incompetent."

O'Shea's face looked as placid as ever, but his eyes hardened. "Cool down, Diaz. We're just working on theories here. The charge may've been meant for someone else—I give you that. Maybe he planned to dance on someone's desk in that recruiting office before pressing the button."

"No one found—"

O'Shea talked over Diaz. "But I still say Horn easily could've set the thing off by accident. Happened on a regular basis in the early days of the Troubles in Northern Ireland. The RUC called them 'own goals'"

"Thanks for the history lesson," Diaz snapped.

O'Shea ignored him. "You guys find any kind of switch with which he might've initiated the charge?"

"No," Kahn said, confirming what Diaz had been about to say. "We would've told you."

"The cell phone," Diaz said, "and maybe it was remote detonation."

"Maybe," O'Shea said. "Either way, I think we've accomplished everything we can sitting in this room. I'll loop you guys in when I got more. I presume you'll do the same."

They sat there for a minute, frowning at one another, not a great feeling in the room. Then O'Shea grinned at Diaz and cocked his head. "With respect, you could lighten up a little, pal. This looks like a high-profile situation right now. I already got two calls from my boss. It won't be your ass on the line if I get this wrong."

Diaz took a breath. "No disrespect intended by me, either, Brian. But instead of your ass or Kahn's here, if this isn't suicide I hope there ain't someone else who's got his ass on the line."

"Like who?"

"Someone out there. Someone we don't yet know about."

O'Shea closed his file folder. "We always hope for the best, soldier."

"YOU DIDN'T TELL ME IT was C4," Diaz said from behind the wheel of the squad car.

Kahn didn't look at him. "I found out right before we left for the meeting. Wanted to see how you guys reacted to that news side by side."

"Side by side. Me and the guy who's *hoping* it turns out all right," Diaz mocked. He knew that wasn't the real reason Kahn had held back. It was punishment for the cathedral thing. "He hopes it turns out all right," he repeated for emphasis. "And I'm the one who's a danger to others. Since when is hope an investigative strategy?"

Kahn looked unhappy. "Brian's a good guy. You seemed pleased that he was on the case when I told you yesterday."

"That was before you and him started railroading this suspect."

"He's not railroading anybody. We're just testing out theories."

"It's not him. How about that theory? He's a victim."

"Why do you think so?"

"The cell phone—"

"Yeah, you mentioned that, like, six times. Did anyone find an SCR tied to the cell phone? No. So why's that any more convincing than the obvious? We know for a fact that the guy had a bomb on him and that the bomb went off. The most plausible explanation so far is that he blew himself up."

"You ever serve in the army, Sandy?"

"Here we go again." Kahn rolled his eyes. "As a matter of fact, no. I served in the marines."

"That so?"

"Does the pope wear a funny hat?"

"You see combat?"

"No. So I guess I'm a pussy."

Diaz nodded silently.

"No disrespect to your prior accomplishments, Manny, but having seen combat doesn't give you the right to run wild or jump rank or put your damned pet theories ahead of someone else's."

"I didn't say it should."

"And furthermore, your attitude sucked in there. Did I not ask you to keep it cool and let the man do his job? Now O'Shea's gonna have a hard-on against you, which means he won't be so happy seeing me coming either. How will that help the investigation? How much trouble do you need to stir up in one week?"

Diaz sat brooding.

"We're not even twelve hours into this investigation and you've prejudiced yourself by defending this guy Horn in an unwarranted fashion. Why? Because you both served in combat? Maybe you don't belong anywhere near this case, Diaz."

"You got it backwards."

When Diaz hesitated at the changing light, a dump truck rumbled by, drowning out all thoughts and belching a cloud of choking black exhaust for good measure.

Kahn absently watched the truck go past, stared a moment at Diaz, and then turned his attention out the window. "This one time when I was in homicide, I had a case where we got called to a crime scene in Brooklyn. Bensonhurst. You probably know that's a solidly Italian neighborhood, but the guy who got stabbed to death in his sleep was a Jewish guy. I saw pictures of him on the piano and he reminded me of my dad, who was then still alive. There was no wife. The son—seventeen years old—reminded me of myself at that age. He had a Camaro on the street that didn't have a mark on it...kept it so immaculate. My partner says the kid cleaned it for traces after murdering the father—quarter million in life insurance on the line, plus the house. I'm like, *No way.* I *know* this kind of kid. He cherishes that damn car is all, saved every penny he had to buy it, begged his father to help him out, took great pride in that machine, always under the hood, adding pieces of after-market equipment every chance he got. That's what I'd done with my Mustang. I knew exactly what it meant to be that kid."

"I still have my legs," Diaz said.

"Okay. Let me finish." Kahn licked his lips and frowned. "Everything pointed to the kid. Motive, means, opportunity. There was a knife missing from the kitchen block. My partner wanted to home in while the kid was soft, nail him before he could re-gather his wits. Me—I felt sorry for the little bastard. Not because he deserved my sympathy but because I could relate to the pain he must be going through."

"Sure, but—"

"And another thing. Here's this Jewish family living in this Italian neighborhood. The kid kills the father for the money? *The money?* No. I couldn't handle that. Because when you're the only Jewish family on the block you stand in for the whole Jewish race. I didn't say this even to myself at the time, but it was back there in a corner of my mind. I was rooting for the kid not to have done it."

"But he did."

Kahn smiled sardonically. "All that cleaning stuff he had for the car—carpet shampoo and whatnot—he used it to make the house spotless before calling for help. Kid did a helluva job, too, would've made his grandmother proud. Not a trace of evidence in the house and to this day I don't know where the knife went. But we found the bloody sponges and chamois a mile away, in a dumpster near a park where the kid used to hang out. My partner broke the case, not me."

"So based upon that story, I'm protecting Horn as a fellow vet and I'm wrong?"

"Don't be an asshole, Diaz. O'Shea's job—and ours—is hard enough without taking sniper fire from your nearest colleague."

Diaz reflected. He understood the story well enough, but as for sniper fire he felt more like the victim of that than the perpetrator. Hadn't he received news of a reprimand via Kahn just this morning? Evidence conveniently not shared with him? And now here was Kahn again riding him for speaking out of turn, emphasizing the pecking order as much as their search for truth.

He planned to keep the story in the back of his mind—always worth learning something and maybe it gave a glimpse into where some of the land mines were planted around Kahn. His own instincts...sure, maybe he related to a vet, didn't want him to be a bad guy. But that didn't mean he'd ignore the man's guilt if someone could prove it.

For the rest, all Diaz could think was how he couldn't catch a break from the sergeant, and yet he had to ride around with him almost every day.

When the phone rang at his desk and Kahn heard it was Burbette of FBI, he considered whether to bring Diaz into the conversation. Diaz had just returned from a false alarm and was somewhere in the building, according to the in-out board. He might be in the john or in the garage or in the break room. He wasn't in the main squad room at the moment, and Kahn decided not to bother.

Check that. Kahn decided he didn't need the added stress of having Diaz on the call, especially when Burbette suggested that they conference in O'Shea, so the Fed wouldn't have to say everything twice. O'Shea was riding in a car on the way to an interview.

"Everyone hear me okay?" Burbette asked.

"Yeah," Kahn said.

"Roger," said O'Shea.

"As you guys know," Burbette said, "the ETK at the scene didn't show anything definitive, but the swab that NYPD took from the crater tested positive for RDX. I just got the results from the taggant trace and it's interesting, to say the least. It's military."

"Confirms our hunch," O'Shea said.

"What hunch is that?"

"Well, just with the guy being a vet that it's a possible self-inflict."

Burbette paused. "Not exactly an earth-shattering deduction, considering the results on the sidewalk."

"Course not. All the same, it's something."

Kahn wondered why he was the only guy not riding O'Shea hard these days. Maybe because he was the only one not having his stones busted by someone from above, Cap being out of commission, too sick even to phone in regularly. With the luxury of space, Kahn thought maybe to give O'Shea a bit of a rescue. "Brian, didn't you determine that Horn was infantry?"

"Roger. Cavalry, actually. Same thing for our purposes, I guess."

"Can you confirm that, Don?"

"Yes, I can. Eighth Regiment. No obvious reason this guy would've had access to plastic, but you never know. I'm gonna try to run that down. Also I'll see whether the taggant can be traced more narrowly to a particular base or a particular service. That'll take awhile. In fact, it could take forever. But I'm on it. What else you got?"

"Bomb parts and body parts," Kahn said. "Minimal shrapnel and some fragments of a cell phone. Also, of course, scraps of the suspect's artificial legs."

"Enough for CSU to reconstruct them?"

"I doubt it. Not completely, anyway."

"Horn was employed." O'Shea jumped in. "Worked just a few blocks away. His boss says his normal commute from work wouldn't take him past the recruitment center. Usually walks a different way to the subway. Plus, it wasn't quitting time. Apparently, he was on his way to the theater, courtesy of his employer. Boss says he was distraught and needed a break. CSU found a pair of *Spider-Man* tickets in his shirt pocket, confirming. He was just a block away from there when the bomb went off."

"Phone records?"

"Not yet. But I got his cell phone out of evidence and the lab made it work. Turned out the battery contacts were just jogged loose. I checked the recents. He seems to be a light user. Last one he called was his sister, not long before he blew himself up."

"You interview her yet?"

"Just a few words over the phone. She's pretty broken up. I have an appointment in a couple of hours."

"I sent an EDC team out there yesterday," Kahn said. "The canine alerted in a few spots in the suspect's apartment, but the sweeper didn't find anything. He must've had the bomb in there, but he didn't build it there."

"So where'd he build it?"

"Good question."

"Maybe someone else built it."

"Well, *someone else* somewhere else—or *him* somewhere else. It may be a crazy world, but I've yet to see a bomb that constructed itself."

* * *

AN HOUR OR TWO LATER, O'Shea called Kahn while he and Diaz sat over pizza on Hudson Street. Kahn had a plain slice and Diaz was tucking into a slice with ricotta, vegetables and sausage.

"How do you eat something like that?" Kahn said.

"I put it in my mouth and chew."

"I mean, it's so heavy. Doesn't it make you feel bloated?"

"What am I, a woman at her time of the month?"

"Ah, youth. You going for the tiramisu for dessert?"

"You tell me how to do procedure, you tell me how to drive, you tell me what to say...now you're gonna tell me what to eat?"

Kahn laughed until his phone rang. When he heard it was O'Shea, he put it on speaker.

"So we tracked down the serial number from that prosthetic," O'Shea said. "It was manufactured by Prosthetic and Sensory Aids Services—part of the Department of Veterans Affairs. Appears to be legit."

"Is it possible someone snuck a bomb in there during the manufacturing process?"

"These things are made one hundred percent in the States, I think. I'll have to get with Burbette, see if FBI can send some agents to poke around the factory—or however that works."

"They should take an EDC team."

"Burbette will know that."

"So we think the bomb was in the leg?"

"That one or the other one. Where else? No evidence he was carrying anything."

"They found the theater tickets, right?" Diaz asked. Kahn had given him a fill on the conversation he'd missed.

"Yeah, they found 'em," O'Shea confirmed. "In his shirt pocket. Why?"

"Just wondering whether his boss's story holds up."

"It does. I was there again today. Any theories on how much C4 this would've required?"

Kahn looked at Diaz, who frowned in thought for a second, then said, "Not much. Half a pound more or less would've done the trick."

"So it's plausible that he had the device hidden in one of the legs?"

"Yes it is."

"Well, I'll be damned. At least, maybe, the guy didn't lack for imagination."

Diaz walked to the station at Christopher Street and Seventh Avenue to catch the Number 1 Train. There was a newsstand there and he noted that tabloid headlines had already moved on from the Times Square bomber to the trumped-up adventures of reality-show celebrities. He bought a Snickers bar and slipped it like contraband into the side pocket of his coat.

The station platform smelled vaguely of urine, always a mystery to Diaz how someone could find the appropriate moment to do that in a place that he'd never seen empty at any hour. Maybe it wasn't a human source. Maybe it was from the accumulated droppings of a million rats.

Having grossed himself out, he decided to consume his snack on the train and not before.

Diaz yawned while trying not to breathe too deeply. The day had been filled with running around, two sweeps, two false alarms, lunch with Kahn. Since the sergeant had chosen to fill him in on the conversation he'd missed with O'Shea and Burbette, Diaz figured maybe he'd begun working his way out of the doghouse. Wanting badly to make a positive contribution, he got back to thinking about the case.

Usually, as every detective knew, the most direct explanation of events was the most likely. If you were carrying a bomb, for example, there was a pretty good chance that you knew you were carrying it. They called them suicide bombers because someone with an IED strapped to his chest didn't expect to report back to the safe house. Yet, as every detective also knew, sometimes things out of the ordinary did happen. Betting on the odds wasn't the same as finding the truth.

In the Horn case a couple of things didn't add up so far. Say the suspect makes up an excuse for leaving the office early. That puts him in control of the timing, for one thing, no matter whether he planned it weeks in advance or made a decision ten minutes ago. And if he's on the verge of blowing himself up, how much of an excuse does he need with the boss? He's not in a jail at 1440 Broadway. He can walk out whenever he wants. A suicide isn't going to worry about getting his next paycheck docked for skipping work.

Plus, it didn't go down that way, from what Horn's boss had said. Supposedly he'd offered Horn the tickets at the last minute, claimed in fact to have pushed them on him. This could mean that the boss was involved, but why make up that whole story? Again, why not just have Horn walk out the door, down to the recruiting station and press the button? So Diaz couldn't help but presume that Albert Horn didn't know beforehand that he was minutes away from blowing himself to smithereens.

Of course, he might've been awaiting inspiration, and just when he looked up and saw the recruiting station, inspiration struck. It seemed to Diaz a strange way to go about things, though, to carry around a concealed bomb, awaiting a moment of opportunity, and then blow yourself up in futility out on the sidewalk with no good target in proximity. It could be that O'Shea was right—and maybe the simplest explanation was that an accident occurred while carrying the bomb in the direction of the recruiting station. But, still, it bugged Diaz to think that here's the recruiting station a couple of blocks from Horn's office all the while, yet he waits for the moment when his boss gives him a pair of tickets to *Spider-Man* before executing his plan. People weren't always rational, but this just seemed too screwy to Diaz.

Now, on the rocking train, he unwrapped his Snickers bar and his mouth watered at the smell of the chocolate. He bit into it, chewing slowly.

What if Horn was being chased? Diaz thought. Perhaps the boss set him up by sending him on an errand to the theater with someone on his tail. Horn saw his pursuer and feared him, so he triggered the explosion out on the sidewalk rather than allow himself to be taken.

Right. Diaz rolled his eyes to himself. The guy was in the middle of a John le Carré novel. He blew himself up to avoid getting stabbed by the poison umbrella.

Diaz shook that thought from his head and tried to think where the core of this case truly lay. Set aside the locale—which wasn't all that unusual, federal installations being natural targets for terrorists—and concentrate on the unique aspect of this thing, which was the artificial legs.

Just before he'd left the station house, Kahn told Diaz that CSU had reported some more information. What they could piece together from the legs, they said, showed one with more burn marks than the other.

Diaz thought of the serial number that he'd found. It made sense for the manufacturer to have put a serial number on every device, for the same reason manufacturers slapped serial numbers on so many things. But Albert Horn had two prosthetic legs and they'd so far discovered only one remnant with a serial number on it.

That left three possibilities. Either the piece with the second serial number had been obliterated. Or despite their best efforts they'd failed to find the part out on the street. Or the part of the leg where you'd normally find the serial number had been tampered with to the extent that the serial number wasn't on that leg at all by the time Albert Horn passed in front of the recruiting station.

Therefore the most obvious explanation was that the leg without the serial number contained the bomb. And—though CSU hadn't said so—Diaz was willing to bet that the parts with the most damage came from the leg without the serial number. If he could confirm that, he'd be far from knowing everything, but he'd know something. He'd know for sure which of two legs carried the bomb. And that would be a start.

TICK, TICK, TICK, TICK, TICK, TICK,
TICK, TICK, TICK, TICK, TICK

4.

DAY TWO: DARK

AT SIX O'CLOCK IN THE EVENING, Brian O'Shea and Detective Second Grade Adeela Payne pulled up in front of a small, detached cottage on 210th Place in Hollis, Queens. It was a solid middle class neighborhood of well-kept houses, modest street trees and patches of lawn—winter brown in the cold—which were adorned most commonly with only a bush or two near the foundation.

O'Shea had recruited Payne to join him for reasons that under other circumstances might be classified as discriminatory. Even presuming that Albert Horn's family would view the proceeding as friendly, O'Shea figured, the sight of a freckled redhead cop and, say, another straight-laced white guy in a suit might not yield maximum cooperation. A black woman detective, on the other hand, in this neighborhood would likely tease out higher quality interaction.

You never advertised this kind of thinking, of course, but it was a given in the department. For a case with a Haitian angle, you solicited a Haitian cop for help when possible. When you were dealing with religious Jews, you grabbed a guy who was a member of that tribe. You didn't have to explain why to your colleague. Everyone just got it. In fact, not long ago Payne had invited O'Shea into an arson investigation involving a group of Irish immigrants. Like attracted like. It wasn't racism, just the way of the world, the path of least resistance in support of the common good. Cases got assigned at random, but within reason the lead detective could then pull in whatever help he needed. Their choice wasn't always ethnically motivated, but race or ethnicity could be a factor in the calculations more times than they'd generally like to admit.

Kyle Butterworth, the brother-in-law, greeted the detectives in a white t-shirt and baggy jeans. He lingered a few beats too long behind the storm door before pulling it open, O'Shea thought. With only peremptory words, Butterworth escorted them several feet into a modest living room filled with upholstered furniture too large for the space and dominated on one wall by a giant flat-screen television. They had the local Fox News station playing, but the daughter, upon seeing the cops, used the remote to turn it off. She looked angry as only a teenager could, in a way that seemed to reduce someone else's misfortune to little more than a matter of her own embarrassment or inconvenience.

Albert Horn's sister, Lydia, on the other hand, appeared genuinely distraught. Wearing office clothes, she didn't seem to be crying just then, but she held a fistful of tissues as big as a baseball and dabbed her rheumy eyes a moment after shaking hands with the detectives, as if shielding herself from the reality in front of her. She had the look of a trapped animal about to be pounced upon by predators, like she was working every minute to hold her viscera inside.

"We're sorry for your loss," O'Shea began, making a point of directing his attention to all three people when he said it.

Butterworth, a muffin top hanging over his belt, rested his butt on the armrest beside his wife, who sat on the couch. Their daughter, introduced as Shawna, occupied a reclining chair off to one side.

O'Shea, by prior arrangement, allowed Payne to take the lead. "Would it be okay if we sat?" she asked.

Lydia said sure, but there were only two spaces—the cushion next to her and an open chair. Payne, much to O'Shea's relief, sat right next to Lydia. He took the other spot and did his best to blend into the background, just observing.

"We realize," Payne began, "that this is a tragedy for everyone involved."

"When are they gonna give us back Al's body?" Butterworth asked.

Payne made brief eye contact with O'Shea. "We don't have control of that, exactly, but we'll look into it for you."

"Thank you," Lydia said. "We'd like to bury him soon." She wiped her nose and dabbed her eyes.

"That's understandable," Payne said. "I have to get one thing out of the way. I have to ask about all of your whereabouts yesterday."

They found out soon enough that Shawna had been in school all day, Butterworth had been at work, and so had Lydia.

"We were on the phone together, though," she said. "Me and Al." She related their conversation, his feelings of discomfort the past month or so, his alienation from work. "Then it just cut off." She gasped.

"Did he say he had to go?"

"No. He was, like, in mid-sentence. I thought the call had just dropped."

Payne looked at O'Shea, sharing a thought across the middle space. No cry of "Allahu Akbar" on this one.

"So he was feeling upset when you spoke, but he didn't mention anything about hurting himself or others before the phone cut off? Can you tell us anything else about your brother's state of mind recently?"

"Grumpy," Butterworth interrupted. "Not himself. Didn't want to talk much."

"Was he usually more talkative?"

"Not really," Butterworth conceded.

"I'd say he was down," Lydia said, "maybe even depressed. He told me he was getting flashbacks from combat."

"Was he acting out, doing anything to suggest violence?"

"No, ma'am. He was fundamentally a gentle sort. I know that seems strange to say—"

"Don't worry about how it seems."

"You'd think someone who joins the army would have a more accepting attitude toward violence, is all I mean. Al didn't. He hated it."

"Never would talk about the army, not to me," Butterworth said.

"Did he have friends?" asked Payne.

"Not many," Lydia said.

"Any new ones recently? Anyone suspicious or who might give you concern?"

"You mean who would've sought to do him harm?"

"That or who might have held a grudge against the government of some kind."

"Terrorists?"

Payne nodded. "Maybe."

"Uncle Al a terrorist!" Shawna exclaimed. "This shit is just crazy."

Lydia paused for a minute to hush her daughter with a look. She returned her attention to Payne. "I could understand why you'd ask that, but no, there was no one."

"Did he receive any packages recently?"

"Not that I know of."

"Okay." Payne placed her hands on her knees. "Do you mind if we look around the house?"

Butterworth stood. "They came through yesterday with the dog."

"We're not looking for explosives. Just for clues to why he might've—to why this might've happened to him."

"Suit yourself," Lydia said. "We got nothing to hide." She folded forward and began quietly weeping.

"Don't mess anything up," Butterworth said. "You can see that we keep a neat house."

Payne stood up and O'Shea followed her lead. In the doorway to the kitchen, however, he stepped ahead, putting her between himself and Butterworth. Payne understood the signal. She stopped in her tracks so that Butterworth nearly bumped into her.

"If you don't mind, Mr. Butterworth, we find it's best if the people living in the home don't follow us around. If we got a warrant, that's how we'd do it. And with your consent we'd like to proceed the same way, being as respectful as possible with your things, of course."

Butterworth hesitated, but just for a moment. "Okay," he said, and retreated back to the living room. He looked uncomfortable but not nervous. O'Shea didn't think he had much to hide, maybe a hash pipe or the footprints to a few porn websites.

They began in the attic and worked their way down, not finding anything pertaining to Horn at all. Half an hour later, they returned to the living room and asked to see his apartment. The family had the television back on.

"It has a separate entrance," Lydia said. "Outside. But there's a door through the kitchen." She went and opened it for them, but didn't follow.

Inside they found two rooms and a bathroom. The curtains were drawn and the place smelled musty. Only a handful of outfits hung in the clothes closet. The bookshelf featured mostly self-improvement books, easy paths to wealth and happiness, that sort of thing. O'Shea pulled out three books at a time to look behind, but found nothing. A montage of family photos hung on a wall, everyone smiling.

"He was a good looking guy in his youth," Payne said.

"His youth?" said O'Shea. "The man didn't make it out of his thirties, poor S.O.B."

On the night table rested a bottle of Ambien, and in the space below stood three flask-shaped bottles of peach brandy, one half empty.

"Brandy and sleeping pills. Heckuva combination," O'Shea said.

On a wall to the side of the bed hung a frame with four medals. O'Shea recognized two: the Purple Heart and the bronze star. The Purple Heart—okay, you could get that for a scratch, though of course Horn had suffered much worse. But the bronze star didn't get bestowed upon a man who merely went along to get along. This man had performed an act of serious bravery at some point.

O'Shea thought of the conversation with Diaz this morning. These guys who'd once laid it all out there for their country were a different breed, he thought, different even than patriotic law enforcement types such as himself. He should have greater sensitivity to where Diaz was coming from, even while allowing the possibility that the bomb tech could be wrong. After all, even a war hero could lose his oars, maybe especially a war hero, coming back to loneliness, reminded every day that he'd given his legs for a country whose main act of collective sacrifice had been to go shopping. Being a combat vet didn't make you right, but maybe it earned you the kid gloves.

The bathroom had heavy chrome bars installed three feet up the wall, the only apparent concession in the apartment to Horn's disability. O'Shea pictured the vet dragging himself there without his legs attached. There was a soft chair near the other side of the bed. That's where, O'Shea was told, the EDC had pointed. He wondered whether Horn rested his prostheses there when he retired for the night.

Payne went through the dresser drawers. Among the clothing she found a blue butter-cookie tin filled with a few pictures from the army and held them up one by one as O'Shea snapped photos with his cell phone. The tin also contained an oak leaf cluster that Horn had never pinned to a medal ribbon and an old army ID. O'Shea remembered that Horn had had a VA card in his wallet.

In another drawer Payne found a few syringes. "Morphine," she said. "Pretty miserable life, I'd imagine."

"Pain...discomfort—yes. But if the guy was angry, there are no outward signs."

"There's a stain on the sidewalk in Times Square," she said.

They went to the side yard through the outside door. Making a move to close it, O'Shea noticed that the wood by the strike plate had a fresh splinter.

"Hmm. Could've been jimmied," he said. "And not long ago."

Payne lifted her dark eyes to meet O'Shea's. "Maybe he locked himself out recently."

"Yeah." O'Shea frowned. "That's a possibility."

THE CANDY HAD DONE NOTHING to improve Diaz's energy level, so he decided on a nap before dinner. He found Jennifer in the apartment, moving about. They exchanged a few pleasantries and he went to lie down, interlacing his fingers behind his head on top of the pillow. He stared up at the ceiling, thinking of Kahn and O'Shea and the Times Square case, but his eyes felt heavy and he drifted in and out of sleep, vaguely aware from time to time of Jennifer's movements on the other side of the door. He heard cabinets opening and closing, creaks on the floorboards, water flowing...

The water carried Diaz's mind to those puddles that formed on the coroner's tarp. He pictured Albert Horn in his winter coat, hobbling along the sidewalk on Broadway, turning onto Forty-Third Street. He saw him hesitate in front of the recruiting station. What went through the suspect's mind when he saw the sign on that building? Anger? Resentment? Or nothing you could put a finger on?

Although Diaz had spent most of his three tours in Iraq dismantling bombs, he'd also participated in a few firefights. He knew when the violence started that you were no longer fighting for abstract concepts like patriotism or freedom. You fought to save yourself and the soldiers in your unit, and maybe not even in that order, because the only thing worse than having to imagine your own end was feeling responsible when the other guy went home in a body bag. So maybe, thought Diaz, when Albert Horn returned to the States, despite all he gave for his country he carried that survivor's guilt.

A man might want to end his life. Diaz could see that. And maybe he didn't want to do so in a manner where his family would come home to find him. But a bomb on the street that might bring harm to innocent passersby? Didn't an American soldier always risk his own life rather than endanger a single innocent?

The ceiling had an old water stain, looked like a cloud formation to Diaz, or the smoky shadow of fireworks. He closed his eyes as a far-off sound rose in the back of his head, like a bee buzzing, growing closer. It was a tune…took awhile for him to recognize it…"America the Beautiful." A lyric that most people never reach drifted up to Diaz now:

O beautiful for heroes proved
In liberating strife,
Who more than self their country loved,
And mercy more than life.

Mercy. He fell back to sleep with the tune stuck in his head, the lyric repeating.

When he awoke, he didn't know whether he'd been asleep for two hours or two minutes. The bedroom window airshaft, ever cast in dirty darkness, didn't tell him anything. Still groggy with sleep, he stumbled to the bathroom, where the door stood ajar, and pushed in. Jennifer's hand caught the door before it hit her. She was standing in her underwear, topless, one breast flattened under the forearm that held the door, the other one right there in pink glory. The sight of it sent a shock through Diaz, clutched his throat.

"Jesus! Jennifer!"

"Excuse me," she said with nonchalance. She made no effort to cover herself at first. Then, seeing the look on her roommate's face, she snatched her bathrobe off the hook.

By the time she got it on he'd backed into the living room. She followed him.

"I'm finished in there."

"That's all you got to say?"

"I'm sorry. I thought you were asleep."

"I was lying down, doesn't mean I was out for the count. There are two people in this apartment."

"You could knock."

"The door was open."

"Just a little. I was almost done. Anyway, it's only a pair of tits, for God sake. Not World War Three."

"We're roommates, not lovers. I don't need that in my face."

"It was an accident. You don't have to be such a prude, either."

"Goddamn it!" He marched into his room, stepped into a pair of shoes and grabbed his coat.

"You're storming out in anger again? This is getting to be a bad hab—"

Before she could finish, Diaz had slammed the door.

ATTACHED TO HIS APARTMENT IN BROOKLYN, Warren Manis had a workshop that any machinist would envy. It consisted of a series of small windowless rooms in an old factory, the first of these containing a long lathe, a band-saw, a drill press, and a plastic fabricator, among other machines. In the second room, meticulously labeled bins lined a series of shelves, keeping the most obscure hardware easily at hand for Manis's every need. A thick wooden workbench dominated the back room, tools on an expansive pegboard arranged like a planogram, with the most-used within easiest reach and the least-used hanging farther away. Finally, a closed-circuit monitor rested on a shelf, covering each form of ingress and egress.

He'd salvaged all of it over several years, down to the high-backed cushioned stool he found in a restaurant's trash. That was the easiest to repair of all. It had only required a few screws and some fresh solder.

Manis lived visually. He had little sense of smell or taste, and his damaged hand, while not unfeeling, distorted his sense of touch. But he saw everything instantly in three dimensions, even vague concepts sketched out flat on a napkin. And if he could see it, he could build it. He was a walking CAD machine.

Pictures hung taped to the two short walls on either side of his workbench. To the right hung photos of the love of his life, the sexiest woman alive, the honey pot where his every waking thought got stuck. He wished she were here now, would never tire of her as long as he lived. Why couldn't she be with him always? She said he was too intense, that she loved that about him but she couldn't do it all the time. Their lovemaking was like an explosion that would leave them stunned and exhausted with their ears ringing. She needed time to recover from that, to rebuild, to refresh the accelerant. *The accelerant, yes, the dynamite.* They talked like that to each other sometimes, in their own code.

Manis looked at her pictures now and felt an overwhelming jealousy. Who did she let visit her nether regions when he wasn't around? Who got to see that perfect ass? That perfect—He couldn't even say it to himself. Did she wear the uniform when she gave it up to other guys? Did she give them anything different from what she gave him? Sometimes she said she gave them less—that there was no comparison—but then she'd leave hints about novelties he hadn't experienced, torture him with her innuendos. It had always been this way between them, almost from the time of their reborn beginning, but it made him angry—though he knew that she liked that part, too. And that made him angrier still and caused him to do things that excited her.

It was all like a hall of facing mirrors, the illusion of depth with no exit. And yet, even though he knew it could be illusory in that way, he felt the anger rise in him now.

He had a multitool in his grasp. He flipped the blade out and ran the dull side between the space where the index and middle finger had been on his left hand. It felt cold in that sensitive, erogenous place. Made him horny. Stoked his anger.

On the wall hung a picture of her in leather, the bad girl. He approached it and held the point of the knife to the black fringe of her red panties, clutching his own crotch with the other hand. He wanted to pull those panties down with the knife right now, but she was far away. He scratched at them futilely, ink and paper fibers flaking off, felt a surge of bile rise in his throat, spun in a rage and flung his knife into the opposite wall.

He'd taped pictures of all the scumbags there. Now, as always, he saw them in three dimensions, their bright eyes, their animal physicality. The knife had embedded itself two inches into the wall, missing all of the pictures. Manis walked over and yanked it out. He scraped the plaster dust from the knife with the edge of his workbench, thinking that one day the methods of violence he'd chosen would not spare these men the way the knife had just missed their pictures.

FRIGID AIR HAD SETTLED OVER MANHATTAN, and puddles from the previous night's rain showed it—shallow puddles frozen solid, a layer of veined ice glazing the tops of the deeper ones. Where water sat on the parkway, the relentless thrumming of car tires had deposited the ice in a filthy frothy slick. Walking along the greenway path, Diaz sensed moments of driver panic in each thud and skid through those potholes, watched them wrestle their steering wheels back into alignment. He wished he were driving on that road just now, feeling the thrill of recovery from that momentary loss of control.

Was that what the bomber thought, just before the blast seized him—that somehow with that final act control would arrive? Whether he pressed the button himself or someone else did, was that feeling the same in the fractured moment?

Diaz thought about having opened the door on Jennifer. He'd seen plenty of women that way before. So why did seeing her there half dressed make him feel as if everything was slipping? Why did he react in anger to a simple misstep like that? She must think he had a short fuse by now, and he supposed she was right. He'd lose his roommate if he weren't more careful.

Traffic was light on the Henry Hudson. Diaz, still thinking of Jennifer, felt the air seep out of him. He stepped over the jersey wall and began walking along the edge of the parkway, losing himself in the rush of passing cars.

A few minutes later, down by the Ninety-Sixth Street ramp, a Crown Victoria swung around him and screeched to a stop. Cop in an unmarked, blinkers going. The guy jumped out, tall and strapping.

"That you, Diaz?"

Shit. It took him a minute to recognize the guy, Peter Hernandez, another detective on the squad.

"Yeah, hey, Pedro."

"This is no place to be, my man, hardly any shoulder. What're you doing out here—car trouble?"

"Nah. Just taking a walk."

Hernandez pointed to the park. "That's what the path is for."

"I know. I—I thought I saw something."

"What?"

"Turned out to be nothing. Funny coincidence, you being here."

"I spotted you from the other side. I did a U-turn. You want a lift?"

"No, thanks." Diaz climbed back over the divider. "I needed the fresh air. Had a fight with my roommate, if you wanna know the truth. Better to walk back, cool off."

"Okay." Hernandez hesitated. "Be careful out here. They fly on this road."

From the greenway Diaz watched him get back into the Ford and pull away. His tires spun out when he first hit the gas.

Diaz squinted into the night. He stuck to the park path on the way back home.

A WIND HAD PICKED UP in Crown Heights, and the cold made Warren Manis's eyes water, reinforcing his alertness. This was another big night. Adrenaline streamed through his chest, and his heart thrummed with excitement.

He'd had to wait only half an hour for Littel's bedroom light to go off. Then another hour, walking up and down the block, keeping moving not only for the cold but also to remain as inconspicuous as possible on a quiet neighborhood street. Yet he couldn't go far because he couldn't allow his eyes to drift away from Littel's window.

When the time came to act, Manis settled his black backpack on his shoulders, walked with authority toward the house, flipped one leg then the other over the low fence, and disappeared under the stoop. He peered through the glass of the basement door, seeing no sign of movement, just the blue-green glow from the night-lights. It took a matter of seconds for him to jimmy the door. He closed it behind him most of the way but didn't allow it to latch.

Inside, he slipped off his shoes and set down his backpack and slid open the zipper, leaving the backpack closed just enough not to let it splay apart. He hooked it over one shoulder and in stocking feet climbed the stairs to the hallway outside Littel's room. He listened at the open door, heard Littel wheezing in sleep, and proceeded down the hall to the bathroom.

There it was: that beautiful machine, resting on the towel. Manis shucked the backpack off again, setting it down atop the vanity. He slipped his hand into the pouch and closed his gloved fingers around the familiar curve of the replacement prosthetic arm. He had lived with the parts of this arm for so many hours, tightened and rechecked every screw, tested every micro-motor, shaped the plastic to match the original by every measure. Most important, he'd carefully reduced the essential core to its most elegant basics, managing not even to include an entire cell phone, just the parts that he needed. Being lighter, this arm was more of a challenge than the leg. He had many fewer grams to work with, and if his calculations were off by even a couple percent, Littel would immediately notice. To make room for his load Manis had to make the casing extra thin, the mechanisms less sturdy. It wouldn't hold up to much abuse. In a week it would likely crack or begin to malfunction. But long before then it would already have served its purpose. He knew the most likely route that Littel would follow tomorrow.

Manis removed his masterpiece from the backpack and set it down gently on the rug in front of the toilet. He lifted Littel's prosthetic arm off of the towel and just for a moment attempted to judge whether he'd gotten the weight right. It had taken many measurements of the photos and many calculations in order to estimate the weight of Littel's arm and replicate it within a fraction of a gram. Now, weighing it in his palm, Manis felt proud of his accomplishment.

But wait! There was a smudge of dirt around the collar where the mechanism attached to the remainder of Littel's real arm. Manis was prepared for this, too. He quickly extracted some grease pencils from his pocket, carefully judged the color of the stain, and replicated it precisely on the new arm.

Now he was ready to go. Listening for Littel one more time and still hearing his snoring, he placed the original arm in his backpack and set the replacement arm on the towel just as he'd found it.

He paused in the bathroom doorway only for a moment. That arm had been such a feat that he almost felt sorry to see it go.

EARLY IN HIS CAREER AS a police officer, Detective Second Grade Peter Hernandez came across a dirty cop. It happened in a bowling alley far from home and far from where Hernandez then walked the beat. That night—an all-important third date—the woman with Hernandez had broken a fingernail in the third frame of the first game and never got over it, which perhaps the gods meant as a sign for Hernandez to cut his losses.

If so, he missed the sign. Instead of taking her off for a more nail-friendly evening, he convinced her to stay and at least bowl a couple of games—they'd already paid for an hour. She whined most of the rest of the night, and pretty soon Hernandez realized the relationship had no future. As a consequence, his attention began to wander.

He made three trips to the bar, returning with beer and pretzels and hot dogs, trying to make the most of things, and on each trip he happened to look down the line and see a bunch of greasers partaking of their sleazy fun. He knew they had to be up to no good. But what the hey, Hernandez was off duty and more concerned with salvaging his night than projecting himself onto a situation in someone else's precinct.

Then a guy he knew from police academy walked through the door. He was also out of uniform, and Hernandez quickly turned away.

Big mistake there, he later reasoned. Seeing a fellow cop would've surely forced the other guy to abandon his bad intentions for the night. Instead, the cop made a beeline for the sleaze in the corner and proceeded to undertake a rather blatant transaction involving cash and some small waxy envelopes—Hernandez guessed crystal meth.

It might've ended with that, but Hernandez tossed and turned on it for a month, wondering whether to report the other cop to Internal Affairs. He convinced himself that he hadn't seen enough evidence to be definitive—didn't get a close look at those envelopes, after all—so he chose at long last to do nothing. But a few months later, the cop turned up dead, and Hernandez felt of two minds about that. First: Good riddance. Second: If he'd acted maybe he could've prevented a tragedy.

This was the prism through which he fretted about the case of Manny Diaz. Driving home to Rockland past midnight, he wondered: *What the hell is a guy in the squad doing out on the parkway, tempting fate?* This was unstable behavior, and instability in a Bomb Squad tech was about as welcome as a taut tripwire beside an IED.

Hernandez kissed his sleeping kids and climbed into bed with his wife, who was down with the flu. She had a skyline of sodas on her night table and a basketful of used tissues on the floor next to the bed. He turned his back on her and pulled the sheet over his shoulder, thinking that he didn't want to bust on Diaz, but he also didn't like the feeling he got from the sight of Diaz on the parkway.

All in all, it made for a lousy night's sleep.

TICK, TICK, TICK, TICK, TICK,
TICK, TICK, TICK, TICK, TICK

5.

DAY THREE: LIGHT

BEFORE A RAY OF SUNSHINE HAD filtered through the drawn shades, the cordless phone on Capobianco's nightstand roused him from congested sleep. Eyes still closed, he reached across the bed to feel nothing but crumpled sheets. Jill was in the shower. He picked up the phone, reflexively barked, "Cap here!"

"You sound like you swallowed a frog," Gowen said. "Am I calling at a bad time?"

"I feel like I swallowed a *pond* full a frogs, tell you the truth."

"You going to the precinct today?"

"I doubt it."

"But you're in the loop, right?"

Capobianco hated this. The police radio was off and Kahn hadn't called him all night. He could only presume that nothing broke while he slept, but he didn't know for sure. "In the loop, yes," he said, "if you mean my squad. What do you know, Hank?"

"The mayor feels anxious and the chief feels anxious."

"So now it's my turn."

"Precisely. It flows downstream. Can't repeal the laws of physics. So how can you help make them feel better?"

"Hold on." Capobianco sat up, ran a hand through his sticky hair and took a few gulps of water. The change of position made his head pound, but at least he didn't have to run to the bathroom for the four hundredth time. He put on his reading glasses and scanned his cell phone for new texts and emails. Nothing earth shattering.

"I reported everything I know to the assistant chief yesterday," he said.

"That was yesterday. This morning, the press is all over City Hall. They want a sign of progress, some reassurance that we're not sitting on a powder keg."

"Who does?"

"Everyone." Pause. "Well, the press probably doesn't care. They just want a story. We know that. Maybe a powder keg is an even better story. But the best story of all is the mayor sitting on a powder keg and his minions too stupid to realize it. You and I both know they'll eat that for lunch."

"I can't predict the future, but nothing we have now points in the direction of a wave of violence." He gave Gowen a fill on the evidence—at least as much as he knew from Kahn yesterday. "I have our best man on it," he concluded.

"Agree with you there," Gowen said. He'd been the one to recommend that Kahn apply for the squad years ago. "I don't suppose you'd think it wise for the chief to go public with the serial number thing?"

"A guy named Gowen once told me that information is neither good nor bad, but leaking makes it so. The one who has it controls the game. So why broadcast anything to the world right now?"

Cap heard Gowen breathing, thinking. He threw off the covers, feeling warm and stuffy. "We have very little, at this point, to suggest motive. But Kahn tells me that O'Shea of A and E says the man was in a fragile emotional state for weeks before he blew himself up. That doesn't sound like a terrorist cell to me. You?"

"No. So why'd he choose the recruiting station?"

"Isn't it obvious? The sorry bastard lost his legs in Iraq. Does the press have that?"

"I don't think so. The administration hasn't even released the suspect's name."

"Let the chief give that to them—the name and his status as a disabled vet. They're bound to find out soon, anyway."

"Better just to release the name. Let them dig up the leg thing on their own. Give them something to do."

"Good call, Hank."

"Listen, I know the hardest thing is when your only suspect lies dead. What's your instinct on this?"

Capobianco already knew, but he paused for effect. "Last act of a lonely desperate man."

"Yeah, me too, if it means anything to you."

"Sure, it does. You're the master. But make sure City Hall knows that we can't prove anything just yet. We're still working it from all quarters."

"Commander of A and E says the same."

"That's a relief."

"Feel better, Cap."

"Yeah, thanks. Stay safe and keep your ass covered."

"Hah!" Gowen laughed. "Always do."

Kahn barely had half his coffee and egg sandwich down when Patti Morris patched through a call he hated to take: Andy Stoltz of ATF. He grabbed another bite of the sandwich before picking up. Let Stoltz know he was interrupting breakfast, as if the dolt could read a clue.

"Kahn—Stoltz here."

"What's up, Andy," Kahn mumbled through the kaiser roll.

"Thirty-six hours and no one called me, that's what."

Kahn chewed and swallowed, immediately tore off another bite of his sandwich. "Called you about what?"

"You know *what,* Kahn. We were still part of the Task Force, last I checked. Why didn't you notify me?"

Because you're a dickhead, Kahn wanted to say. Instead he said, "I got enough bureaucracy to satisfy within my department without getting involved with more initials. You're on the JTTF, you should already know what's going on. FBI's your source by the book, aren't they? Call Burbette if you want to bust balls."

"Well, what's going on?"

"We got a vet who lost his legs twice. For my money, it's a lone nut, shouldn't involve the whole federal government."

"That's not for you to decide."

"Didn't say it was, but I got work to do. You need anything else, Andy?"

"That's all you have?"

"What else do you want? If I come across some guns for your Mexican drug lord friends, I'll let you know. Deal?"

"Fuck you, Kahn." He hung up to get the last word and Kahn gave a smug grin to no one in particular.

He finished his sandwich and chuckled to himself. Stoltz was the kind of guy who showed up at a championship game in the ninth inning, last into the stadium but first into the picture when they hoisted the trophy.

No doubt Burbette felt the same way about him, which is probably why he forgot to call him accidentally on purpose. That was a mark in the FBI's favor, so far as Kahn was concerned.

He picked up the phone and called Capobianco.

Jill answered. She passed it to Cap and Kahn heard her say, "Five minutes." Protective of the lieutenant.

When he came on, Kahn said, "ATF was just poking around."

"That's all they ever do. Beats real work. Don't worry about it."

"Your wish is my command."

"Anything since last night?"

Kahn looked at the clock on the wall. "It's not even nine a.m., Cap."

"So?"

"It was quiet, from what I hear."

"They're pressing us down at City Hall now."

"What for?"

"Because their boss is an elected official and must appear to be in charge at all times. Do I have to tell you? And—part and parcel of that—they want to know there isn't another bomb out there."

"There's always another bomb out there...eventually."

"Cut the crap, Sandy. You got anything reassuring?"

"Since what I told you last night, no. But a couple guys are on the board this morning who haven't been seen for a while. Maybe the flu epidemic's receding. You coming in soon?"

"I wish. My wife's got me chained to the bed."

"I'll call if I get anything new. I promise."

Capobianco started to say something, but instead gave a cough and kept coughing. By the end it sounded like he'd hacked up a lung.

"You all right, boss?"

"Shut up, Kahn."

NO SOONER HAD KAHN HUNG UP the phone than he saw Peter Hernandez cross the room in a cardigan sweater and faded jeans.

"You look positively grandfatherly, Pedro. What are you—undercover or something?"

"I'm not on duty till four, came in special to speak with you."

"Oh?"

"Diaz around?"

"He's due but I haven't set eyes on him yet."

"Mind if we take a walk? I don't want—"

Kahn held up a hand, getting that this was sensitive. "I don't have time for a stroll just now," he said. "We can use Cap's office."

Hernandez slipped his hands into his pockets, looking hesitant.

"We can close the door, pull the blinds."

"Someone might see us come out."

"That bad?"

"I'm not sure."

"Aw, hell. Let's go get a bagel at that place on Hudson. I've only had one breakfast so far this morning."

They didn't make it to the bagel store, though. In front of a veterinarian's office, Hernandez stopped and pulled Kahn aside. There were beautiful black-and-white pictures of dogs in the window.

"That golden lab in the picture, you think it's one of ours?"

"Popular breed. Had one of them as a boy."

"Never been much for animals myself. But I'd bet you wouldn't let one get into trouble, would you? I mean without doing anything about it?"

"Course not. What the hell's this about, Hernandez? I'm short on patience this week."

"It's Diaz."

"You said."

Hernandez told him what he'd seen on the parkway last night. "Weird—risky behavior like that. What's the word—gratuitous. Like we don't have enough danger in this job every day."

"Hmm." Kahn bit a lip.

"Anyway, I thought you should know, Sarge—being kind of his partner and the most senior guy in the room, what with the lieutenant out."

Kahn rubbed his chin. *Diaz playing in traffic? The guy must be coming unhinged.* But it wasn't his place to share these concerns with one of the detective's peers. "Thanks for telling me," he said with as little emotion as possible. "You did the right thing."

Hernandez nodded and let out a sigh, clearly relieved to have it off his chest. "That bagel," he said. "I'll buy."

"Never mind. I don't need it."

"You'll keep this between us? Diaz won't know?"

Kahn rested his hands on his hips. "I can hardly do that if I have to act on your information, can I? It was direct contact, after all. You said you got out of the car and everything."

"I had to make sure he was all right."

"Admirable enough. But if I have to discuss it with him, I can hardly say a little birdie told me."

"I hadn't thought about that. Maybe don't say anything after all."

"That'll be for the lieutenant to decide. You did the right thing, Hernandez. From here we'll have to play it as it lays."

Kahn left him standing on the sidewalk and headed back toward the precinct house. He had no bandwidth for handholding Hernandez just now, felt the downward tug of managerial responsibility like a weight on his back. No wonder Cap had gone gray at the temples in just nine months on the job. Maybe they should give these guys psych tests before taking them into the squad.

He walked slowly, staring at his feet. Diaz had always been a little too much his own man, but since the Times Square bombing he seemed to be growing an enormous chip on his shoulder. No—Kahn caught himself—it started before that with the package by the steps of St. Pat's. Deep down Kahn knew that Diaz meant well, had passion, cared about what he was doing. But if the detective had begun to go rogue, it would be Kahn's job to rein him in before someone got hurt.

Lewis Salinowsky was slicing potatoes when Father Igor strolled into the church kitchen. He liked the deacon, who wasn't an actual priest but whom Salinowsky insisted on calling Father out of respect. Father Igor ran the charitable end of St. Euphrosyne Ukrainian Church. In that position, he'd given the vagrant a lot of breaks in the past year, paid him a little sometimes for his "volunteer" kitchen work, made sure his bunk in the shelter kept him away from the creepiest individuals. Now Salinowsky was eager to ask another favor of his benefactor.

"You're at it early," Father Igor said, brushing a shock of blondish gray hair off of his own forehead. He had a clipboard in his other hand, had come to count the stocks.

"Too cold this morning for panhandling," Salinowsky said truthfully. He set down the knife, wiped his hands on his apron, and pointed to the mound on the chopping block. "That's thirty pounds there, in case you were wondering."

"Well done, Lewis."

Salinowsky's shoulders hurt. He'd been sitting, and the stainless steel counter was too high for sustained work from there. Now he stood, a little shaky.

Father Igor reached out to catch him, but Salinowsky steadied himself without assistance. The blister in his stump was bad, though. He did his best to ignore it. "That methadone clinic you turned me onto," he said, "I'm planning to go this week. Check it out."

"I'm glad to hear that. You deserve better for yourself."

Salinowsky nodded, knowing he'd raised the subject of the clinic only to suck up a little. "You've been very kind to me," he added.

"Nothing you wouldn't do for me if the situation were reversed." Father Igor blinked slowly, as if letting a split-second of meditation pass.

"I never volunteered for anything in my life except for the army," Salinowsky conceded.

"That was enough. No one's keeping score."

"I am, though. I owe you big time, Father, and I have another thing to ask."

"Oh?"

"Someone's been messing with my stuff."

The vagrants slept in a big room, thirty cots lined up like checkers with a small locker at the foot of each. They couldn't leave anything outside the locker when they left the premises in the morning. That's why the ones who traveled heavier never came to stay at St. Euph's. They used the City shelters or slept on the street.

"Here or outside?" Father Igor asked.

"I'm not sure."

"You're missing things?"

Salinowsky shook his head. "I don't know. It's more of a feeling." He scratched his arm, getting the creepy-crawlies just to talk about it.

Father Igor studied him. "Tell you what. You promise me—*promise me*—that you'll go to the methadone clinic this week and I'll make a space for your things."

"It's a deal." Salinowsky rocked in his eagerness. "Can I go get them?"

Father Igor nodded. Salinowsky felt eyes on his back as he hobbled out to his regular cot and gathered his possessions from the footlocker. There wasn't much, just two armfuls. He hugged them to his chest.

"There's a place in the pantry with some room," Father Igor said. "I'll show you."

DIAZ ENTERED THE SQUAD ROOM while Kahn was on the phone. Since last night, a feeling of resolve had settled in his gut. He accepted the incident of Hernandez seeing him out there on the parkway as a wake-up call. The time had come to stop allowing his emotions to rule him so. What had gotten into him of late, he didn't know. He'd been reporting to work under a cloud of dread for weeks, like the department was going to crush all life out of him, like he had to flail just to get his breath. But he now hoped being caught out last night by Hernandez would serve as a tap of the reset button. No more indulging his instincts, good or bad. Keep the head down, do the job, get on with it.

"Detective Diaz," Morris called. "I have Donald Burbette of FBI on line three. He asked for Kahn but said he'd settle for you."

Settle. How was that for a fresh start? Diaz swallowed hard, forced himself not to go straight from being settled for to second-class citizenship. Of course he was second choice. The detective sergeant outranked him. "Sure, I'll take it."

He went to a free desk and picked up. "Diaz."

"What happened...Kahn out for donuts?"

"I dunno. He's on the phone. How you doing, Don?"

"Peachy. Trying to spread the info around here, in case someone besides O'Shea is capable of an insight."

"I'm game."

"Lucky for us the army's trying to be better about controlling its most dangerous weapons. Or maybe that was just the cause of the week when this batch of C4 came through. Either way it's my good fortune to report that they were able to track the taggant from Horn's device specifically to the Grafenwohr Army Training Center in Germany."

Diaz nodded to himself. It was a one-in-a-hundred break, but the history of law enforcement was rife with them. "The seven-oh-second EOD is there. Any known connection to Horn?"

"Negative."

"Engineers? They have access to C4 sometimes."

"Well, we know our man is cavalry, so no."

"He passed through Germany, though. All the seriously injured do, coming out of the Middle East. They fly them into Ramstein and patch them up at Landstuhl Medical Center."

"You been to any of those places, Diaz?"

"All of them. Not as a patient in Landstuhl, though. Went to visit friends a couple of times. It's pretty surreal."

"All war is surreal."

"This is like dying and going to heaven. One day you're eating dust and getting shot at. The next day or soon thereafter you're lying in this sterile environment, crisp clean sheets, people being all civil to you and shit. But, just like heaven, no one wants to go there voluntarily. Know what I'm saying?"

"No doubt our man Horn didn't choose that stop for himself. The hospital, I mean."

"Who does? Some of these guys would be better off dead. I had a guy beg me to shoot him once, put him out of his misery."

"Did you do it?"

"Course not. I called over the medic. Guy's living in Indiana now, has a decent job. It hurt worse at the time than the damage turned out. Sometimes, though, it's the other way around. They save more guys in the field today than ever before."

"Modern medicine."

"One way to look at it. Or maybe it's so the politicians can see lower numbers on the KIA report."

"Hell, that's cynical, Diaz. Maybe we need you in the FBI. Any theories on how Horn might've gotten a hold of the C4? Not like they keep a few bricks in the dispensary of Landstuhl."

"No. Any reports of a theft?"

"You kidding? There are so many moving parts in the army. They probably lose ten million bucks worth of crap every day and don't know it."

"You don't have to tell me. I remember them giving cash out to the Sunnis. You had guys earning twenty-five grand a year carrying around trunks with half a mil. Someone wants to make a bomb and sees some bricks of C4 piled up in a warehouse...he probably can't resist temptation either."

"And Albert Horn couldn't resist temptation?"

Diaz bristled. "I didn't say that. My gut—I still don't like him for this. I don't know why. Maybe someone tricked him or something. Anyway, pretty hard for a serviceman to bring C4 home to the States from abroad. Vast majority come home on commercial airliners unless they're in super bad shape."

"Maybe he took special medical transport, given his condition."

"Probably did, but there would be a ton of people around, and he wasn't exactly mobile at the time, probably snowed on drugs, too."

"I see what you're saying. You know what would help us, Diaz? If you have any old army connections you could exploit."

"I don't understand. How'd you get your information?"

"Through channels, but that's all I have. It's not like interviewing men on the street—get my meaning? It's as if I had to solve a murder in the corporate headquarters only by interviewing the people in the communications department."

"You want me to do an end-run."

"I wouldn't call it that and it's up to your superiors. But it strikes me that you might have a few friends who would be willing to go off the reservation in the interest of justice. If I'm out of line—"

"No." Diaz's mind started chugging. "I do know some guys. I'll think it over."

"All right. I'm still working my end, of course. Pass along the information to Kahn, will you? And lemme know if you turn over any rocks and find something underneath."

* * *

At ten o'clock that morning, Warren Manis returned from an early outing with a spring in his step. It had taken a long time to locate his third victim, a homeless veteran named Lewis Salinowsky. This wasn't like Horn or Littel, where the stalker could work from knowledge of an office or a home address. It was more like catching a single fish in the vast ocean, and Manis felt damn proud for having gotten this far.

It helped that he had a flexible schedule due to his own disability. Though educated as a mechanical engineer, Manis had most recently worked as a union machinist until the belt of a grinding machine seized and mauled his left hand. He lost two and a half fingers in the accident—the ring finger and middle finger and half of the index finger. As a consequence he now had persistent phantom feeling in the two wholly missing fingers, an erogenous zone in the notch, and disability checks for life. He also worked as night watchman for the warehouse attached to his apartment. He got the apartment for a nominal rent, took in a small paycheck, and had no one looking over his shoulder so long as the place didn't burn down or get robbed.

The ground-floor apartment, which once served as the manager's office of a Nineteenth Century sailing loft, had old wide-board pine floors and red brick walls. Manis hung his coat on a peg by the front door, walked across the large open room, and plugged his digital camera into the computer on his desk. Within minutes the printer spit out a series of crisp photos of a prosthetic leg that attached to a transfemoral amputation.

Manis seized the pictures and opened the padlock to his secret workshop. He spread out the photos on his workbench and proceeded to study them. Salinowsky had a relatively simple prosthesis manufactured from space-age materials. A soft high-tech foam lined the socket, Kevlar reinforced the harness, and carbon-fiber composites made the pylon especially light. The challenge would be getting the replacement leg to weigh close to the same while still being able to support half of Salinowsky's body. Manis had some ideas for improving the harness in a way that would create the illusion of lightness. Also working in his favor was the fact that Salinowsky was a psychotic drug addict. If he noticed the discrepancy at all, he'd probably attribute it to his distorted mental state. At least, Manis hoped so, because this one was going to be tricky.

A moment after hanging up with Burbette, Diaz sat staring into the middle space, thinking of who he might know stationed in Germany. He made a few phone calls to old buddies, picking their brains about mutual acquaintances, and finally got the perfect name: an army guy, formerly EOD, who'd burnt himself out in that MOS and gone on to become a captain in the MPs. He was still based, someone said, at Grafenwohr. In a few more minutes, Diaz had the captain's mobile number.

He set down the phone and gathered himself just as Kahn, across the room, did the same at his own desk. Kahn got up and walked past Diaz, nodded a good morning, but kept going, headed for the break room. There was something in Kahn's look—something a little uncomfortable, a little mysterious—that made Diaz decide not to share what he was doing just then, see whether he got anything first, see how it played out.

The guy in Germany was named Victor Nunez—pronounced Noons. Diaz's source had made a point of saying that there was no tilde over the n. Nunez picked up on the second ring and immediately said, "Hold on."

When he finally returned Diaz launched right into dropping names and established his bona fides as former EOD himself. "What can I do for you, Lieutenant?" Nunez said.

He had a southwestern accent that struck Diaz as almost too carefully cultivated, like the dropping of that tilde. Never mind. Diaz wasn't exactly Señor Español himself.

"It's not 'Lieutenant' no more. 'Detective' now."

"Oh. Busted?" Nunez laughed.

Diaz had already explained that he'd left the army. He tried to laugh back but couldn't put his heart into it. "Not busted, just climbing a different silo these days. You got a minute to talk?"

"Tell you the truth, I'm jammed up, couple of guys in the office here. Can I call you later?"

"With all due respect, I'd rather not. We have a situation here. Can't say yet whether it's national security, but it involves a bombing in New York, possible terrorism."

"No shit. Hold on, then."

Diaz waited a moment while Nunez cleared his office. He came back quicker this time.

"You called my personal cell. Any chance you can call me on the land line?"

Diaz shook his head, though of course Nunez couldn't see that. "Not to start off all negative on you, but I'd rather not. What I'm about to ask you…it may be better kept off the grid."

"Oh? Okay. Go on, then."

Diaz gave an overview of what transpired in Times Square. He explained that Horn was former army. Paused for effect. "The main charge," he said, "was C4 tagged to a United States Army batch that was delivered to your base."

"Wow. How long ago?"

"FBI found out yesterday."

"No. I mean, when was the C4 delivered to the army?"

"That's an interesting question. I don't know."

"It would have to be the past five years. I don't think they tagged that specifically before then."

"Can we narrow that down further?"

"I doubt it. What else can I do for you?"

"What are the chances that someone could've stolen C4 from the army?"

"High, I'd say."

"Really? Ain't that stuff under lock and key? It was when I was there."

"Sure it is. So's a lot of things. Doesn't mean they don't turn up missing. These days especially, all these outside contractors with their various clearances coming and going. Do you know how much stuff the army has? My guess is the bean counters don't even know."

"But we're talking about C4 here, one of the most powerful explo—"

"I understand. Let me give you a hypothetical. Army engineers need to raze an old structure of some kind to make way for a new road. So they go to the secure vault where the explosives are held, fill out some forms, remove the material. Say for argument's sake that it's fifty pounds of C4."

"Fifty pounds." Diaz already knew where this was going.

"At the site, not only are the engineers there, but also the logistical guys, maybe a platoon of regulars for protection, outside contractors, even could be questionable friendlies, if you know what I mean, guys who got their uniforms yesterday morning. Not like blowing up a building to make way for a road would be a high-security need-to-know operation, right?"

"Fifty pounds," Diaz repeated.

"Now, you've been EOD. I don't have to tell you how accustomed you can get to all this shit. Guy who never saw a plug of C4 is pissing his pants just to have it in the same room with him. Meanwhile, these engineers, they've gotten so complacent that they're using it to stop a leak in their gas tank."

"Never saw it used for that, but I get your gist."

"I'm speaking metaphorically, Diaz. Point is when that fifty pounds of C4 is on the truck they're not watching it every second, right? Maybe one guy goes to take a piss while the other one goes to have a smoke. They come back and the next time they check—which could be never—there's only forty-nine pounds. What do they do—raise Cain? I doubt it. Unless they have a reason to suspect someone right there, they figure they miscounted at the vault. Am I right?"

Diaz thought back to his army days, all the shortcuts you took in the oppressive heat, just not to have to move another inch. "Probably."

"You bet your ass. So...what? They're gonna go back and report it, make a revision to the original form, risk getting called on the carpet, having to fill out more reports? Screw that. Hell, there are nuclear missiles that the air force has mislaid this way, entire tanks. They're more dangerous than a brick of C4. A little C4 never hurt anybody."

"Sure it has."

"Are you smoking dope, Diaz? I'm not saying it hasn't. I'm explaining how it gets rationalized."

"Okay."

"Now, a pattern of theft, that's a different thing. That may get caught eventually. But a little skim here or there. Don't kid yourself. I'd bet it happens all the time."

Diaz reflected. "Well, let me ask you this, Captain. Do you have any record of a theft?"

"Not off the top of my head, but I could check. Albert Horn was the soldier's name?"

"Yes, but he's out four years. As far as the theft goes, anyone could be the culprit. What would help me most would be a list of names: everyone who's authorized to remove C4 from storage. Going back as far as you can."

"Should be doable but I can't do it covertly."

"No sweat. FBI might be asking for the same info through channels. I'm only going outside to expedite things, not because we got anything to hide."

"Roger that."

"Call me any time," Diaz said. "Sooner the better."

Gavin Littel overslept, waking bleary-eyed in Brooklyn at half past nine. He called his assistant and said he'd be late. She told him he'd better hurry or he'd miss the 10:30 meeting. Just another day for another mid-level office grunt.

Within half an hour he'd done everything any man must do in the morning. The one exception being that he also strapped on his prosthetic arm and flexed the fingers to make sure he had it aligned properly. It wasn't responding as usual, so he took it off and put it on twice more, but there was no help for it. He'd have to make a phone call later—couldn't deal with it now or he'd miss his meeting.

A balky arm, however, was better than no arm at all. He knew that from experience. So he had it attached when he left his house a few minutes after ten.

Wearing a pinstriped suit and a foulard tie, Littel walked down his block and turned south onto Utica Avenue, moving along briskly. He had the *Wall Street Journal* tucked under his arm—home delivery. Some of the stores were just opening, shopkeepers cranking up their awnings with long poles or rolling up the gates in front of their windows. Other establishments had been open for hours.

Littel stopped into the bakery between a shuttered Caribbean music store and the fresh fish store, where an employee stood hosing down the sidewalk, steam rising. Inside the bakery, he bought a morning glory muffin and a cup of coffee with cream and light sugar. He walked out clutching the bag with the muffin and the newspaper in his balky prosthetic hand. With his good hand he sipped the coffee.

Pretty soon he came to a point approximately sixty feet from the intersection of Utica Avenue and Eastern Parkway. Right across the street from a ground-floor Subway sandwich shop with a US Armed Forces Recruiting Station upstairs, something happened. Bag and muffin took flight in a rush of decompressing air. The forearm of Littel's prosthesis disintegrated, puncturing his chest with shrapnel while the mechanical hand flew diagonally across the street.

On the sidewalk, the explosion perforated the left eardrum of a seventy-five-year-old woman on her way to the grocery store, a flying ball bearing punctured her left eye, and more shrapnel caused contusions of her neck and face. A twenty-year-old man lost his left testicle to a fragment of titanium, traveling near the speed of sound. The owner of a bodega, standing outside having a smoke, lost part of his right hand.

The blast threw Gavin Littel onto his back on the sidewalk like a rag doll, one leg splayed across the curb, his foot coming to rest at an unnatural angle in the street. He lay there twitching while blood spurted from his chest.

By the time the paramedics arrived, he'd bled to death from a tear in his heart.

* * *

Kahn called the lieutenant as he and Diaz screamed to the scene in an unmarked squad car. Diaz could hear Cap cursing through the phone.

"We don't know anything yet," Kahn said. "Just that it's another rather small explosion, one dead again, presumably the bomber from preliminary reports. And there's a recruiting office right there."

He paused and Diaz heard Cap barking again.

"Okay," Kahn said. "I'm hanging up. We're there."

This time they'd beaten Burbette to the scene. Cops from the local precinct had cordoned off the area for a block in each direction and the injured were being loaded into ambulances. A team from the coroner's office and CSU had only begun to evaluate the corpse, so the two Bomb Squad detectives didn't get too close to him at first.

Sun shone up Utica Avenue—an egg-yolk yellow February sun, low in the sky. Diaz shaded his eyes with his hand in the middle of the avenue and looked around.

"Once again, minimal property damage," he said, as Kahn returned from his own brief tour.

"Yeah," Kahn said. "Look at what one of the POs noticed."

He escorted Diaz over to the front window of a Bank of America branch office, where the prosthetic hand, having penetrated the glass, hung like a missile that had suddenly lost thrust.

"Something out of an action movie," Diaz said.

"Make sure the photographers don't miss that," said Kahn.

"Roger. Who's joining us?"

"Cai and Higgins."

Diaz fetched a spindle of string from the car and began to mark off quadrants. The assistant ME was still working around the corpse when the detective approached. She handed him the suspect's wallet and he slipped on a pair of gloves and took it from her, removing the driver's license.

"Nice of these guys to carry identification," he said half to himself. "This one lived right around the corner."

"Jesus, look at that," one of the photographers said. "Blew his arm clean off at the humerus."

"No." Diaz bagged the wallet. "That happened some time ago and a world away."

"How do you mean?"

"Take a closer look. See around the stump?"

"I'll be damned." The photographer resumed shooting.

"Gavin Littel," Diaz muttered. "Tell me. Why did this happen?"

Littel's mouth gaped open, silent. His tongue had slid into the back of his throat and his jaw had been pierced with shrapnel. His right ear was torn off completely.

O'Shea arrived just as the body went off in a bag. "Whaddya know?"

"Same shit, different corpse."

"Prosthesis?"

"An arm this time. And right there's the recruiting station. Very little property damage. A few more injuries than last time, nothing life threatening, I'm told." He handed O'Shea the wallet. "Dude lived in the neighborhood."

"I'd better go check it out. You'll send a response vehicle?"

"Already radioed. They'll meet you there."

Soon as he left, Burbette walked up. "One of the witnesses says black smoke."

Diaz nodded knowingly. High explosives.

Burbette helped him finish laying the quadrants, and by the time they did so the whole team was there in their Tyvek suits. In three hours they found something like what they'd found around Horn, prosthetic parts and some of the interior workings of a cell phone.

Stoltz of ATF arrived, but no one would give him the time of day. When he stalked off, Kahn turned to Burbette. "You called him?"

"Had to."

"What a dick."

"Don't get me started."

Burbette crouched down and used his ETK on the burn in the sidewalk. He held up the test tube and confirmed. "RDX. That means C4."

No one looked even mildly surprised.

With the day nearly finished, Kahn glanced at his watch. He'd let too much time pass but the lieutenant hadn't called him to yell. That was strange. He took himself away from the group and dialed.

Jill answered.

"Hey, sorry to bother you. How's the patient?"

"Asleep. You need him?"

"Afraid so."

"Something big?"

"Sometimes two smalls make a big."

Cap came on quicker than Kahn would've expected. Maybe the ringing phone had already awakened him.

Kahn didn't waste any time. "It's the same pattern, Lieutenant."

"A guy with no legs?"

"One arm this time. The rest fits the same."

"What kind of explosive?"

"C4."

There was a long silence on the line. "Aw, hell. I just told Gowen this morning that it looked like a lone nut."

"That was a reasonable working theory, Cap."

"Reasonable but wrong."

"Not necessarily. Could be two nuts stirred up with the same inspiration."

"And they share a supplier?"

"Maybe."

"Their very own blind sheik?"

"Could be."

"Gowen's gonna brief the chief, who's gonna brief the Commissioner, who's gonna brief the mayor. Who's gonna brief the press, no doubt. What do I tell him?"

"One bomber signifies a lone nut and three makes a pattern. Two—it's possible that could be no more than coincidence."

"No, it isn't. Not with prosthetics and C4 at the center of two bombings over less than seventy-two hours."

Kahn twisted his lower lip between two fingers. "Truth be told, I didn't believe it as I was saying it. Let's see. You could tell them we're doing everything in our power."

"Great, Kahn. And you'd better be." Kahn heard him swallow hard. "I'm gonna go take an aspirin."

For the lieutenant's sake, Kahn hoped he could keep it down.

TICK, TICK, TICK, TICK, TICK,
TICK, TICK, TICK, TICK

6.

DAY THREE: DARK

THAT NIGHT CAPOBIANCO SAT EXPECTANTLY AT the kitchen table for his first meal in three days.

"Here you go," Jill said.

He looked down at a bowl of steaming dark water with some dry toast on the side. "What is it?"

"Beef consommé."

"You're kidding, right?"

"You have to ease your way back into it."

Capobianco took a cautious sip of the soup and a bite of the toast. He chewed slowly and swallowed. "How am I supposed to gain enough strength for work eating like this?"

"You're not going to work tomorrow and you know it. Doctor says another forty-eight hours."

"I'll be mad by then."

"Not as mad as I'll be if you sneak out earlier."

The phone rang. Jill looked at the caller ID and handed it to him. She mouthed the word: "Gowen."

Capobianco held it to his ear. "Hi, Hank," he said. "Calling to see how the patient is feeling?"

"You wish. But I can tell you how the mayor is feeling."

"Disappointed?"

"And then some."

"Let me guess. He's scheduled a press conference on the site of one of the bombings."

"I talked him out of that. It would only inflame people. We're keeping it low-key for now, urging the press and the public not to jump to any conclusions."

"That makes sense."

"All of the NYPD is on high alert for the next one, and the Commissioner will ask the public for any information."

"If you see something, say something."

"Insert copyright notice here."

"Let me ask you a question, Hank. Anyone pissed that I'm out sick while this is going down?"

"They're big boys. They know people fall ill sometimes. But, you want my advice, get back to the precinct before patience wears thin."

"I hear ya. Unfortunately, I'm under house arrest here. Went to the doc this afternoon and he says I'm in danger of pneumonia if I don't take it easy another couple of days. Nurse Jill confiscated my car keys."

"Don't worry about it, then. I'll cover for you."

"You're a pal, Hank."

"Hell, I'm the one always telling these guys you're the right man for the job. Don't screw it up and prove me wrong."

They hung up and Capobianco looked across the kitchen at his wife. "If you have a heart, you'll let me put the police radio back on. Doctor didn't say I couldn't use my brain."

* * *

Diaz didn't go straight home that evening. He exited the subway at the 181st Street station and stopped at a worn-out bar on St. Nicholas Avenue for dinner and a few pops. The place was dark and quiet, and some not-so-new cop flick played on a television that sat on a shelf beside bottles of Bushmills and Tullamore Dew.

"What movie's that?" he asked as he settled onto a stool.

"Um, Kevin Spacey. Whatchamacallit. *The Usual Suspects*."

"Oh, right. Saw it. Keyser Söze. The bad guy wins."

"Don't they always?"

Diaz threw him a look. The bartender was an ex-con who'd served a few years for B and E a long time ago. Now he was as straight as anyone could be in a cash business.

The detective placed a twenty on the bar and tucked one corner under a water-stained paper coaster. He didn't expect to see any change, but if he went over budget he didn't expect to have to reach into his pocket again, either.

"That Bushmills is calling to me," he said.

The bartender held the bottle while Diaz downed the first shot and refilled him without asking.

Dinner was a Jamaican meat patty from the warmer. It reminded him of his youth, all those stale greasy dinners alone with his brother in Bedford-Stuyvesant while his parents worked overtime. They were a rare intact family in that neighborhood, and he should've been grateful, but instead he felt jealous of the drama out on the streets every night—gang wars, people being shot at. Halfway through college he joined the army. Being mechanically inclined, he'd have been a natural for repairing Humvees and such, but there was no danger in that. Then some corporal told him how you cut a path to EOD.

The movie ended and another came on. For dessert Diaz had a fifth or sixth shot with a Killian's Red chaser. He felt loose in the joints when he left the bar around eleven.

A few minutes later he found the apartment dark. He removed his pullover, slipped out of his shoes and settled onto the couch to watch the Knicks play the Kings in Sacramento. He never made it to the fourth quarter, passed out right there in a fetal position still wearing his cell phone and gun holsters.

Deep into the morning, still more than half asleep, Diaz heard a suspicious sound and felt someone in the room. He opened one eye and saw a man's legs in suit pants. Black socks covered the feet, and the toes faced him. Beyond the range of his vision, Diaz sensed that the intruder was doing something with his hands. The intruder took a small step forward and the floor creaked.

Diaz, now fully awake, reached for his Glock. He swung his feet to the floor and stood up as he withdrew the gun and leveled it at the man, whom he now saw had his pants open and was fussing with a cuff of his shirt.

"Whoa!" the man said, raising his hands. "Don't shoot!"

"Who are you?" Diaz said.

The man was of medium build. He had brown hair and a five o'clock shadow and wore wire-framed glasses. "I'm with the woman."

"Jennifer."

"Jennifer. That's right."

"Close friend?"

The man smirked. "That's some roommate you got there. I had a roommate like that, I'd have a chronic case of blue balls. I'd be in the bathroom all night with a roll of paper towels."

"How's that your business?" Diaz lowered the gun to his hip but didn't put it away. "You should be careful sneaking around here."

"She said you were a cop. We just didn't want to wake you."

"Yeah, you did a great job of that."

Jennifer appeared in the doorway, barefoot in a long nightshirt, smiling at first, hair mussed. When Diaz saw her he did his best to look nonchalant while he holstered his gun, but he knew that the sight of it in his hand like that would freak her out. Sure enough, she strode between the two men, facing Diaz with her arms spread.

"Don't hurt him, for cryin' out loud. Manny. Manny! You okay?"

"Yeah." He felt the glaze lift from his eyes. "Just surprised."

"Sorry if we disturbed you." She turned to the other guy. "You better go."

Diaz scratched an eyebrow as she escorted him out the door. She was in such a hurry that she had to open and close it twice, just to get the man his shoes.

"Awkward," Jennifer said without mirth, locking the door.

"The guy snuck up on me." Diaz adjusted the strap of his holster and wiped the remaining sleep from his eyes.

"You could've killed him."

"I doubt it. I kept my finger off the trigger."

"That's small reassurance."

"There are six break-ins a day in this precinct. You might've told me ahead of time that you'd be home with someone."

She brushed back her hair with all five fingers. "I didn't know. It was—um, spontaneous."

Diaz nodded slowly, his energy receding into his diaphragm. He made a move toward his room but she cut him off. "We have to talk."

He didn't want to argue so he collapsed to the couch again. She sat on the chest that they used as a coffee table, her bare knees sealed together. When his eyes dropped, she stretched her nightshirt over them. "I can't have you pulling guns on people, Manny. For the first time, I'm really wondering if rooming with a cop is going to work out."

"I told you. He surprised me. When I fell asleep, no one was here. I wake up and there's a guy standing over me."

"We saw you there earlier. We did a good job of being quiet."

"Too good." He paused, feeling a surge of unexpected sadness. "Honestly, when you said you'd start bringing guys back, I didn't know it would be right away."

"And I didn't know I needed your permission." She caught herself and lowered her tone. "You're on a knife's edge lately. Want to talk about it?"

He frowned. "Pressure at work, that's all. Bombs going off. I thought I wanted that—a little action—but it has everyone in the squad on a short trigger."

"I wouldn't use that term after what just happened."

Diaz shook his head, as if to clean the slate. "I'm jumpy. I admit it. I'm sorry. Tough days at the office. I got a reprimand just yesterday on top of everything." He took a deep breath, at that moment realizing that he needed her. Not for the rent, mainly. He needed this person here, this source of stability—and more than he'd ever known. "I'm really sorry, Jennifer. Don't go."

She searched his face and he looked into her eyes. The sparkle there said that she knew there was something more to it, something more than the events that make up a few bad days. She rested a hand on his thigh and ran her palm in a circle.

"We don't have to be strangers, you know. We can be there for each other."

Diaz closed his eyes and saw the man who'd just left, heard again his comment about the blue balls. An asshole like that, probably one of those Upper East Side guys who thought he was better than everyone else. Dude flashes some cash and a couple of wry jokes—not a care in the world—and in a few hours he's bedding this hot chick within feet of Diaz. Diaz—a different kind of guy. One of those guys who spend their lives keeping America safe for assholes to screw beautiful women in peace.

Opening his eyes and looking at her moving hand in disgust, Diaz blurted, "What the hell? You're offering me sloppy seconds now?"

Jennifer let out a cry at that. She took her hand back like it was burnt, stood abruptly and said, "Screw you, Manny. You don't deserve me as a friend!"

When the door slammed he thought: *She's probably right.*

HER TRAIN WAS LATE.

Manis paced nervously in the bustling Amtrak hall of Penn Station, back and forth from the big board to the Hudson News store. The *New York Post* had a special late edition headline: AN ARM AND A LEG. Manis bought a copy and controlled every muscle in his face as he read the story standing up. The cops had nothing on him, every fact and word of the article inferring smalltime homegrown terrorism or veterans losing their minds. He'd diverted them all, just as he'd carefully planned. And now there were two targets down with only one to go.

He stuffed the paper into the nearest trash bin and looked around. The train had finally arrived and passengers streamed up the escalator from the platform below. When he saw her auburn hair, the erotic shuffle of her feet in those cute red canvas sneakers, he sucked in a breath to calm himself.

"An hour sitting in New Haven," she said. "What a rat fuck." She barely glanced at him. "Take my bag."

The bag, a small leather weekender, wasn't heavy, but she handed it to him so abruptly that he almost dropped it.

"Let me look at you," he said.

She ignored him and began walking toward the exit. In close-fitting jeans her butt looked tiny, almost boyish. She was lithe, wiry, small-boned—always had been. But Manis wasn't interested in hips. Her smallness made her secret places that much more private. She exuded sensuality, and when he concentrated hard he could convince himself that she saved the best only for him.

He jogged a few steps to catch up. "I made a reservation at that place you like. I've had to change it twice, waiting for you."

They rode the subway in silence, one or two feet apart, hanging on to the overhead rails as the train jostled them. Manis felt her aura like a physical force, penetrating him, though whenever he tried to ease closer that force seemed to push her away like matching poles on a pair of magnets. She met his gaze a few times, though. Those bright violet eyes of hers with the gravitational pull of planets—he could get aroused just looking into them.

At the restaurant in downtown Brooklyn, they sat at a table for two in a corner banquette, knees occasionally brushing. He tried to let his leg linger in her direction, but she pulled away, turning her hip toward him. When he reached for her delicate, alabaster hand, she pulled that away, too.

"You're acting like it's been so long," she said.

"It has. It's been thirty-eight days."

"You *know* that?" She sniffed. "How many minutes?"

"Let's see." He cocked his head, calculating.

"You're pathetic."

Manis smiled through his bushy gray beard, the one he'd worn since before they'd become reacquainted as adults. That he'd controlled her once she didn't ever acknowledge. And he couldn't remind her, for fear of losing her forever. She was like a stray dog who'd come home to a different house, and you never knew how much of the world the bitch had seen while she was gone, how much she now understood. But, in spite of that, he still claimed ownership rights, though he couldn't articulate them after all that had happened. If only she knew how much power he had, how much he'd done for her. "I missed you."

"I'm not your wife. Buy a magazine. Surf the Internet. Get yourself off."

"It's not the same."

"Then find a warm friend."

"I want *you*."

"Stop being so weak."

But she was here on his territory. She'd come to him. He must have something to offer her.

"I've been working at talking like them."

"Like who?"

"What you like." He put it on. "I took duh dawg to duh cah pahk."

"Sounds more Boston than New York. I can get Boston whenever I want."

He dropped his chin. "I'll keep working."

"You're pathetic."

"Why do you keep saying that?"

"Because you are. Isn't that what your mother always told you? She was right."

"She only told me that when she caught me spying on her. It was worth it, though. I learned a lot from that spying. When I was done, when I achieved manhood, she got hers."

"I thought you said that was an accident."

She had her hand around the stem of her wine glass. He tried to take her fingers but she withdrew again, placing her hand in her own lap.

Manis said, "I picture us dying together in a fiery explosion, you and me. In complete ecstasy. Like my mother with that soldier."

"He wasn't a soldier. He was a security guard."

"Oh, right. You got that right. I'm sorry."

"Don't apologize. You're like—you're desperate. Not me. I got laid just this morning."

"I don't want to hear it. Don't tell me."

"This guy was so fat, he would've crushed me."

"Shut up."

"I had to go on top. But you know how much I like that."

Manis reached over and pinched her hard on the thin skin that stretched across her upper ribs.

"Ow!" she said. "That hurt."

He reddened. "See what you made me do."

She looked at her butter plate. "Get the check."

* * *

When they stepped through the door of his apartment, Manis dropped the bag and wrapped his arms around her before the door closed behind him, but she shucked him off. "Let's have a drink."

"Champagne?" He went to the refrigerator and took out a bottle.

"What brand is it?"

"I don't know. Something Italian."

"It isn't even champagne, then."

"The cork still pops." He let it fly, at first intending to hit her but flinching away at the last second and missing.

"You're always popping off too soon," she said, laughing at his expense.

She poked around the apartment as she drank from the flute he'd handed her. It was heavy, not fine crystal, another salvage item that some restaurant had thrown away. But combined with the dinner wine it had started to loosen her up. Manis could see it in the swing of her arms.

He snuck up behind her and took her shoulders and buried his face in the crook of her neck, inhaling deeply. She smelled antiseptic.

She threw her head back to drain her drink, and it made the voice box stick out on her sinewy neck almost like a man's Adam's apple. She wore a stretchy knit sweater with a plain round-neck collar. He began kissing her and reached around and slipped his gnarled hand down through the opening, getting just to the top of her bra before she twisted away and slapped at him.

"Not like that!" she said, tossing her glass in the air toward him and making him catch it. She gave a cruel smile when he fumbled it and went and sprawled across the bed.

Manis set down the glass and followed her, aching for her. He lay down beside her, feeling her resistance, unsure what she'd allow him to do. Once he'd been the dominant, controlled the entire transaction. But that was a long time ago.

She had her bony back to him and he spooned with her, burying his face in her hair, rubbing against her, reaching a hand around between her legs. She didn't push him away for once, but she lay there in her jeans, unmoving and unreceptive.

"I want you so bad," he admitted.

"Not like this," she said. "I'm not ready."

"What do I need to do?"

"You know what."

Manis sat up, squeezed his eyes shut, and pressed his fingers into his forehead. "Why?"

"Because it turns me on. It turns you on, too."

"No, it doesn't."

"You just won't admit it."

He wanted to cry, almost felt sick to his stomach. "Which one?"

"Let's talk about Albie today."

Albie. He let out a small sigh of relief. At least Albie was one who could never have her again.

"He was handsome," she began. "Even when they wheeled him in, pale and unconscious, I could see that." She stood up abruptly. "Get yourself undressed, Warren. Get yourself undressed and get under the sheets."

"Okay." He obeyed. His manhood, ready to burst a minute ago, had shriveled.

As he lay there, covered to the collarbone with nothing but a sheet, she walked to the bed and rested a hand on his chest. She resumed her narration.

"He had curly, kinky chest hair, like all African-Americans. Not much of it, but for weeks as he lay there I ran my fingers through it with no one around, pinched his nipples, pinched my own. Want me to show you?"

Cowed into not speaking, Manis nodded silently.

"Of course you do," she said. She pulled off her shirt and unhooked her bra.

Manis licked his lips as she toyed with her small breasts.

"Like this," she said, throwing back her hair, her eyes closed. "And this." She pinched and prodded with one hand, still resting the other on the sheet over Manis's chest.

"When he woke up," she continued, "we got to know each other a little. That's when I heard that accent, like something from an old longshoreman or something, all wyes, dirty and sensuous like the street."

Manis flushed. He knew he couldn't compete with that. Hadn't he just proved himself an utter failure in the restaurant? He'd lost that which he'd once acquired with no effort. No amount of trying would get that accent back.

"At the beginning," she continued, "I fed him when he was too weak. Fed him with a spoon, then a fork." As if she could taste it herself now, she ran her red tongue over her front teeth, then stuck it out, leaned over, and dangled it an inch from Manis's dry lips. Her breath smelled of alcohol.

"I could tell right then that he wanted me, but he wasn't ready—too much pain. He would cry at night over the legs, cry when he didn't think anyone could hear. But one quiet night I went to him and held him. I wiped away his tears with my fingertips"—she ran them now across Manis's cheeks—"and I licked off the salt like this." Her tongue lapped up the imaginary tears.

Manis felt the sweat forming in his underarms, beads stippling his forehead. He started to shake his head to stop her, but he felt paralyzed, still would endure anything to have her tonight. So many times he'd ruined it and she'd cut him off, stormed out. After so many days, and all that he'd done for their relationship, he couldn't face something of that nature just now.

"After two months," she said, "Albie Horn's strength began to return. The legs still hurt but the inflammation had gone down and the operations had ceased and they'd started withdrawing more of the morphine. The next time I drew the late shift, I cranked the dose down a little more. I wanted him to feel. Do you know what I wanted him to feel, Warren?"

"N-no." He stared as she peeled off her jeans. Her panties were white and not at all sexy, which for Manis made them all the hotter. At times like these he perpetually thought of her as a girl.

"Ooh," she moaned. "It was time for me to show Albie that he was still a man. I still had my uniform on—you can use your imagination for that, can't you, Warren?"

He shook his head, but not to deny it. He was aroused again.

She touched him through the sheets. "Before I even got my undies off he was hard, just like you now. I turned away from him, pretending like I was shy, and slipped them off just like this."

He watched her do it, using both hands, the white undies around her ankles, that small tight ass finally exposed. But the story—it was getting to the point where he could no longer stand it. He knew that was what she wanted—for him to live on that cusp of desiring and not desiring.

She turned around and came to him, slipping her hand under the sheet for the first time. "Ooh, he was so hard. Imagine that, Warren, all the trauma, no sex for months.

All his hopes dashed and now to know he was alive again, not fully mutilated."

Without warning she slipped two fingers into the crotch of Manis's damaged hand, rubbing back and forth. It made him tingle in places that shouldn't be connected at all to that scar.

"In spite of everything that happened, he was still a beautiful, strong black man. I went and locked the door—you can imagine that part, Warren. Then I pulled down his sheets and his stumps were there, bandaged but clean. His thighs with those curly little hairs. I slipped onto his rod like this."

She straddled him and slid him inside her. "Ooh, his cock was on fire."

"Shut up," Manis said, though he couldn't help pumping.

"It was harder and hotter than any cock I've ever had."

"Shut up!" Manis screamed. He began to writhe. She was holding his arms down at the wrists, but she was a wisp of a thing, shouldn't be able to control him physically.

"So big and strong he still was, Warren. His thick, hot—"

"No, you bitch!" Manis broke free and reared up and threw the back of his hand across her mouth, feeling her teeth caught by his knuckles. He flipped her over and began beating at her as he exploded inside her and she moaned in pain and pleasure.

When he'd finished she used the sheet to dab at the blood of her split lip.

Manis went to the freezer and got an icepack for the cheekbone, which already had begun turning black and blue under her left eye.

"See what you made me do," he said.

She laughed like the devil at that, dabbed at her lip and looked at the blood on the white sheets. "Oh, what will the girls say when they see me like this? Understand why we have to keep our distance from each other most of the time?"

"You're not normal," he said.

She arched an eyebrow, reached out, and pulled hard on the beard of his chin. "Oh, and you *are* normal, Warren," she mocked. "*You* are."

TICK, TICK, TICK, TICK,
TICK, TICK, TICK, TICK

7.

DAY FOUR: LIGHT

SALINOWSKY AWOKE ON HIS COT IN the big church shelter room feeling achy and twitchy. His nose was running and tears filled his eyes. Like an allergic reaction, he thought, though he knew this was no allergic reaction. He fetched the artificial leg from beneath his cot and grabbed the soap from his locker and hobbled to the communal showers, placing the leg on a bench in the anteroom and using a plastic stool that Father Igor had provided to assist him.

As the warm water ran over him, Salinowsky ignored the others who were showering near him and thought about all that he needed to do. The symptoms meant he'd require a fix in the next twelve hours or things would start to get ugly. But he was out of heroin again—in truth had no idea what had happened to his bundle from two days ago. Wasn't that supposed to last the better part of a week? Maybe the girl who cooked up his last trip had stolen the rest. Or maybe the dealer had. You couldn't trust those people, but then again Salinowsky couldn't even trust his own memory.

He yawned and a shiver ran through him. It didn't really matter what happened—the bundle was gone. He was twelve hours from the cramps and pukes, and he'd promised Father Igor that he'd break the cycle and hit the methadone clinic within a week. He had the card in his pants pocket and everything, the place run by some Catholic nun lady.

That clinic beckoned but so did the street. Father Igor said it would be a nice day today: sunny and around fifty. Salinowsky's grandfather always advised him to make hay while the sun is shining, and no matter what path he took Salinowsky knew he was nearly out of money again and still days away from cashing his next benefits check. As the soup kitchen wasn't open on weekends, he'd have to starve or beg for the next forty-eight hours just to get by, and he couldn't very well ask Father Igor for extra food after all he'd already received. At some point, a man must make his own way in the world. Fortunately, Lewis Salinowsky had a plan to start saving his benefits checks instead of squandering them, and to use his experience helping in the shelter kitchen to land a real kitchen job in some restaurant, maybe as a dishwasher, maybe something better if he could talk them into it. The main thing was that after all these lost years he'd begun to see a way forward. Even if, as usual, the path ran through a thicket.

That kind and pretty nurse at the rehabilitation hospital...hadn't she told him when he said he couldn't go on that everyone in life had the same challenge—just to put one foot in front of the other? And it didn't matter if they were your own two feet or someone else's because it was just an expression. He and the nurse had laughed about that together.

It had been a long time since Salinowsky shared a good laugh with anyone. As he dressed he thought back to his days growing up in the Bronx, playing softball and roller hockey on fenced blacktop. He knew himself to be an impressive specimen back then, off to college on a baseball scholarship, entering the army after ROTC as a second lieutenant. He loved the physical challenge of the army, would willingly take extra weight in his pack just to motivate his platoon. In the beginning, it wasn't physical pain that he used drugs to escape from—wasn't pain at all, truth be told.

They'd raised a camp on a barren hill overlooking a small village on the Afghan side of the Hindu Kush, human beings clinging to the crags like ants in a hailstorm. They felt like sitting ducks at first, holding the hill every night, calling in Apaches, then waking up to count the dead enemy through their binoculars. But after a while a fragile equilibrium had established itself. The attacks didn't stop, but they became fewer. The Americans began taking patrols out to the enemy, but only on a selective basis, not every night. So fear-driven adrenaline often gave way to utter boredom. How much time could you spend digging latrines and trenches?

It was one of the soldiers in his platoon who turned Salinowsky on to black tar. When your whole world was the top of a barren hill, when you lost four men in three months to ambush, when you got tired of playing video games on a television wired to Humvee batteries, when a change in the wind made the whole place stink like piss, a snort now and then seemed like a reasonable indulgence. Later, of course, it was a different calculus. When you'd had your limb blown off by an IED and only morphine or similar could dull the excruciating pain in your leg and your heart, a needle every day became your savior.

By the time he landed at St. Euphrosyne Church, he knew he'd been saved more times than he could count, and yet he still needed saving. Salinowsky knew he couldn't—or shouldn't—go on like this. But when he thought what life would be like without those moments of ecstasy that the heroin gave him he could picture nothing but unbroken misery. The highs were not everything but they counted for something. The streets were mean and cold and empty of love. You needed to take flight from that now and then just to keep your sanity. Had he kept his sanity?

Oh, it was a squirrel cage, he knew, round and round. He just couldn't decide how or when to climb down from it.

Salinowsky made sure the lady's card from the methadone clinic was still in his pocket as he got dressed and strapped on his leg. He stowed the remainder of his things in the pantry cabinet that Father Igor had ceded to him and walked out into the winter sunshine.

In a public trash bin on the corner Salinowsky found a paper coffee cup. He pried off the travel lid and—finding it one-third full—sniffed the contents. *Still fresh enough.* He drank it down in two gulps, working his tongue across his palate to make the sweetness linger.

In a cold puddle by the curb he washed his cup, then walked with it upside down to dry. He found a piece of cardboard soon enough in a space between buildings, used his Sharpie to scrawl a message: HOMELESS DISABLED VETERAN PLEASE HELP. You'd hardly know he was college educated, he thought, but what else was there to say? These guys who wrote essays on their signs... they didn't pull in any more than the ones who cut to the chase—sometimes less. Because the details creeped some people out. The average pedestrian didn't really want to know how human you were. It only reminded them that the space between you and them was narrower than they ever hoped to believe.

With his sign and his cup in hand, Salinowsky limped down Mulberry Street to Columbus Park. He eased to the sidewalk and propped himself in the sun against the bubbling paint of a wrought iron fence. Finding a bottle of Thunderbird in his coat pocket, he took a couple of swigs and screwed up his courage. Three years on the street and he still had to settle that pit in his stomach before holding out his cup. In many ways, the barren hill in Afghanistan had been easier.

A SHOT RANG OUT, WAKING him. *Shot?* Or was it a bomb going off?

Something like that—something that threatened.

At least that was his first reaction.

By the time Salinowsky realized it had only been a box truck taking a pothole hard, he was sprawled on his stomach, his prosthetic leg on the concrete behind him. Now he remembered that he'd removed the leg for effect, had laid it across his lap—more productive than any cup or sign.

He scrambled back to the fence, still feeling jumpy, his insides as much a wreck as his outsides. He flinched at everything. Every shout from a stranger on the street he heard as advice to take cover, every stray whistle as danger flying through the air. His lip trembled. The loud noises just shredded him, went straight to his brain like reliving the explosion that had claimed his leg. Hands shaking, he looked into his cup. Just four bucks plus change there so far, and the sun had moved. It was warmer out but he felt a chill in the shade like something close to defeat. He needed angel wings and he needed them soon.

Salinowsky strapped on his leg and decided to move to a different street—maybe try Canal Street, just a block up.

When he got there he settled onto his butt before a vacant building, this time putting a piece of folded cardboard under him for insulation before finishing off the fortified wine with two deep swigs. He'd only just removed his leg and laid it across his lap when a young woman slipped a ten-spot into his cup, looked a little embarrassed, and kept walking. Salinowsky said "thank you" to her calves. He was feeling too strung out to smile, but if this kept up for a few hours, he figured, he wouldn't go to the methadone clinic today. His nerves were shot and he couldn't remember his plan for turning around his life, but he knew where to score another bundle.

And that was something.

Never mind the MO of the previous two attacks. Now that one isolated incident had become a pair, the public began seeing suspicious packages everywhere, most notably, as one might expect, in front of armed forces recruiting offices.

Kahn and Diaz did two RSPs on two packages in Queens, using the Wolverine once and the bomb suit another time, following procedure to the letter. One turned out to be a box of old CD's. The other, three bags of dry plaster in an abandoned knapsack. *Dead weight.* Diaz wondered. *What the hell is someone doing carrying that on their back?*

But never mind. They were in the response truck again with the robot stowed and heading back to the precinct house at half past eleven, Kahn writing up the incident reports on his lap.

The voice in Diaz's head spoke to him. It said, "Our hero Manny Diaz on the move, villains and creeps quaking in their boots on the street at the mere sight of him. But Diaz is too focused on the big case to notice."

He zoned back in and turned to Kahn. "Something don't smell right about this," he said.

Kahn kept his eyes on his report. "Yeah? How's that?"

"The basics. Veterans blowing themselves up. I don't buy it."

Kahn looked through the windshield. "They have a much higher rate of suicide than the general population, which is understandable, going from all the stresses of combat back to the dullness of domestic life. Plus the economy sucks. Only thing that makes it worse for the vets is coming home to no job, no means for providing for their families."

"But our two suspects had jobs." Diaz paused. "You sound like you're writing a brief for the prosecution. You've studied this?"

"I've been reading up at night, trying to figure these guys out."

"A little bit of knowledge can be dangerous. Ain't that what you told me? Quote unquote: a danger to himself and others."

Kahn set down his pen. "Okay, Diaz. What's your theory?"

"I don't have one yet—not a complete one. But I don't see a sane veteran blowing himself up on the street."

"Sane, no. Who says these guys are sane? They're the exceptions in society, like all bombers. In this case, they're probably suffering PTSD."

"Guys I know with bad combat stress can barely wipe their asses. Friends of mine with that can't get through the night, spend all their time just trying not to drive away their last family member, if they can even think that far ahead."

Kahn gestured with his pen. "These two guys—both lived alone."

"Horn had his sister and she seemed to care for him. He had his niece, something to live for."

"Maybe he just snapped."

Diaz twisted his mouth to one side. "Snapped and happened to have some C4 lying around? These guys with PTSD ain't big planners. They're just trying to get through the day. And you can't hold down jobs like these two had with more than a mild case."

"So they had a mild case."

"I'm telling you, Sandy. You don't commit an act of violence like this with a mild case. Maybe you punch someone out in a bar, but you don't blow yourself up."

"Says who?"

"Says me. These ain't spur-of-the-moment explosions. Someone had to plan these things, like any bomb."

"So maybe it isn't combat stress. Maybe it's political."

"Nobody's issuing any statements, though."

"Their acts are their statements. The recruiting stations."

Diaz shook his head. "Neither one went inside. Littel was across the street. Why would you do that? Can they be that stupid? It almost seems like spontaneous combustion."

"Yeah," Kahn agreed earnestly. "Their limbs blow up and their own human lives just happen to be in the way." He scratched his chin. "Maybe they really don't want to hurt anyone else. Like those Tibetan monks who set themselves on fire to make a point."

"So what's their point?"

Kahn counted on his fingers. "War is bad? Life sucks? The army didn't treat them right? The Veterans Administration isn't doing enough to help them?"

"But there's no record of either of them holding a gripe. O'Shea says Littel's ex-wife didn't report anything that would lead you to believe the man would commit premeditated violence. She said the guy was pretty well adjusted. In fact, she was the one who had the affair that caused the marriage to bust up."

"Maybe that made him bitter and he didn't share."

"Right," Diaz said sarcastically. "The shy and retiring type who turns violent."

"Don't knock it. Fits the profile of a lot of bombers. Think Ted Kaczynski."

"He's sitting in his cabin writing manifestos, though. These guys are going to work every day, keeping their heads down. They didn't leave behind any signs."

"The work thing could be a cover, like I said before."

Diaz continued to think aloud. "It could also explain why someone's choosing them. They're less likely to arouse suspicions. They're blending in."

"Still, even if they're being chosen that doesn't mean they also aren't complicit. Osama chose KSM, who also chose himself."

"Maybe it's blackmail. Maybe they know something and they've been persuaded to take what they know to their graves."

"What—like black ops?"

"It would explain why nobody's creating propaganda around it."

"Conspiracy." Kahn shrugged. "That's always one possibility. Or, more likely, Littel was just imitating Horn's actions."

"With C4? On such short notice?"

"I admit that line of thinking is thin. But that doesn't mean they aren't directly involved in their own destruction."

"But it doesn't mean they *are* involved—that's all I'm saying—other than as victims. I know I got a bias, but if these guys just want to check out with a political statement, why not commit suicide and leave an angry note? O'Shea said Horn has the bronze star—a friggin' war hero. Both of them, they're American soldiers, and American soldiers are trained to avoid civilian casualties at all costs."

Kahn closed his report folder. "There you go again with that army idealism. You heard about that American soldier—right?—the one who walked through the Afghan village and murdered more than a dozen women and children in cold blood?"

"That guy snapped."

"Maybe these guys did, too. Snapped a long time ago, acquired the C4 or were persuaded to acquire it, and now they're finally acting on it."

Diaz bit his lip. Could he be that far from the truth on this one? Could preconceived notions about a soldier's sense of honor be interfering with his judgment? He thought of last night, pulling the gun on Jennifer's date. Hell, he could've killed the S.O.B while the jerk stood their buttoning his cuffs. He was on a hair trigger sometimes—couldn't these other guys be, too? But not with an IED. An IED wasn't even like a grenade—something that someone else made and that you could buy on the black market. These guys were hiding bombs in their false limbs—custom-made bombs.

"I'm not buying it," Diaz said. "There's something else going on here. I don't know what."

"I'm willing to listen, Manny, if you figure it out before the rest of us. I'm willing, but—" Kahn broke himself off.

Diaz watched the sergeant's mind wander and come back inside the truck and settle again on the report in his lap. Self-editing. Why? Diaz couldn't know for sure, but he suspected it had something to do with the reprimand.

He'd given himself a reputation with that damn package by the steps of St. Pat's. Now every minute Kahn expected him to run off the rails.

Despite the bright sun, Manis had his coat closed against the chill as he sat on a low wall of black polished granite in front of 26 Federal Plaza in Lower Manhattan. A post office resided inside the Social Security building there, and Manis watched its patrons come and go. One of these patrons, he hoped, would be a homeless man named Lewis Salinowsky, subject of the third picture on Manis's workshop wall and the only one left whose face he hadn't yet crossed out with a big red X.

More than two years ago, Salinowsky, motivated by love or by some similar delusion, had penned a long letter to Sallye Ritchie, a nurse who now worked for the Veterans Administration in a hospital near Boston. Salinwosky hadn't been aware of the nurse's current location, so he'd addressed the note to her last known workplace, the Landstuhl Regional Medical Center in Germany. It had taken the letter nearly eight months to catch up to Sallye's forwarding address, and five months ago she'd carried the note to Brooklyn in her purse with the sole purpose of using it to taunt Manis. That note had set Manis on his path of revenge, the post office box number written with a trembling hand in the return address field. And that note, he hoped, would now lead him to the man Sallye had always described as most virile of all her paramours.

Manis had been staking out the post office for the past two days, knowing that the federal government mailed most veterans' benefits checks around the first of the month. He'd left Sallye asleep in his apartment, presuming she wouldn't climb from bed until noon, when the post office would close for the day—Saturday.

It didn't take long for his bet to pay off. At a few minutes past ten, a lanky man in grimy clothes limped toward the front door and Manis followed at a safe distance. He watched the man go to the proper mailbox, but apparently he found nothing inside except junk. Salinowsky couldn't hide the disappointment on his face as he dumped his mail into the trash bin and wandered toward the door.

Unlike Horn, he had a pronounced limp. He pulled at an eyebrow and then fell into a trance before recovering himself, exiting the post office and heading up the street. He walked east and Manis followed—Worth Street to Leonard, up from there to a bench in Columbus Park with a cup and a sign.

Manis waited awhile until Salinowsky got comfortable. The park was quiet, despite the improved weather. In half an hour, the beggar had garnered no more than a few coins.

At eleven o'clock, Manis went up to him with a dollar in hand. "Nice day to be outside," he said, stuffing the dollar into the cup.

"Unless you got no choice," Salinowsky said. "Be cold tonight."

"You have nowhere to go?"

"I didn't say that." For the first time, Salinowsky looked up. Nothing in his face suggested any suspicion that the man in front of him wished him dead. But his cheeks twitched as if demons ran through his skull. He was too busy battling threats from within to perceive any from outside.

Salinowsky had what appeared to be several days' growth of blondish-gray beard, but his hair looked reasonably clean, Manis thought. His bloodshot dull blue eyes, however, betrayed premature age and unhealthiness.

Manis reached into his pocket and produced a five-dollar bill. This was no time to be stingy. "I wonder," he said, "where does a man like you sleep most nights?" And when Salinowsky looked quizzical he added quickly, "I'm looking for a cousin of mine who lives on the street around here."

Salinowsky squinted. "What's his name?"

"I'd rather not say. I don't want anyone tipping him off." Manis waved the bill. "Do you stay someplace with other people who're in your situation?"

"I do," Salinowsky admitted. He cast his gaze down again, which gave Manis a chance to study the lower part of the artificial leg that poked out between his pants and his dirty brown shoes. He'd seen the leg before, surreptitiously photographed it on the street when he'd tracked Salinowsky once before to another begging spot before later losing him. At that time, the vagrant had it displayed across his lap while he slept. Salinowsky got more pictures than he'd ever need. It was the same prosthesis, he was sure. Now he only wanted the address to plan an overnight visit and place his device.

"Please," Manis said, lying easily. "He's a veteran and he's fragile, my cousin. I want to bring him home."

"Maybe he doesn't want to go home. My sister wants me to go home, but I won't."

Manis took a stab. "He sent a request to me from some city shelter."

"That dump's up on Stanton." Salinowsky shook his head. "I won't stay there. I stay in the church shelter most nights, St. Euph's over on Allen Street."

"Ah, no." Now that he had a location, Manis sought quickly to bring the conversation to its conclusion. "I'm sure he won't be there. He doesn't believe in any church."

"You don't have to believe to go."

"All the same. Thanks." Manis practically choked on the word. He slipped the fiver into Salinowsky's cup and turned to depart.

"No atheists in the foxholes," Salinowsky said behind him.

Manis didn't turn back around. He repeated to himself, trying to get the accent: "No ate-ee-ists in da fox-oles."

When he rounded the corner, he immediately typed St. Euph's into his smart phone, lest he forget it. Not every day you came across a name as unusual as that. He'd look it up after Sallye left town and plan a visit there real soon, maybe skip showering as early as tomorrow morning in order to blend in when the time came.

AT THE BOMB SQUAD OFFICE, Diaz took a pile of photos and set them aside on the big break-room table—the same table where the guys on duty took most of their meals. Between the epidemic of flu and the epidemic of bomb calls, he had the place to himself.

The pile contained the crime scene photos from the Horn and Littel cases. In two days they'd become so familiar that he could no longer milk anything from them, couldn't look at them fresh. But some new pictures had arrived—the super-close-up lab photos taken with that static camera set-up they had at the lab.

In the old days, he was told, the bomb techs used to spread out the evidentiary fragments on this very table, trying to reconstruct the bomb. Nowadays, with the demands of modern forensics, the techs couldn't touch the evidence. So, other than rare occasions when they visited the lab, they had to confine themselves to pictures.

He spread out the new ones on the table and began poring over them. They showed every piece of the device that had survived the explosion and every fragment of Albert Horn's artificial legs, even his shoes.

Rather than sort them by left and right leg, as CSU had arranged them, Diaz decided to sort them based on whatever common elements he could discern. So he put shots of the feet next to one another, for example. CSU had photographed the feet with the shoes both on and off. They'd organized the rest of the legs on a tray like shards of pottery from an archaeological dig, arrayed as they thought they might fit together. Diaz placed pictures of the upper parts of the legs in their own pile and sorted out what the CSU techs took for the middle portion.

Altogether, it added up to a lot of images, every angle of every piece included. If you weren't looking for something in particular, the repetitiveness might make you space out real quick, but Diaz had something specific in mind. He was looking at the serial number on a piece of composite from one leg and trying to locate the matching piece on the other leg. Presumably the manufacturer stamped the serial number in the same place on every leg. So if he found the matching piece without a serial number, it would tell him which leg had contained the bomb.

He hunched over, resting the index finger of each hand on corresponding spots and peering from one to another, and he was so deep into it that he startled when Morris called, "Mariah Primm for you, Manny!"

Diaz straightened up and headed for his desk. "Mariah?"

"Senior tech at CSU?"

"She asked for me?"

"Sergeant Kahn is out. She says it's about the veterans case."

"Oh, okay. Roger that." Diaz picked it up and said his name into the phone. There was no small talk, Primm being the clinical type.

"We've had some success reconstructing the Littel bomb. As you probably know, like with Horn there are some cell phone parts but not enough to suggest an entire phone there."

Diaz's heart sank. "So…no remote detonation?"

"I didn't say that. Something very interesting is going on here, apparently. On site your team located a blasting cap, an SCR, an arming switch. All very minimal."

"Power source. We found a battery, too, right?"

"Yes, but not a cell phone battery."

"Yeah, we thought it was too big for that. If it's not from the cell phone, I'm guessing it was part of the prosthetic, the battery that powered the arm."

"Precisely, a six-volt."

"Hold on."

Diaz jogged back to the break room and gathered up the photos. He rifled through them at his desk. He'd been focused on the serial number issue, but this was far more important. Now that he looked carefully at remnants of the wiring in Littel's device, something jumped out at him.

"Whoever made this bomb wired it to the battery that was already in there," he said.

"Yes. Clever. Have you ever heard of anything like that?"

Diaz reflected. "I've seen car batteries used, radio batteries, flashlight batteries. Cell phones, of course. Can't say I've seen anyone use the battery from a mechanical limb. Dr. Primm, do you know exactly what it's doing in there—in normal circumstances, I mean."

"It powers the sensors and, more importantly, it needs that capacity to work the motors that bend the arm and fingers."

"Oh, sure. Makes sense. And, from the perspective of a bomb maker, plenty of juice to set off the C4 as a bonus. So what's with the cell phone parts—did it power the cell phone, too?"

"It's not remote detonation, Detective. No sign whatsoever of a receiver."

So for sure he'd been wrong. "There goes one of my theories."

"What theory is that?"

"I've felt pretty certain from the start that this wasn't a suicide. So I figured it had to be remote detonation."

"Not by cell phone, Detective. But from what we can tell, this bomb wasn't detonated by a direct application of force on the part of Littel, either."

"You're saying it's not remote but, at the same time, he *didn't* pull the switch?"

"That's correct. Maybe there was no switch to pull. It seems that the main trigger here is the GPS module from a cell phone. As I said, there's no receiver. Our working theory is that the precipitating factor was Mr. Littel walking into some GPS coordinates."

"You mean it was programmed to go off in a particular geographic spot?"

"Seems that way. The cell phone parts are part of the bomb, but it's not remote detonation by phone call."

Diaz broke into a broad smile. If it proved out, this meant he was right about the veterans after all. He'd have to get this to Kahn stat. He repeated for clarity, "So the guy carrying the bomb hits preprogrammed GPS coordinates and the bomb triggers."

"Simple as that. At least that's our theory. Our digital team is still trying to crack the code for how this device was set up. They're poking around inside the chip, which is delicate, as you can imagine. They don't want to corrupt it."

"No matter, doesn't sound like suicide to me."

"Me neither, Detective."

Just then Diaz saw Kahn come in. He tried to catch his attention, but the sergeant walked straight to Morris, said something Diaz couldn't hear, went into Capobianco's empty office, and closed the door.

"What all this means, if we're right," Diaz said into the phone, "is that there's a perp still out there."

"And if he hasn't run out of victims," Primm affirmed, "he could be building another bomb."

KAHN SAT BEHIND THE LIEUTENANT'S desk, door closed and blinds drawn, staring at the telephone. He couldn't picture Capobianco lying in bed, could only see him in shirtsleeves with his tie undone, standing by the couch in his living room, red in the face. Maybe he didn't need to hear about this now—about a cop in his squad who might be heading for trouble. No one had been hurt yet, after all, and maybe no one ever would be.

On the other hand, one thing Kahn could see clearly in his mind was Diaz strolling up to that messenger bag in front of the cathedral like he knew exactly what was inside—and he couldn't have known. Kahn saw him produce the Leatherman knife. He saw him hesitate when Kahn called to him in anger, hunch up his shoulders, then drop to one knee and proceed as if a superior officer hadn't just advised him to stand down. He heard Diaz explaining what he'd looked up in the dictionary, which concerned

Kahn more than anything—seemed to suggest a detective on the hunt for nothing but an excuse to go his own way. Then Kahn's thoughts coalesced around the voluntary report from Hernandez, this most troubling news of Diaz walking fine lines within feet of speeding traffic.

Suicidal? Maybe. Reckless? Most definitely. And Kahn kept thinking: *not on my watch, not on my watch.* He had a responsibility here. If Cap were back in the precinct house, easy enough to punt Hernandez to him. But that wasn't how the situation shook out. He picked up the phone and called the lieutenant.

"Cap here."

"You sound more yourself."

"It's good to hear your voice without my ears ringing, Kahn. And I'm damn sick of sitting around. It has me feeling marginalized, tell you the truth."

"Then I can help."

"News on the twin bombers?"

"Not exactly. Between us and A and E we've hoovered up enough evidence in the past three days, but it doesn't lead anywhere so far."

"Confirmed C4 with a military taggant, right?"

"Yes, sir. Burbette's trying to run down the source."

"Find an NSN number or IMEI on the phone?"

"No, Cap. We got cell phone parts but none of the right ones for that."

Capobianco started to say something else, hacked, got out a few words, and went into a full-out coughing jag. When he'd recovered, it seemed like a good time for Kahn to change the subject.

"I'm thinking of taking Diaz off the case."

"Diaz? Why? The reprimand wasn't enough? Breaking procedure again?"

"Not precisely." Kahn told him about what Hernandez had reported, the detective out in the middle of the night, playing in traffic.

"You shitting me?"

"I wish."

"Last I saw him he seemed fine. Now—is he that far gone?"

"This case strikes close to home, I think. It's dredged up something in him."

"But St. Pat's was before this case."

Kahn once thought he'd want Capobianco's job in a few years. Now he wasn't so sure. "Maybe the kid had a premonition, Cap. I dunno. I have no experience with this kind of thing. But I'm beginning to think he could need a psychiatric evaluation."

"We can put him in for that," Capobianco thought aloud. "Probably requires giving him leave. Can it wait until the squad's back at full force? Still got a lot of people out sick."

"Your call. I'm just sharing the facts. The kid's got a short fuse of late, arguing with me, arguing with O'Shea."

"Well, is he arguing about the case or about the weather?"

"About the case."

"That doesn't seem so bad. Everyone has their own style."

"True enough. It's walking at night in the middle of the West Side Highway that has me spooked."

"He's walking in the middle? I thought you said on the shoulder."

"Middle...shoulder—"

Just then the door burst open.

* * *

Sallye Ritchie sat brooding over a cooling mug of coffee in Warren Manis's apartment, her senses dull, her thoughts diffuse. She had her elbows resting on his small kitchen table, and she held the mug up to her mouth too long, her lower lip clinging to the hot ceramic near the broken skin where he'd hit her. It stung, and she pulled away, setting down the mug and pondering. This time last year he'd given her a shiner that she couldn't hide for weeks at work, had to concoct a story about hitting her face on the steering wheel in an auto accident. The other nurses looked at her cross-eyed for a while, but she had few friends close enough to press her. More troubling, those few who did know her well also knew that she'd acquired this measure of abuse on a trip out of town. They didn't know how or why, but they had to suspect something more than her lame explanation.

Now the split lip. She'd be back among the nurses tomorrow morning peddling another bullshit story to save face. But this time memory of the last incident might make their inquiries more insistent. All of them—including Sallye—had been trained to spot domestic abuse. For patients who came through the emergency room door, all were mandatory reporters. For a colleague, however, they'd have to tread more lightly. Still, Sallye knew it couldn't go on much longer. She'd have to rid herself of the obsessions that she'd allow to creep into her life, into her long relationship with this strange man.

Strange but not a stranger. She'd known him so many years now. How odd to carry on with such intimacy yet with so little depth of understanding.

She set down the coffee mug and cruised the apartment perimeter, opening cabinets and drawers, browsing books, seeking clues to the creature who Warren had become. For if she'd ever known him, she suspected that she no longer did. He'd morphed under pressure the way a diamond emerges from coal, but he hadn't turned into a beautiful gemstone, just into something misshapen, deformed. Yet she remained fixated on him, the same way a person couldn't easily avert her gaze from a bad car accident, wanting to set eyes on that appalling thing while also wanting not fully to see it. The exception being that she'd had a hand herself in this particular wreck.

The inside of the apartment showed few hints of Manis's inner self. Nothing unusual in the books or the few pieces of bric-a-brac. There were two photographs on display: a faded picture of his mother in front of a ranch house and one of Sallye holding a non-alcoholic beer in the lounge on the Eskan Village Air Base in Saudi Arabia. An army brat, she felt as comfortable there as anyplace—which wasn't necessarily saying much. She'd never felt an attachment to physical locations. Home wasn't four walls or a bed or a geographic spot. From her earliest days it was her father's lap, her mother's, or the knee of one of their friends. She felt warm and safe there and she yearned for it even after she'd grown up. That desire had become something deviant, she knew, this thing she did to men when no one was looking.

Deviant, yes, society would say so, but the behavior was nothing that she could help.

Behind a beaded curtain in Warren's apartment, she located the door that she'd seen many times before but had never passed through. The doorknob was locked and a padlock hung closed in place at her eye level for good measure. She'd asked about this door before, even tried to suss out the size of the room on the other side when they sometimes wandered the empty warehouse next door. But he wouldn't tell her what was inside. Now she rested a hand on the doorknob and put a hip to the door, but it was solid, unyielding. She jerked the padlock. Nothing.

Warren's behavior had changed of late. She still appeared able to lead him around by the nose whenever she wished, but something under the surface had shifted, like a fault line that you couldn't see just yet but that you could feel, could sense in your viscera. A workshop, he called it, but what made it secret? What he had in there, she thought...it meant something to him. Something, after all this time, that she now felt compelled to learn.

In a kitchen drawer filled with junk she found a large paperclip. She worked it around in the doorknob lock, prodding and twisting. The knob rattled but the paperclip didn't catch anything inside that she could lever. She tried the padlock and found it even more resistant. She needed something stiffer, went to her bag and found a cuticle trimmer in her manicure kit.

She tried the padlock again, got a little more play but couldn't make it trip open. Encouraged, however, she inserted the tool into the doorknob. It went farther in and she seesawed it while wiggling the knob. Pop! Suddenly the knob turned freely. The surprise of it made her spine tingle. *Halfway there.*

Sallye walked the perimeter of the apartment, listening for him. He was a volatile fellow and she couldn't predict how he'd react if he found her in the forbidden room. If she got the padlock open, she thought, she'd have to be satisfied with a quick gander inside, then get out of there and know she could go back anytime if the contents interested her.

Returning to the door, she parted the beaded curtain and began working the padlock again, pushing and pulling the block as she jammed the tip of the cuticle trimmer around inside. She was sweating now, some beads of the curtain sticking to her neck where they lay across the dampening skin, tugging ever so slightly at her as she moved her shoulders, prodding with the tool.

She felt like she was getting somewhere, the tumbler succumbing slightly, the tool going a little deeper, achieving a bit more angle. She sensed the trap of her own tunnel vision as she vigorously twisted at the keyhole, the lock inches from her face, but the danger had receded to the back of her mind. She could hardly feel the beads of the curtain tapping upon her neck one moment, then lifting off of her skin, almost of their own accord. Meanwhile Sallye prodding the lock, twisting, probing…

A voice from behind froze her. It came from Warren in an unfamiliar tone. Sonorous, penetrating her skin. It said, "What do you think you're doing?"

DIAZ IGNORED THE LOOK OF SHOCK on Kahn's face. Kahn had had his feet up on Capobianco's desk, and he dropped them to the floor like he'd been caught humping a freshly dead jellyfish.

"I knocked," Diaz said. He was too excited to retreat. "There's a break in the case."

"How do you mean?" Kahn said, still with the phone in his hand, still discombobulated. "They collared someone?"

"No," Diaz conceded. "Nothing like that. A technical break."

"Let me get the lieutenant on." Kahn set down the receiver and pressed a button on the desk set.

"Diaz," Capobianco said through the speaker. "Still got all them fingers?"

"I'm sorry about the cathedral thing, Lieutenant. No excuses."

"Forget it. It would've been your funeral, not mine. Don't do it again, though. It makes Kahn nervous. And he'd hate having to inform the next of kin." He chuckled.

More supportive than Kahn, more magnanimous, Diaz thought.

"Thanks, Lieutenant," he said. "I promise." He could practically see Capobianco winking at him.

"So...the breakthrough, Diaz."

He told them about the conversation with CSU, how the likelihood seemed high that the bombings were initiated by GPS coordinates. Bottom line: suicide not probable.

"Explains why the devices aren't so packed with shrapnel," Kahn said. "Maybe they're not meant to kill anyone else. It's flat-out assassination."

"How'd the bomber know what coordinates to put?" Cap asked.

Diaz said, "I guess he could've programmed every army recruiting station into the chip."

"Every one in America? Or—more likely..."

"The bomber is tracking the movements of his victims."

"That's what I'm thinking," Capobianco said.

"Worth a look," Kahn said. "And sort of like what Manny's been saying all along."

Finally a word of support from Kahn. Diaz thought it was too hard-earned, but he'd take it.

The conversation wrapped up. Through the speaker, Capobianco said, "Get back to work, Diaz. You're officially out of the doghouse."

Feeling more satisfied than he had in a long while, Diaz took himself to lunch at an Italian red sauce joint on the corner of Hudson and Jane Streets. He ordered a bowl of stracciatella, chicken parmigiana, and a side of ziti. As he sopped up the last of the sauce with a crust of bread, he thought with satisfaction that the new theory had come back around to his position, vindicating his faith in the two alleged perps—at least for the moment. Then he thought of the bomber possibly tracking his next victims. And for the first time in a week the voice in the back of his head repeated, "Danger lurks."

He caught the waiter's attention and called for the check. The waiter, exchanging glances with his boss, shook his head. "It's on us, chief." They knew they'd just fed a cop.

Diaz was placing a twenty on the table anyway when the phone rang, a blocked number. He picked it up. "Hullo."

"Detective Diaz?"

"That's me."

"Nunez here. How you doing?"

"Great, but I'll get better. You find anything out?"

"Sure as shooting. Your two boys—Horn and Littel—both passed through Landstuhl Hospital within a year of each other."

Diaz stood to go and glanced at his watch, phone cradled against his shoulder. "That's it?"

"What did you want in two days, for me to solve your case for you? It's a start, isn't it?"

"Captain, don't most amputees from Central Command pass through Landstuhl?"

"Sure, okay."

"So, much as I appreciate the news, I probably could've guessed as much without you telling me."

"You could've guessed but now we know for sure. You're asking for favors and all of a sudden you don't like what I'm giving you. You know, Diaz, I got a pile of paper on my desk two feet high and none of it has anything to do with the NYPD."

"Hold on. No offense, Captain. I'm just a little pumped up. We're starting to narrow this thing down."

"So you don't need me anymore."

"We need you more than ever. We're pretty sure there's a third party out there blowing up these veterans. He's hiding the bombs in their prostheses somehow."

A pause. "In their new limbs? They didn't suffer enough? Sick bastard."

"Good if we could end his streak. Help me think this through."

"Okay." Despite his protestations, Nunez seemed to be enjoying this. He jumped right in. "Landstuhl's one common thread, maybe. If the C4 also came from a base in Germany, then it has to do with a point of contact that these guys shared. Maybe it's someone they pissed off."

"That someone is in the States now, so it means he got discharged from the army and came back home."

"Or he was a contractor. Don't count out that possibility."

"Special Ops?"

"Those guys are usually inside. Besides them, only types I know with authorized access to C4 are EOD and combat engineers. Doesn't mean he was authorized, of course, but that's most likely, unless someone just went and lost a load. The sappers might use contractors. Or, like you said, he'd been inside and got discharged."

"How you doing with that list of everyone in the area who had access to U.S. Army C4?"

"I'm getting to it. Bound to be a long list."

"We'll narrow it down once we have it."

"Okay, Diaz. Give me a few minutes to get back to you."

"That quick? You meant a few days, didn't you, Captain?"

"A few minutes...a few days. Hell, could take a few years. But I'll see what I can do."

Diaz had second thoughts. "Here's another idea, then. Can you get the patient charts from these two men?"

Nunez hesitated. "That's confidential information, Diaz."

"They gave up their privacy rights when they died."

"Hmm. I like the way you think."

WHEN THEY MET AGAIN IN O'Shea's office in Alphabet City, Diaz felt more like a part of the team, and it relaxed him. He leaned back and levered his chair on its two back legs.

"So maybe it's not suicide," O'Shea said in a conciliatory manner.

Diaz appreciated that, because he knew it had been said for Kahn's benefit.

"Looks like assassination now," the sergeant agreed. "And Diaz has a bit more that he's been saving for us. Wouldn't tell me in the car."

"Out with it," O'Shea said into Diaz's smile.

Now, for the first time, Diaz revealed that he'd been having conversations with a high-up military police officer in Germany. Kahn may have suspected as much, but O'Shea looked impressed.

"If the C4 came from Germany and the victims both passed through Germany," he said, "seems like a high probability that there's a connection there to the bomber."

"Exactly," Diaz affirmed.

"So who touched both these guys at Landstuhl?" O'Shea asked.

"Lots of possibilities," Kahn said. "Doctors, nurses, security guards, cleaning staffs."

"Physical therapists," O'Shea added. "Shrinks."

"I don't think these guys get much physical therapy until they arrive stateside," said Diaz. "Shrinks are a possibility, though."

"The place is probably a beehive. How do we narrow it down?"

"I got the MP working on a couple of fronts."

O'Shea leaned back in his chair, ran his fingers through his red hair, blew a breath at the ceiling. "Damn far from solving this thing and the bomber's still out there, could strike any minute. There'll be hell to pay if another one of these guys blows up."

"I hear the governor has called in the National Guard to stand in front of every recruiting station," Kahn said. "They should be hitting the street right about now."

"Like they would've stopped either of these two guys?"

"Must be quite a few of those offices."

"More than a dozen in the five boroughs."

"That's not so bad. We can suggest they turn the entire block around each one into a no-go zone."

"Yeah, that'll really make people feel safe. And all the bomber has to do is reprogram the device so the GPS gives it more leeway. If it's assassination, this nut could tweak his MO easy enough, doesn't have to blow up these poor suckers right where he did before."

"He may blow his cover along with it."

"How do you figure?"

"He wants us to think these guys are terrorists, take the attention away from where it really belongs."

"So, now that we know that they're not terrorists, how does that help us? I think it makes our job harder in some ways. We're looking for a lone maniac."

Kahn shrugged. "Our job is no harder than it ever was. But now we got a working theory that the maniac has a connection to Landstuhl. What's Burbette doing these days? Isn't he officially supposed to be working that angle?"

"He tells me he's getting nowhere," O'Shea said, "caught in the sticky tape of bureaucratic inertia. It's on your MP, Manny. Back channel."

"My specialty," Diaz said. He looked at Kahn, who rolled his eyes. But the grimace on the sergeant's face had a smile peeking through it.

After Kahn and Diaz left, O'Shea went into the next room, where four of his investigators sat at a large folding table with dueling laptops. He'd recomposed himself for their benefit, but deep down he felt an unusual level of concern. He thought of the lab results and Diaz's army connections and couldn't avoid the conclusion that this investigation may be getting away from him. There was no harm in his having been likely wrong about the suicides. In this business, it didn't matter where you started—only where you finished. But O'Shea didn't feel like he was driving his own bus anymore. Diaz's initiative was carrying the Bomb Squad well into AES territory, and if O'Shea ended up with a back seat in his own investigation, Capobianco's squad threatened to rob the investigations squad of its glory.

Not that O'Shea cared much about the credit himself. He liked his job, and for all intents and purposes he was exactly as most people saw him: not stupid or uncaring, but not a conniver either, just naturally relaxed under pressure. No matter the case, he went home and slept well every night. But he couldn't say the same for Ray Fisco, the commander of AES. Fisco, a striver, always had an eye on the next rung of the ladder. When you're in that position, you have to look out for danger from above and from below, which put you on full alert every second. Lately Fisco had been fielding too many unsolicited calls from the guy whose job he wanted, Inspector Rex Brennan. Didn't help that Joe Capobianco, head of the Bomb Squad, reported to the same guy.

O'Shea walked around the table, picking up papers and peering at them, sneaking peeks over everyone's shoulder. While Diaz and Kahn were off chasing glory, he and his team had undertaken the mind-numbing scutwork that led to most arrests. They had reams of information listing every armed services veteran who received disability benefits in the New York City area, looking for some common pattern that also fit Horn and Littel. It would've been nice if some dweeb in Washington had ever produced a list of veterans who were missing limbs. Then O'Shea's team would only need to cross-check that with the benefit recipients to find a manageable group. But no such luck. They were having to dig for every individual detail and create their own database. At least, O'Shea thought, they'd had the good sense early on to filter out anyone who'd left the armed forces before the first Gulf War.

And now they had the Landstuhl connection—but it wasn't like the Veterans Administration had that stamped next to anyone's name, either. O'Shea thought with a sigh that he'd have to report soon to Fisco, and what would he tell him.

He watched one of his men stand from his chair with his hands laced behind his neck, stretching. Must've been catching because within seconds the other three cops emulated the first. They looked like a bunch of college kids who'd just pulled all-nighters, hair mussed and eyes bugging out of their heads. O'Shea had read recently that being too sedentary could kill a man. Who said a desk job at the NYPD wasn't as dangerous as walking the beat?

* * *

MANIS DIDN'T HIT SALLYE, DIDN'T raise a finger to her right then. He took forceful hold of her upper arm and pulled her away from the door, grabbing a strand of the colorful curtain as he did so, beads clattering to the floor. They crunched underfoot as she turned around.

"What are you doing?" he repeated.

She started to apologize but caught herself. He'd scared her for a change, but all she had to do was re-establish the pattern. "You've got something to hide in there. I don't like you keeping secrets from me."

Manis let go her arm. "Come live here. I'll clean out the workshop and that can be your space."

"You'd do that?"

"Only for you."

"You're pathetic."

"Am I? Give me that!" He snatched the cuticle cutter from her hand. In one motion he took it into his fist, wrapped the other arm around her waist, and held the sharp instrument within an inch of her right eye. "How's it feel?"

It didn't feel good. She blinked and her eyelashes brushed the pointed end, but then she managed to twist away and push past him into the center of the room.

"That lock," Manis said, tossing the cuticle tool to the table, "it can't be picked."

"Where were you?" she asked.

"Out on an errand. I thought you'd sleep later. You usually do."

"Something got me out of bed early." She didn't want to tell him about the bad vibe he'd been throwing off, how it had risen in intensity all year, how it was beginning to scare her. "What kind of errand?"

"You're a needy woman, Sallye. It's not so easy to satisfy you. Takes a lot of groundwork." A thought crossed his mind. He added, "No ate-ee-ists in da fox-oles."

Sallye furrowed her brow. "What the hell's that supposed to mean?"

"I'm re-acquiring a New Yawk accent. Isn't that what gets you excited?"

"That's a joke, not an accent. You sound like one of those kids from *Our Gang* or something, not like the big strong men who walk the streets around here."

"Most of them don't have it either."

"That's why I'm selective. So sue me."

"Why does it matter, anyways, the way a man talks? I've never understood it."

She walked to the photo he had of her, picked it up, stared into her own younger eyes. "They make me feel like a girl again, that's why. I lost my virginity at fourteen to a guy in my father's platoon. A guy from the Bronx. You remember him."

That cut him deeper than she expected. He dropped his voice. "You were a virgin, eager to move along. You wanted it."

She set down the photo.

"I couldn't control myself."

She shrugged. "I was nearly full grown. But also a baby with a deep yearning to be touched. That note my mother sent, when you were in the sick bay and my father and the rest of the platoon had shipped out... What did it say?"

"You never read it?"

She shook her head. "I was a good girl."

"Your mother gave you to me. She saw me as your salvation."

"She was always off somewhere, probably getting her own."

"So was your father. She hoped I'd grow you up."

She snarled. "You did a job of that, didn't you?" Then suddenly she wanted to drop all of it, get away from the subject. She asked herself aloud, "Why am I revisiting this anyway?"

Manis set his jaw. "Same reason you tell me all your other tales. Because it turns you on."

When he said that she knew she'd miscalculated. For some reason, the story had helped him recapture something he'd misplaced. It made him bolder. He reached out and touched her hurt lip, forced his thumb between her teeth. She pushed him away. "It does turn me on. Makes me hornier than the sight of you today ever will."

"But you're here, aren't you? And the man I was—he's in the past. No ate-ee-ists in da fox-oles."

"Stop saying that. You sound like a turd."

"I didn't back then?"

"That man, Warren... He caressed me down to the *bone,* made me come *alive,* made me..." She stopped.

"Made you what?"

"Made me feel at home. Then you shipped out, you bastard."

"Not by choice."

"By the time he came back, I was a different person. We both were."

"I wish I could have that girl again."

She watched Manis rake his eyes over her. He reached for her robe but only got the belt. It detached as she spun away, and she clutched the robe closed.

"I said it's no longer the same," she said.

That seemed to give him a pang. He grimaced like he had a stitch somewhere. He went red in the face.

She crossed her arms in front of her chest and shivered, longing with every fiber of her being for that which she'd lost.

"You've never mentioned me to anyone, have you?" Manis asked. "Then or now."

He had her there. She'd never told a soul about him—not here, not in Boston, not in Germany. Their relationship was like a small fire in a dangerous place. One draft of oxygen and it might spread out of control.

She said, "Did I ever tell you about Lewis?" She saw him flinch. That reaction she'd seen before. The name caught him like a bullet to the gut.

"Only a thousand times."

"He was the closest I ever had to the perfect lay, you know." She closed her eyes. "A real man, he was, solid as a rock. All of him. And he had that accent, too. Not like you do it—"

"No ate-ee-ists in da fox-oles."

"Would you shut up already with that!" She had to go soon, would put herself on the night train to Boston. This thing they had between them, it was heading for the danger zone, would reach that point one day soon and she'd regret that she let it get that far. But not yet. She couldn't resist using him. Passion stirred deep within her.

She sauntered over to the unmade bed, rested the tips of her fingers on the balled comforter. "I can see him there."

"So can I," Manis said.

"Not an ounce of fat on him. Not like you, chubs. A real man, firm and hard and well endowed." She closed her eyes. "Take off your clothes and lie down, Warren."

"I won't do it this way again with you. I won't."

She walked to him and took hold of his belt buckle.

"Unlike the others, Lewis knew from the start that I wanted him. He was awake. Alert."

"What difference does it make?" Manis said. "You'll never have him again."

"How do you know?"

"He's dead. He will be."

"All of us will be. So what! He's alive in me now. Do you want to do it or not? I'll tell the story different this time. Give it all to you." She dropped her robe to the floor, placed one foot on the edge of the bed, and stood there in all her scrawny sexuality, showing him her womanhood.

Seeing his anger grow evoked the old pattern for her, made her yearn for the violence that would follow—the ecstasy and the explosion.

She went into a trance, thinking of the old Warren and all he'd meant to her, of his fine eyebrows—Manis now had scars where his eyebrows should be. Of his five o-clock shadow on her soft young skin—the dark rough stubble as opposed to when she met Manis again on the base, years later, his new bushy beard already showing gray in it. Of the enormous feeling of Warren inside her those first few occasions when they'd lain together.

But at the same time that she was thinking of the old Warren, she narrated to the new one the story of her secret romps with Lewis in a room on the second floor of the hospital, how she got him, half dazed, to prop himself up on his one good leg and hold her up with one arm while his other hand grasped the handrail of the bed, how she'd allowed him to rediscover his manhood and violate her in every orifice. And how she'd cried out in pleasant surprise, almost getting caught by the supervisor.

Oh, how I'd cried out, thought that very moment would be the end of me.

She was crying out now, something calling from her viscera, the hurt and the pleasure and the loneliness. She writhed underneath Manis. Afraid. Tried to escape the blows that she'd invited, but it was no use.

Then she lost consciousness.

When she opened her eyes in the apartment in Brooklyn, she hurt up and down. It was early evening. Her eyebrow was cut and her nose was broken. Blood had dried all over the sheets, and Manis was gone.

Then she realized where to find him—back in the secret room.

Its padlock hung unlatched, but the handle wouldn't budge. Light splashed under the closed door, and through the seams she heard a shuddering high-pitched whine. It sounded like power tools.

Around five o'clock, the temperature dropped and clouds rolled in. A clipper system blew down some snow, but not enough to stick, just the right amount to dash the hopes of anyone who dared to anticipate spring. National Guard troops paced the sidewalks in front of every recruiting office within seventy-five miles of downtown Manhattan, with the governors of New Jersey and Connecticut getting into the act, ignoring the fact that no one had any evidence of a threat within their states.

Generally speaking, Bomb Squad detectives had no time to process the high drama quotient that had begun to weigh on this case. That afternoon, members of the squad got summoned to fourteen suspicious package calls in three hours, two of them falling to Kahn and Diaz. How Diaz had squeezed in the leisurely lunch, he didn't know. Now he sat dog-tired in the break room, waiting for the microwave to cook his ramen snack. He'd gone off duty ten minutes ago, but he needed a fillip before hitting the street.

Through the doorway he heard someone say, "Manny still here?"

He jumped up and went into the squad room. It was the phone for him. Nunez.

Diaz looked at his watch. Second call in less then twelve hours and ten o'clock at night in Germany. This had to be good news.

"You're a hard worker, Captain Nunez."

"You told me it was a matter of life and death."

That response made Diaz miss the military, where they'd bury you in paperwork to replenish your pencil supply but when lives got put on the line everyone snapped into action. Not that his Bomb Squad colleagues didn't take their jobs seriously, but Diaz just didn't always sense the balls-to-the-wall urgency. An abundance of caution seemed to hang over every action.

Nunez cut right to it. "Got the patient charts we talked about."

"That easily?"

"Took some doing, some sneaking around. Let's just say this conversation is deeply off the record."

"Confirmed."

"Also couldn't help myself so I crunched some of the data for you. Your men Horn and Littel...eight persons involved in their cases overlapped."

"That many?"

"Hospital only has a few hundred rooms. Of the eight—all doctors and nurses—one is deceased, five are still at the hospital in Landstuhl, one male doctor has now been assigned to the Sternberg Army Hospital in Luzon, Philippines, and a female nurse works stateside at the VA Medical Center in Bedford, Mass."

"The five who still work at Landstuhl, they take any leave lately?"

"I'm checking on that. According to the work schedules I've seen so far, it seems unlikely that any of those five would've been able to blow someone up in New York over the past two months. Maybe if the devices were manufactured and placed well in advance..."

"I doubt that. It's hard for me to imagine that they were stable enough to take the punishment of daily use for too long without going off on their own or malfunctioning."

"So most likely we can rule out the ones still working at the hospital."

"The one who's deceased—"

"A plastic surgeon."

"We know he's dead for sure?"

"A she, not a he. Fifty-five-year-old woman in the middle of a shift. Complained of stomach pains and three minutes later keeled over with a massive coronary. It all happened in front of six colleagues. I'd safely posit that they're not all in on a conspiracy to fake her demise."

"Man, it's gotta be pretty bad if you collapse right in the hospital and they can't save you."

"Maybe they were all waiting for an appropriation from Congress," Nunez deadpanned.

Diaz made sure that the MP heard him laugh. "And the doc in Luzon?"

"I have a call in. Rather not give his name unless there's something there, considering how I got this information."

"Okay. What about the nurse in Massachusetts? You got a name and address?"

"No home address, no. She calls herself Sallye Ritchie."

TICK, TICK, TICK, TICK, TICK, TICK, TICK

8.

DAY FOUR: DARK

DIAZ HAD HIS APARTMENT KEYS IN his hand when he heard a thud. He cocked his ear to the closed door and listened with more care. Two voices. He was sure one belonged to Jennifer. The other had a deeper pitch. It took him only a second before he concluded that it belonged to the guy from last night.

Now he heard more thumps, softer, a rhythm to them. Giggling. Soft talking. Moaning. He pictured two legs of the couch tilting up and falling back with each thrust. He could barge in and catch them both bare-assed, watch the arrogant guy retreat, have another uncomfortable conversation with J-Fo. What the hell would that accomplish? She'd chosen this guy, and Diaz had no designs on her. It was an inconvenience, sure, but after what had already transpired, why not let the woman have her fun?

He slipped the keys back into his pocket and retreated, taking the stairs down. The voice in his head said, "On nights like this, Manuel Diaz wondered whether the only kind of luck he ever had was bad luck." Hell, he'd been wearing a smile on his face when he reached the door, best mood that had possessed him in weeks, ready to show his roommate that he could be as pleasant as the next guy, not just all negative. Why this night of all nights does he have to come home to the sound of Jennifer's lovemaking?

Before long—he didn't plan it—Diaz's feet had carried him back under the bridge, to the path beside the parkway. He knew he shouldn't be there, that it was drawing him like those women from mythology—what did you call them?—sirens. *Oh, yes, sirens.* That was funny. How did it come to be that sirens now meant something that drove you out of the way?

He thought all those things in earnest, with hints of self-awareness, but yet he stepped over the concrete barrier anyway.

A cold wind had picked up. It flapped his coat with a certain violence as the cars roared by, made him wonder how close the fabric was coming to those headlights. Had a Range Rover just clipped him or was that a whip of the wind?

Another car went by, real close. Crazy close. If his coat caught in a bumper, it would mean the end of him. *This is nuts,* Diaz thought. *I'm nuts.* He saw Hernandez in his mind, jumping out of the car. "You okay?" The look of surprise on his face—surprise mingled with a kind of consternation—a narrowing of the eyes that said, "I don't need this shit." Of course, because that's how they rolled, thirty-eight guys all in this thing as a team, you drop a banana peel and it's not some stranger who lands on his ass, but one of your buds. Why was that so hard for Diaz to grasp these days? He'd sure known it in Iraq.

He thought of the bozo in his apartment right now, putting the wood to Jennifer. Wasn't it Gandhi who said, "Hate the action, not the man"? *Something to that,* Diaz thought. Sort of like by making the world safe for women and children, you also made it safe for some jerk to stand inside your own kingdom and bend your roommate over the couch, and no one could separate the two actions because they both fell on some kind of continuum. *Hell.*

The cars flew by. Diaz thought about those two guys on the street with their limbs twice blown off, their bodies penetrated by ball bearings, how they fell to the sidewalk with their eardrums punctured, once and for all cut off from the world's pain but also from its love.

An aspect of that image snapped Diaz back from the dark place he'd been inhabiting. He stopped in his tracks and turned to face the cars and became scared of his own stupidity, looking into those headlights in the growing darkness.

In one quick motion he leapt over the concrete barrier, back to the safe side. He returned to the walking path and found his way to the bar on St. Nicholas Avenue.

"Usual?" the bartender asked.

Diaz frowned. "Just a beer." He had to kill time but he wanted his head to stay clear.

He looked at his watch. After eight o'clock. Give her another hour and then she'd have to understand, if she didn't already, that it was his apartment, too. But Diaz no longer had it in him to be angry. He was willing to figure that she just mistimed her little romp, lost track of the hour, or had expected him later. There could be a million explanations besides her rubbing his nose in it. And why would she intend to do that, anyway?

The bar had another old cop movie playing on the television tonight. Diaz didn't pay it any mind. He thought of the TV news crews that forced themselves onto the scene of every bombing, of the twice-daily press conferences at City Hall, people staring at the National Guard troops from across the street. They all ate it up. Deep down they all wanted something to happen, to remind them with the threat of death that they were all alive. And the voice in Diaz's head intoned, "Is it any different for Manny?"

THE GUY WAS GONE WHEN Diaz walked into the apartment, Jennifer on her bed in those terrycloth short shorts and a printed t-shirt with sparkly gold lettering. She was freshly showered, and soapy steam permeated the living room air.

Diaz called hello to her and changed into sweatpants and a torn button-down shirt. With the heat pipes knocking, he sat on his bed and propped himself against the wall on some pillows and broke into the middle of a fitness magazine that he had lying around. *Really should get back to work on those abs.*

"Penny for your thoughts." Jennifer stood in the doorway with her arms folded across her chest.

"I was thinking that I need to hit the gym more," Diaz said truthfully, tossing the magazine to the floor, atop a pile of several others.

"Those pictures aren't real, you know. Airbrushed."

"What's next? You gonna tell me that *South Park* is just a cartoon?"

"That's right. Tom Cruise didn't really come out of the closet."

"I'll be damned."

"Can I sit?"

When Diaz nodded she perched at the foot of the bed. Even without trying, Diaz thought, she looked sexy as hell. She was wearing no bra, and her bare legs glowed like well-oiled weapons.

"You're home on the late side tonight. More trouble in paradise?"

"There's always trouble, whole city on high alert, running around all day x-raying empty packages. But I got home around six. You were occupied so I took off for a while."

She blushed then. He wasn't sure he'd ever witnessed that before.

"I'm not seeing that guy anymore."

"That was quick. You sounded like you were having a good time just a couple of hours ago."

"It started out that way but he turned out to be a jerk. He's a dentist, you know, has an office in the Chrysler Building."

"Are those three things related?"

"I warned him that we had to be quiet out of respect for Manny."

Diaz wanted to say that it's hard to be unobtrusive when you're screwing on the living room furniture, but he let it go. The new him.

"So he produces this contraption," she went on, "some kind of anti-tooth-grinding mouth guard with padded, like, cheek things. It resembled a—" She circled her hand in the air, searching for it. "One of those things you put on a horse."

"Like a bit and bridle?"

"Yes, for a carriage horse or something. He wanted me to bite down on it, like he was going to ride me. Made me feel like an animal—and not in a good way. Asshole."

She looked down at her hands and Diaz adjusted himself on the bed and studied her some more. Her ears were small and they directed the eye straight down the curve of her neck to her collarbone. Her arms had a hint of baby fat and her breasts looked plumper and more seductive through the t-shirt than they had when fully exposed to him. In spite of himself, he tried to picture that moment again, to freeze it in time, but the details had already faded. Only the awkward feeling remained.

She caught him looking at her, didn't move but said, "Why do men have to be such jerks? Half of them want to drag a woman into the gutter and the other half want to preserve her in amber."

"And your last real boyfriend, which kind was he?"

"First one kind, then the other. I was nothing but arm candy after a while. He always wanted me looking perfect. Like a butterfly in a case."

"Which is dead."

"What?"

"The butterfly in the case is dead."

"Exactly."

Manny felt philosophical. He said, "Beauty is best when you only see parts of it, like the butterfly flitting around. In real life, you don't often get a full look. In the display case, it's just too much. It overwhelms your senses and makes itself trite. The specialness goes."

She looked pleased. "I didn't know you had this kind of wisdom, Manny."

"I'm surprising myself. But I was just thinking—" He caught himself. "I don't want to sound like one of those jerks."

"You won't. Just tell me."

He took a breath. "When I saw you the other day in the bathroom, sounds insane but it was only one breast and the other was hidden behind the door. The hidden one made the other one that much more beautiful, because it left something for another time, something unknown.

Same just sitting here. You're ten times sexier with your clothes on."

"Are you coming on to me, Manny?"

"No."

"It sure sounds like you are." She touched the arch of his bare foot. "You know, I really like you, Manny. Maybe not just as a friend."

He reached out a hand and they interlaced fingers. But when she twisted herself onto her knees and began crawling to him, he stiffened his arm, holding her off. There'd been a time, not beyond memory, when he'd have begged the gods for what she was offering him. Now he just pebbled his chin and met her beautiful liquid eyes.

"The thing is, J-Fo...I can't get it up."

"Huh?"

"I'm impotent."

There it was. She flinched, stunned, like he'd just hit her across the bridge of her nose with a stick. He had to laugh at that.

"So you're joking."

"Not at all. You just looked so gobsmacked. Why's it so hard to believe?"

"You're so—so virile, I guess. Is it a war injury?"

"You could call it that if you want. It's nothing physical. My mind just don't want my pecker to go on alert anymore. It's retired."

"And it won't ever come out of retirement?"

"I don't know. Not any time soon."

"How can you tell for sure?"

"Let's just say I've tested it on more than one occasion."

"Maybe they weren't the right girls."

"I don't think that explains it."

"So when you saw me the other day..."

"Nothing."

"Is that what made you angry?"

"Could be. Or something else. I got a lot on my plate right now."

"But what could be more important than this?"

"Lots of things, Jennifer. A whole heap of things."

TICK, TICK, TICK, TICK, TICK, TICK

9.

DAY FIVE: LIGHT

DIAZ HAD A FRIEND WITH AN old Nissan that rarely got used. It sat out in the elements on a vacant lot in Harlem, paint faded, dashboard cracked. But there was air in the tires and the engine always started on the first try.

The radio worked, too, still the original one after all these years. Nobody stole car radios in New York anymore. Diaz had his theories on that.

At half past five on Sunday morning, he opened the creaky driver's door and climbed in behind the wheel. By six-thirty he had it gassed up with the fluids topped off. At a few minutes after seven he accelerated onto the Harlem River Drive, heading for the Cross Bronx Expressway. Despite the sense of crisis, Kahn had insisted that he follow his schedule and take the day off, making Diaz wonder whether all of his progress with the sergeant over the past day had been illusory. Either way, the case of the veterans ate at him. With nothing else to do and J-Fo heading to her parents' house in Jersey for the day, he couldn't bear sitting around the apartment. He'd decided on a working weekend.

As usual, a good bit of I-95 by the Connecticut border resembled a parking lot, though at this time of year you couldn't blame beach traffic. *Maybe skiers,* Diaz thought. Once he got past New Haven, snow lay on the ground in the shadows of roadside trees.

At nine he followed the blue signs and pulled into a Burger King parking lot. He took out his phone and called Nunez. "Hey, I need a favor."

"You didn't solve that case yet?" the MP jibed.

"I'm a slacker. Can you help me out?"

"I'm beginning to feel like part of the team."

"You're one of the good guys, Nunez, no question. But still unofficial. Our A and E man is a cop named O'Shea. One of them redhead types. Lanky and old school."

"Don't tell me. His grandmother used to run guns for the IRA."

"I hadn't thought of that. Maybe she made bombs. Maybe he's doing his penance on Avenue C."

Nunez laughed. "I could come to like you, Diaz. So what about O'Shea?"

"He's point man and I'd like you to fax him something, if you don't mind. That nurse who's stateside—Sallye Ritchie—and the doc who went to the Far East—"

"The surgeon's a dead end."

"That right?"

"Turns out he's been promoted to colonel and he has some big job in PACOM. He's got more on his plate than a sumo wrestler at dinner. No way he's got time to moonlight building bombs."

"You sure?"

"Maybe if this was going down in Hawaii there'd be an outside chance. But not in New York. If he's set foot in that city at all in the past few years he'd be surrounded by half a dozen aides."

"Okay." Diaz let out a breath. He thought about telling Nunez where he was headed, but decided against it. "Is the nurse still a possibility?"

"I'm neutral on that."

"Fine. What I'd like O'Shea to have is a list of all her patients while at Landstuhl. Can you pull that together for us?"

"Take a bit of work but I don't see why not. Probably in a computer file somewhere. If not, they'll have paperwork, patient records."

"I got a notion that O'Shea's team can cross-check her patients against vets known still to be in New York. Maybe we can anticipate his next victim."

"Good idea," Nunez said. "I'll do it."

Diaz hung up and hit the Burger King drive-thru, working his way through an artificial-tasting breakfast as he rode along. The highway had opened up, so he made good time the rest of the way, arriving in Bedford just before noon.

He stopped into a diner in an old clapboard house on Great Road, left a pee and took a sweet coffee to go. Although he had the address of the VA hospital in his phone, he asked directions of an elderly woman on the sidewalk. Easier to get it from a local than to drive around with his eyes off the road.

Before he headed to the hospital, though, he dropped into the police station, which had been wisely located next to the high school, an open admission that teenagers were the source of most trouble in a town of this small size. He introduced himself to the officer in charge, acknowledged that he had no warrant, but said out of courtesy he just wanted someone to know he'd be poking around.

"You got a gun?"

"My service weapon," Diaz said, pulling back his overcoat and showing the holster.

"Okay," said the officer. "If there's a bomb involved, though, that'd be the state troopers."

"I doubt it'll come to that," Diaz said, though he doubted his own doubts. "But I appreciate the heads-up."

In a few minutes, he'd pulled into the cold, bleak parking lot of a sprawling brick federal facility. The old part reminded him of a Nineteenth Century mental hospital and the new part looked like every plain municipal box of the Fifties and Sixties, before the government decided to make its buildings even uglier. He knew places like this—had spent half his life within their walls—and he also knew that the people inside rarely lived down to the bleakness of their surroundings. Against all percentages, the human spirit wanted to rise.

Without identifying himself as a cop, he told the receptionist he was looking for Ms. Ritchie. Was she on today? The elderly receptionist kindly called someone in administration, who informed her that the nurse should just be getting off shift.

"Does this involve one of her patients?" the receptionist asked.

"No," Diaz said. "It's personal, but I'd really like to catch her. Where would she get out?"

The receptionist didn't show a hint of suspicion, maybe because Diaz had chosen to don a suit and tie for the occasion. If she did become suspect, he'd show his badge, but he'd rather not cause people to talk. She directed him to the employee parking lot and he hung around by the door, asking anyone not too old whether she was Sallye Ritchie.

At twelve-thirty, a nurse with bandy legs and an open wool coat stepped out the door and began walking toward the parking lot. She was remarkably thin and she still wore her uniform.

"Excuse me," Diaz said for the tenth time, "can you help? I'm looking for nurse Sallye Ritchie."

He saw immediately that he had her. And she also must have known by her hesitation that she'd given herself away. "That's me," she admitted. "Who is it wants to know?"

Diaz showed her his badge and introduced himself.

"What's this about?" she said, clutching her coat closed against the chill.

"I'd like to—" It was then he noticed the bruises. She'd done a good job with the pancake makeup—to a point, anyway—but you'd have to be blind not to see that someone had beaten her up, and not long ago. One eye still had bad swelling around it and the white was mottled yellow and red. The bridge of her nose was swollen, too.

"Listen," Diaz suggested, "can we sit down somewheres? Get a sandwich and a cup a coffee?"

Her eyes darted, looking for a way to evade him, but Diaz decided right there not to make threats that would turn her more skittish. His instincts told him to play it soft. "Please," he said. "I drove all the way straight from New York City this morning."

She wouldn't look directly at him, but she gave a strained smile. "That where you got that accent, Detective?"

"Born and bred in the city, ma'am."

Ritchie chewed the inside of a lip and shrugged. "My car's just there. Can you follow me?"

Diaz readily agreed. He supposed she could bolt, but there'd be no point, now that he knew for sure where she worked.

He watched her climb gingerly into her navy blue Ford Focus, her white sneaker the last thing to disappear.

Before he started his car, just to be safe, he wrote down her license plate number.

IT WAS A LEISURELY DRIVE, Diaz figuring that the nurse drove slowly to gather her thoughts. But he wondered what those thoughts contained. She'd just had a visit from an out-of-state cop and she had no idea what he wanted. Or maybe she did have an idea.

He followed her to a place outside town, a greasy spoon toward the end of a strip mall farthest from the road. She parked between a car and a handicapped space. Diaz pulled through an open spot in the middle so his grille faced out. He was turning off the ignition when his phone rang, O'Shea calling.

Ritchie paused with her hand on the door to the restaurant, sensed that Diaz wasn't behind her, and turned around. He held up the phone and pantomimed, getting the point across that he'd be right there, and she entered without him.

"What's up, Brian," he said.

"I got that fax from your friend."

"That was fast. Anything there?"

"She treated both of our victims in Germany, but we knew that already."

"You don't think it could be coincidence."

"If it is, I'm pitching for the Yankees tonight."

"It ain't baseball season."

"It ain't coincidence, either."

"You got anything else?"

"We cross-checked her patient list with known veterans in New York."

"That was fast, too."

"Thank God for computers. In addition to our two vics, only one guy comes up, lives in a post office box—our luck."

"What's his name?"

"Lewis Salinowsky. Got a few guys on the street already looking for him."

"Good." Diaz wrote it down.

"I called you right away," O'Shea said, "seeing as you've been out front on this. We're also tracking down an address for the nurse."

"Don't bother with that."

"Why?"

"I'm about to buy her lunch."

She already had one thick ceramic cup on the paper placemat in front of her when he walked in. Plus one for him. She'd even added the cream. She nodded to it.

"Drink up. It's getting cold. I ordered you a BLT. Whole wheat toast."

"Thanks. Do you know why I'm here?"

"I'm guessing my nurse friends called you."

"Why would they?"

She reached for her bruised cheek. Her arms were also black and blue. "They don't miss much. A few of them voiced their concerns today."

"I'm a New York cop."

"I visited there recently. They know that."

Diaz shrugged. "Assault and battery ain't my jurisdiction. I'm with the Bomb Squad."

He watched that register. It didn't seem to set off any alarms. She sipped her coffee. "What's that got to do with me?"

"We've had a pair of bombings in the past week. You hear about them?"

She shook her head. "I don't follow the news much. It's too depressing."

"I'll say. These two guys—army veterans—got blown up within a couple days of each other." He told her the names. "Mean anything to you?"

"No." She frowned and shook her head. Diaz noticed that her face had little affect, but he supposed that could be a tool of her trade. You might learn to disguise your feelings to protect the feelings of your patients. It was a valid theory, anyway.

Don't jump to any conclusions. Just keep pressing. "They were both patients of yours at Landstuhl."

"Oh? That's strange. But, then again, I had so many. When?"

Diaz pulled out a pair of photographs. He laid them on the table. "Does this refresh your memory any?"

She slid them toward her end, looked down, and smiled gently. "Yes, it does. This one's Gavin and the black guy's Albie."

"So you do know them."

"It was a long time ago."

"How about Lewis Salinowsky?"

He caught her with that. Something changed in her face, but she shook her head. "You have a picture?"

"No."

"Did he get blown up, too?"

"Not to my knowledge. How do you know him?"

"Like you said, he was a patient of mine," she admitted. "They all were."

There was more to it than that. He could see it flash across her eyes. Something devilish. Consciously or unconsciously, she was suppressing an emotion that wanted to rise inside her of its own accord.

"It's no joke, ma'am. Like I said, two of them are deceased. And by violent means."

"I'm not laughing. Not at that, anyway. Just that I have fond memories. Is there a law against that?"

"Depends what those memories lead you to do."

"You don't think I'd hurt them!"

"Crazier things have happened."

She put a hand on her breastbone. "I'm a nurse."

"That doesn't disqualify you."

"What I do is help people, Detective, not hurt them."

Diaz took a sip of the now-cold coffee. He found it watery and flavorless. He added two packets of sugar but that didn't help. When he set the cup down for the third time, he said, "I'll give you the dates of the bombings. Please tell me your whereabouts at that time."

He used the calendar on his phone, just to be sure, even though he had the dates seared in his memory.

She rocked her head back and forth. "Those are weekdays, aren't they?"

"Yes, last Tuesday and Thursday."

"I was here, working."

"At the hospital?"

"Correct."

"Their records will corroborate that?"

"Of course."

Diaz studied her as he ate his sandwich. He knew never to rule out anyone based upon their appearance or livelihood. And there was something strange about her. On the other hand, her alibi was too easy to check. No one trying to cover up would claim to be working in a hospital on those days. Working at home alone, maybe, but not someplace where you signed in and a hundred people saw you during the course of the day. Then again, there was the GPS angle. Whoever did this may have set events in motion days ahead.

"So, how'd you get that shiner, Ms. Ritchie?"

"The shiner?"

"The eye. The cheek." Now that some lipstick and some cover-up had worn off, he could see that she had a scab at the bridge of her nose and a split lip, too.

She looked into the plate with her half-eaten sandwich. "Tripped and fell down the stairs."

"At home?"

She shook her head. "In a New York subway station."

"You report it? Anyone assist you?"

"In the big city? No. They're all out for themselves."

He stared at her.

"Is there a law against not seeking help?"

Diaz further gave her the silent treatment.

"I was embarrassed," she finally admitted.

"Your husband, huh?"

"I don't have a husband."

"Your boyfriend."

"I didn't say that. I'd rather not talk about it."

Diaz filed it away. Looked like domestic abuse, but who knew. Maybe she was a member of a gang involved in these bombings, got beat up related to that. He took the pictures off the table and held them at his waist like a pair of cards.

"A person in your field...how many patients? Thousands?"

"I never counted them."

"Thousands. Yet you came up with the names of these two right away." He slipped the photos back into his jacket pocket.

"Those two soldiers were in bad shape," she said. "Memorably so."

"What did they have?"

"Concussion. Multiple contusions. Missing limbs. What does it matter?"

"Horn and Littel had their missing limbs used against them. Bombs in their prostheses."

She closed her eyes an extra moment, as if something had just washed over her.

"You know something about this, don't you, Ms. Ritchie? Wanna share?"

"You can call me Sallye, Detective. I'm a person, not just a nurse. I don't only know things. I feel them. There's something about a wounded soldier. Have you ever known a wounded soldier?"

"I've been one myself."

"Really?" That perked her up. "Then you know that some wounds are hidden."

"So what?"

"So there's more to it than changing the dressing on a contusion. You have any invisible scars, Detective?"

"More than I can count."

"How about visible ones?"

"Those, too. A few."

She squirmed in her chair. "Where's your biggest physical scar?"

"Right here." He drew a line across his ribs.

"Let me see."

Diaz noticed that her eyes widened in anticipation, ready to drink him in. She licked her broken lip. *Very strange.*

"I don't think showing you would be appropriate just now," he said. But he wanted to string her along, play off the weakness that she was showing. "I can tell you the story."

"Please do."

"You first. What makes you so eager to hear it?"

She recovered herself. "Professional interest. That's all."

Bullshit! he wanted to cry. There was something more going on here, though he couldn't see what from this vantage point. Still, he had to throw her a bone.

"We were in Iraq, a large town near our operating base. I was an EOD officer and we were looking for a bad guy who was placing IEDs in local roads. We got a tip, had to go into town to check it out. Me and a team went along to disarm and secure whatever we found, but a firefight erupted on our perimeter, pinning down our regulars. I saw the guy we wanted bolt upstairs. Me and another guy sprinted after him, up to the roof. We weren't that high up, but there was a gap between buildings. The bad guy ran across the roof and jumped to the next. I figured if he could do it, I could too. So I attempted to follow. But with fifty pounds on my back I dropped like a stone. Corner of the corrugated roof cut right through my uniform, but I ended up pretty lucky. Landed on the hood of a parked car."

"Just the cut from all that?"

"Also fractured my left wrist and sprained an ankle. Nothing I couldn't deal with. Now it's your turn."

"How's that?"

"What do you know about these bombings?"

"I don't know anything about them, Detective."

"Then you wouldn't mind if I had a look around your apartment."

* * *

She lived in a house, not an apartment. And she seemed too eager to show it to him, Diaz thought. Which could mean one of two things. Either she had nothing to hide and he was just an evening's entertainment for her. Or she was setting him up. He could call for backup, but he was on someone else's territory. It might take awhile, and then he'd lose the flow of the interrogation. A better course was to stay alert. But just to be safe, he texted his exact whereabouts to Kahn.

With the single garage door left open for him, Diaz backed his car into the driveway.

"Manuel Diaz," the voice said in his head, "takes every precaution before approaching the well-disguised heart of darkness."

The house looked a hundred years old but well cared for, clapboard with a small screened porch facing the side yard.

She hadn't waited for him. He rested a hand on the doorknob and then thought better of it. With his index finger poised by the snap of his holster, he used his other hand to knock on the door.

"Come in!" she called.

"No. You open it, please."

After a moment, it swung open away from him and she revealed herself. She'd removed her overcoat and her shoes, still had on the nurse's uniform and the white stockings over the bandy legs. There was an awkward pause and she stepped aside, waving him into a small vestibule that led past a laundry room into a family room and a small kitchen. All neat and tidy.

Diaz scanned for anything that might be dangerous. Then he relaxed a bit.

"Buy you a drink, Detective?"

"It's a little early for that."

"I'm on a reverse schedule. That sandwich was supper."

"I've had that experience." He'd normally say no about the drink, but even though he was on the job, he was off duty. "You got a beer?"

She shook her head. "Some vodka and some white wine."

He thought better of it. "I'll pass, thanks."

She filled a tumbler with ice and poured herself a healthy portion of Popov. He followed her to the living room, where everything was bone white, almost too spotless. He found himself wishing he had a canine to sniff around. Where was Fowler when you needed him? He hadn't seen him in several days. Maybe out with the flu.

"They call you Manuel?" she asked.

"Manny. But best keep it formal."

"Oh, come on!" She took a gulp of the vodka. "Lighten up."

"It would be easier if I wasn't worried about who's going to get bombed next."

"But that's nothing to do with me. I told you that."

"I wish I could agree."

"You don't believe me?"

"It's possible there's a connection you don't know about."

She held the tumbler to her lower lip and looked into the clear liquid. "Those were good men, Detective. At least, when I last saw them."

"When was that?"

"Back in Landstuhl."

"None of them tried to reach out again?"

"A few over the years." She looked down into her drink. "None of the ones that you mentioned. Come sit down."

Diaz took her advice and perched on the edge of a soft chair directly across from her on the couch.

"Do me a favor, Manny."

He raised his chin.

"Say 'unique New York' three times fast."

"I didn't come to do parlor tricks."

"Just do it. What do you have to lose?"

She extended her legs across the carpet so her feet rested between Diaz's shoes. He observed that she had a hole in her stockings between the second and third toes of her right foot, chipped pink nail polish showing through. He said, "Unique New York, unique New York, unique New York." Got the syllables mixed up in the last round. Ha ha. Watched her break into a wide grin.

An idea crossed her face. "Say, 'No atheists in the foxholes.'"

"What?"

"Oh, forget it. That accent of yours. So great. Real." She shivered." A little dirty."

"How do you mean, dirty?"

"You know." She grinned even wider, a twinkle in her eye.

She's crazy, Diaz thought: The only unique New York thing is my losing control of this conversation to a crazy person?

She took another sip of vodka and slid farther down on the couch, bringing her toes now between his heels. She flexed both feet and ran her toes up onto his ankles.

Diaz jumped up and she rose to meet him, reaching for his jacket. He immediately covered his gun and shoved her away. She dropped herself back onto the couch, giggling.

"What the hell's wrong with you, lady? I'm a cop."

"I knew that already. A cop's a man, too, isn't he?"

"You lay hands on me again and I'll slap you."

"I might like that." She touched herself on the lip, lifted the tumbler to her mouth again, and looked up at him with cow eyes.

Diaz had seen enough. He stepped forward and wrenched the tumbler from her hand, spilling the remains of the vodka onto the cocktail table, half-melted ice cubes ticking on the glass top.

"Hey!" she said.

She turned to march for the kitchen and he grabbed her by the wrist, wrestling her down to the couch.

"Let go. I need to wipe that up."

A puddle of clear liquid lay atop the glass of the table.

"I didn't drive all the way here to put up with crap like this," Diaz said, "so cut it out. What was your interest in those dead men? We both know it was more than professional."

She looked at the puddle on the table, met his eyes, and pouted. "I have a thing for guys in that condition, okay?"

Diaz furrowed his brow. Their legs were touching. "What condition would that be? Injured army guys?"

"Like I found them—or they found me. Guys who are missing things—missing parts."

"Like arms and legs?"

"Fingers, flesh, other parts. It touches me, okay? I feel a need to make them whole."

He fell silent, thinking. Her eyes were a little wild, not even counting the mottled bruising. There was something poignant in it.

"Can I see your scar, Manny?"

Not said like she planned ahead to surprise him. More of an impulse.

She had to be involved in this madness. It was inconceivable to Diaz that she was not somehow involved. He felt acutely the responsibility to get through to her, to milk her for more information. It was some kind of force that brought him here, him of all people, a veteran with his own issues. He didn't ever think much about God, but this was like God using him for what made him special, the way some invisible hand had pushed him to resist Kahn and O'Shea early in the investigation.

Diaz stood and she grabbed at his arm, trying to hold him down. He shook her off, crossed the room, and threw his jacket over a chair in the adjacent dining area. He pulled his Glock from its holster, removed the magazine, and ejected the extra round from the chamber, slipping all the ammunition into his pocket, then placed the empty gun in the middle of the polished table. Without further thought he removed his harness and shirt and t-shirt. He turned around and took three strides in her direction.

"Oh," she said. She rose slowly and took small steps toward him with her hand outstretched.

Before he could react, Diaz felt her delicate fingertips running along the thick, dark scar on his torso. With her other hand she caressed his left nipple, but she had her attention on the scar.

"It's beautiful," she said, entranced. "Can I kiss it?"

"No."

"I want to kiss it."

She fell to her knees and he dropped with her, grabbing her by the elbows. "I said no."

"I'm so hot. You're making me so hot."

"You're sick."

She pressed herself into him, but he didn't feel aroused. On his side of the transaction it was like a medical exam. And, anyway, he knew he'd already crossed too many lines. He dreaded what Kahn might think.

"Stop, I said."

Diaz moved his hands up to her shoulders and shook her violently. "Stop. Stop!"

She looked into his eyes. Yearning there. But also a thread of shame. She turned away from him, suddenly back in charge of herself, like someone had thrown a switch.

"What did you do to those guys?" Diaz asked, still standing bare-chested.

A sneer crossed her face. "I fucked them, is that what you want to hear?"

"I want to hear whatever's the truth."

"Seduced them and gave myself to them right there in the hospital room."

She was a lunatic, Diaz realized. But he dared not say it aloud, didn't want to break the spell.

"All three?"

"Of course all three. Albie, Gavin, Lewis. That's why I remember them so well. And I'd bet they remember me, too."

"You're forgetting that two of those guys are dead. They don't have no more memories."

"I did everything I could to make them whole, Detective. Above and beyond the call of duty. They were broken and I proved to them that there was still love in the world. Proved to them that they were still men."

And that you were still a woman, he wanted to add. Diaz noticed that she'd spoken with a tinge of pride, but also with an expression of agony on her face. He reached reflexively for his own scar and knew that she hadn't done what she did just for those men. Without knowing her entire story, he knew for sure that she was broken, too—broken and in need of fixing. Screwing those guys didn't only prove their wholeness, he suspected. The act made her whole, too.

He turned away and dressed himself in silence, feeling her presence behind him, still standing there.

"Don't I turn you on?" she said.

He shook his head. "Do you have anything for me?"

"Only that which you won't take."

He strapped his harness back on and slipped into his jacket. "Those men… In their position, it wasn't a choice. You took advantage of them."

She sniffed at that. "I gave them what they needed. So what if I took back what I needed in return. But I didn't kill them, Detective. I fucked them, but that was years ago. And I didn't kill them, didn't even know they were dead until you told me."

"You have any idea who might've done this?"

She barely hesitated. "A big strong man comes all this way just to find that out. Wouldn't I tell you if I had?"

KAHN WAS AT HOME AT four o'clock when the phone rang. He lived with his second wife and their two young kids in a row house in Bayside, Queens, two rooms on each floor, plus a carpeted basement, which was filled with toys. He was helping them clean it up when he saw Diaz's name on the Caller ID.

"Where are you now?"

"Ninety-five, three hours from home. I made a little freelance visit."

"O'Shea told me. Then I saw your text."

"Right. You ain't pissed?"

"The important thing is, did you find anything?"

"It was way weird, Sarge. The nurse knew both victims but I didn't see anything that ties her to their murders."

"What about the third guy, the one we're now looking for?"

"The nurse admits knowing him, too. But she's ten cc's short of a full syringe."

"What the hell's that mean?"

"She's nuts, Sandy. Stark raving mad, if you ask me. She made me show her my battle scar and it got her all hot and bothered."

"Angry?"

"Horny."

"Don't tell me the rest."

"Ain't nothing to tell there. All three of those vets... she seduced them when they were on their backs in the hospital."

"How is that relevant?"

"It's not, so long as you believe in her good intentions. On the other hand, it must mean something. I just can't figure out what. They find this Salinowsky guy yet?"

"No."

"Maybe he's the perp."

"How do you figure that?"

"Jealousy?"

"Of what?"

"The other two guys?"

"But that was years ago. And how would he even know?"

"Just a stab. She claims herself not to have ever seen any of them since the hospital. My gut tells me she's telling the truth, so far as that goes. Whether they corresponded, she hesitated before denying it. There's a piece missing."

"More than a piece, Diaz. Salinowsky could be the perp, but for my money he fits more into the pattern as the next victim."

"I agree."

"One thing protecting him may be how hard he is to find. If the bomber's working off veterans' records like we are, he's also got the same postal box address as us, no more."

"On the other hand, he's been at this longer—more time to search for him. Can Burbette help?"

"FBI's riding shotgun but they don't have anything we don't. All we're getting from them is a little manpower. Your MP in Germany provided more info than all of Burbette's channels put together. Sometimes you got to go off the reservation. Like you did."

Diaz paused. Kahn knew he was waiting for the thank-you that wasn't going to come. The sergeant worried that his charge had a hero complex, which could cause a guy to act out, already had in this case. With all the pressure from on high, he felt grateful that the kid had pushed the envelope, taking initiative to track down the MP and the nurse on his own. But his approach to the bag at St. Pat's showed that he liked to skirt fine lines and sometimes ended up crossing them. And then there was that bit about walking in traffic on the West Side Drive. Kahn couldn't let himself forget that.

"You're welcome," Diaz said into the silence.

That set Kahn off. "Don't be a prima donna, Manny. This isn't a beauty pageant and there aren't any prizes for trying. Your reward comes when we catch this guy."

Diaz sighed through the phone. "What's our next move?"

"You and I got the rest of the day off. Let the others handle it. If they find Salinowsky, maybe he'll know something. Or maybe, like you say, we'll get lucky and he'll be our guy."

"Can we put someone on the nurse?"

"I thought you said she was clean."

"She may know what's going on or she may not, but there's a piece she's not telling. Someone beat her up recently."

"And she wouldn't say who?"

"She told me she fell down the stairs in a New York subway. But all the bruises appear to be on her face and arms. You'd think she'd scrape her shins or knees in a fall like that."

"You checked her head to toe?"

"Of course not, but she wasn't limping or anything, no casts, no cuts on her hands. Any scabs on her knees should've shown through her stockings, but there weren't any. Sure looked like someone punched her out to me and maybe she put up her arms in defense."

"Punched her to shut her up?"

"That I don't know."

"I'll see if we can get someone from the fibbies to tail her. Is there anything specific we could take to a judge for a warrant?"

"Negative. Just a feeling."

"That won't cut it."

"I know. That's why I'm coming home."

TICK, TICK, TICK, TICK, TICK

10.

DAY FIVE: DARK

When Warren Manis looked in the bathroom mirror he saw a gash on one ear with a fresh scab over it. Sallye had forehead-butted him when she climaxed. *Crazy bitch.* He angled his gaze and stared at the wound from the corner of his eye. Nice bump on the side of his head, too. He cursed her under his breath, cursed that he loved her so much that he hated her. Or was it the other way around? Either way, she was culpable. Despite his early efforts, she'd created a structure in their relationship that he had to rebuild for his own needs. Couldn't go on this way, always getting the hind end. Couldn't walk away, either, because like her he wanted to recapture something that he'd lost. But in order to rebuild the relationship, at first he had to destroy the source of the problem, her connection to those men. Maybe he'd started this thing, but she had driven him to everything he'd done lately, driven him with her manipulation, and the knowledge of that made him angrier with each passing day. What he'd done so far would only be half the payback.

His face...he hadn't washed his hair or trimmed his beard for two days, but that didn't make him look nearly bad enough for his purposes. He wasn't a makeup artist, not going to whip up a plastic face the way people so easily seemed to do in Hollywood movies. This was real. He needed real.

Manis took a scissors and cut some swatches out of his beard, making it uneven. That was better. He flicked a hand through his greasy hair—not much to be done with that. Then he reached for the damaged ear and picked at the scab. It hurt. He dug a nail under the edge and ripped it off, his eyes tearing in the effort, but now he had it bleeding pretty good again. He dipped a finger into the blood and smeared it on his face.

Better.

For clothing he had some old pants and a torn shirt that he'd soiled for the occasion. He had some tattered shoes and an old belt that he pretended to hold together with duct tape. On the street not long ago he'd found a filthy overcoat that smelled of the sewer. He fished it from a plastic trash bag under his workbench and waited until he was outside to slip his arms into the sticky sleeves.

He carried no identification on his person, just a beat-up canvas satchel that he'd stolen from a mason at a construction site. Inside that bag was a replica of Salinowsky's leg, containing the largest charge of C4 that Manis had yet employed. Salinowsky, he figured, would be too high to notice the extra pound. In case he did, there was an anti-tamper switch in this one. Anyone who tried to open the casing would be dead before he knew what happened.

All the way home, Diaz brooded, thinking not just about the case but about whether he'd ever receive his due. Things could get political in the department. Not that he was gunning for lieutenant or anything—not any time soon—but it was possible that Kahn was playing games. Might he be dissing Diaz on purpose, trying to use his underling's shoulders for a ladder? *No fucking way.* Diaz felt guilty even for allowing it to creep into his mind.

He shook himself—groggy from all the driving, not to mention the adrenaline letdown. He felt drained, a few thoughts short of rational, but sharp enough to ask himself what a pat on the head was going to do for him, anyway. He'd seen acts of great bravery in Iraq that barely garnered a medal. With or without the ribbon, you came home broken the same way. Now, all he'd done was make a few phone calls overseas and take a ride to visit a sexually perverse lunatic nurse. Not like he climbed a hill while death rained down in Iwo Jima or something. Meanwhile, the bomber was still out there, more mayhem in the offing.

In the Bronx, Diaz refilled his friend's car with gas out of courtesy. Half an hour later, he parked it in Manhattan and dropped off the keys with a thank-you note. If he ever needed to do a stakeout, the jalopy would be perfect, he thought. It wouldn't stand out like your average Crown Vic. On the other hand, it might go to pieces in a high-speed chase. Everything had its compromises.

He walked the few blocks home in the cold, feeling no temptation to the parkway path, maybe never again. Cap would return to the station soon, he hoped, maybe even tomorrow, and Diaz couldn't look him in the eye if he ever drifted back toward that gratuitous danger.

By the time the dry heat of the apartment building hit him, Diaz felt dog-tired. The hallway smelled of Italian food, making his mouth water. He hadn't eaten since the sandwich in Bedford.

He used his key, but the door to his apartment caught without opening.

"Just a minute!" Jennifer called.

She pushed the door closed and it reopened a second later.

"You're using the chain?"

"Don't look so worried. Just didn't want you barging in."

He saw then that she'd dressed and had makeup on. She wore an apron over the dress, and behind her the table was set for two with candles on it.

The air went out of him. "You got a date?"

"I thought it was time I did something special." She had a look on her face like none he'd ever seen there before.

"What? For me? Why? On account of my being such a sourpuss all the time?"

"C'mon. Don't ruin it. I got a lasagna in the oven."

"You can cook?"

"The recipe came from the Internet. It's not a date, see? You're the guinea pig."

"That's more like it. Should I pick up some beers?"

"We're all set." She looked at her watch. "You have time for a shower."

Diaz didn't argue. He wanted the feel of that nurse off his skin. When he was done, he climbed into his best jeans, braided loafers and a fancy guayabera. He gelled his hair, too.

"You look sweet," Jennifer said.

"It's the least I could do."

He opened the Chianti while she cut two huge slabs of lasagna, then pulled off her apron and tossed it into a corner. She wore a knit dress that clung to her hips, black and white stripes. Diaz looked her up and down and she playfully pirouetted for him. He set the wine bottle down on the table and shook his head.

"Of all the roomies in all the apartments in all the world, she walks into mine."

"Oh, stop." But she laughed with him.

She dimmed the lights and lit the candles. When she sat down, she raised her glass. "A toast to roommates."

"To roommates," Diaz said, and they clinked rims.

By the second bottle of wine, the day felt a little less stressful to Diaz. He said, "Mmm. A lot of work, that lasagna."

Jennifer shrugged it off. "There are shortcuts these days. Not like the way anyone's grandma used to make."

"You look better than anyone's grandma, too."

Hard to tell in the dim lighting, but Diaz had the impression that she blushed. "I was helping my folks reorganize their closets all day. I guess I was still in domestic mode, so I stopped at the grocery store and when I came home I just kept on going."

"Pretty nice of you, after the way I've been behaving."

Her eyes searched his face. "Were you out on that case today?"

He nodded. "Person of interest up in Boston. She has a thing for guys with mutilations."

"Like piercings?"

"Way more than that. She gets off on missing limbs. You ever hear of a thing like that?"

Jennifer shook her head. "Makes me think of that stupid dentist, though."

"This goes way beyond that. I showed her the scar on my stomach and she practically came in her pants."

"You're a sexy guy."

"Not that sexy. I'm not exaggerating her reaction, either."

"Well, why would you do a thing like that?"

"I was trying to get her to open up."

"Sounds like it worked."

"Too well. A flood came out."

"So she's connected to the murders?"

"I shouldn't tell you that, but yes, somehow. She screwed both the guys who got killed. Seduced them in their hospital beds."

"In the hospital?" Jennifer laughed. "I'm picturing that, all those tubes and stuff."

"It's not funny," Diaz said. "She's a real sicko. I mean, what do you make of that?"

Jennifer tightened her jaw, reflecting. "People have all kinds of fetishes. I guess that's as good as the next. It's not necessarily anything to be ashamed of."

"It is if it leads to murder."

"How do you figure it did, Manny?"

"I don't know. There's another guy, a loose end. He's out there somewhere, and it's possible that he did it or that he's the next victim."

"You don't know?"

"We can't find him."

"What exactly did the woman say about that?"

"Said she, like, provided all three with a service that had mutual benefits. Hasn't seen any of them since they left the hospital. She claims to have no reason to have killed them."

"You believe her?"

"Anyone can build a bomb, but these bombs were pretty smart."

"Don't tell me she's just a dumb woman."

"I don't mean it that way. You need to be pretty sophisticated to build bombs like the ones that killed these guys. Not so easily done without a lot of talent or a lot of practice. Preferably both. But I don't make her that way." He paused to think deeper. "She does have a forceful personality, though. She came on pretty strong, like she's used to getting her way."

"Jealousy."

"What's she got to be jealous about? Seems like she's getting what she wants."

"Not hers." Jennifer sat forward. "Think of how you felt when I was with that dentist."

"I wasn't jealous."

"Just think of how you felt. You saw me with my clothes off not long before that. You couldn't have me."

"Correction. Didn't want to."

"Maybe not in your conscious mind, but somewhere deeper. Guys want to possess women. It's fixed in their DNA. I've had gay friends with zero interest in my body who thought they had to protect me, keep me from being touched by straight guys."

"Because you're beautiful. They don't want you to get hurt. This nurse—"

"She's a nurse?"

"You didn't hear that from me. She's not like the nurse of a man's dreams. She's a scrawny thing, not much meat on her."

"Not your type."

"No."

"But someone else's. And if she offered it freely?"

"She did offer, if she's telling the truth. If her come-on to me was part of a pattern."

"But you have an issue right now, Manny. Besides, you were there for professional reasons."

"What's your point?"

"Someone more involved might want to protect her. Someone who's jealous that she's screwing these guys—or once did. Go back to how you felt emotionally when you heard me with the dentist."

"Stop bringing that up." He waved at the candles. "You're ruining the atmosphere."

"See? Multiply it times ten. Or times a thousand. That's how it feels to him."

"What are you, a secret FBI profiler?"

"I just know men and women. Can I ask you something, Manny?"

He went for the wine bottle but found it empty. The second bottle. "Is it about the apartment rules?"

"Uh uh."

"You want me to do the dishes?"

"Later." She reached across the table and ran her fingers over the top of his hand and between his knuckles. "Let's go lie down."

"I told you the score on that."

"I don't mind." She stood up and led him by the arm to her bedroom.

He followed her, half feeling that he owed her something. How crazy this life could be—she so hot and sensual, he made by circumstances into such a reluctant suitor. A few years ago, he'd have killed for this.

Killed. The thought brought him short. He kissed her and her mouth fell open, her lips and tongue like butter. Her dress clung like a second skin. She pulled him down to the bed. Twice in one day he would fail to deliver.

"I want you, Manny."

She guided his hand between her legs, but he pulled it away.

"You know I can't, J-Fo."

"I got that." She kissed him, ran her fingernails through his stiff hair, across his chest. "There are different ways to get a woman off."

She guided his hand down again, this time to her bare thigh and used it to hike up the front of her dress. She placed his palm atop the mound of her underwear, which was warm and damp.

"You still got something to offer, Manny," she said. "Maybe not all the parts are perfect. But I'm not asking for perfect."

"What are you asking for?" He buried his face in her hair. She smelled like hot olive oil.

"Well, you still got the rest of your body, don't you?"

Manis stood by a wire trash bin on the corner of Avenue B and East Third Street. From that vantage point he had a view both of the ornate front of St. Euphrosyne and the plain side door that the homeless men used. They'd started lining up for the soup kitchen at half past four, but the shelter itself hadn't opened until six. Some of the men had wandered off after dinner, but others went back inside only to come out again. He figured they'd copped their squat for the night and wanted to wait until the last minute before entering the shelter for good. Besides, they were passing around some bottles and a few cigarettes.

Keeping count in his head, calculating that there were still plenty of beds available inside, Manis hung back. He didn't worry too much about looking suspicious. Lurking around was typical behavior in this part of town. Despite the cold, there were plenty of people on the street, and any new recipient of church services would naturally be hesitant to step forward out of self-preservation.

By eight-thirty it had grown frigid and the tips of Manis's fingers were cracked and blue. *The things I do for that bitch,* he thought. But there was no point feeling bitter. His goal lay within sight.

Ten minutes later, he watched Salinowsky shuffle across the avenue, oblivious to traffic. Manis ducked his head and pretended to be digging through the trash, but that didn't matter. Salinowsky's glassy eyes seemed to perceive little around him.

High on smack, Manis thought. Perfect.

With the mason's satchel in hand, Manis turned and followed his target at twenty paces. Unlike the other vagrants, Salinowsky didn't pause at the threshold, just marched right down the steps and into the building. But at the next doorway, someone brought him up short, a man with a large kitchen tongs in his hand. The man had a red face that was flushed further from the heat of the kitchen. At first, Manis thought he was making friendly conversation with Salinowsky, but he became more animated as things progressed. Salinowsky, rocking on his heels, pulled out the ashen pockets of his tattered coat to indicate he carried nothing. The red-faced man said something else and Salinowsky did the same with his pants pockets, showing only some small change and a few trinkets. That gesture had little more effect than the first, and the red-faced man denied Salinowsky access to the kitchen.

"I asked your name, buddy," said a voice next to Manis.

He perceived for the first time a young man standing there, short and pale and gaunt with an elaborate tattoo that ran up his neck. He carried a clipboard in his hand.

"Everyone needs to check in."

Manis made up a name.

"You got ID?" the man asked.

"I got mugged this morning. They took everything."

"What's in the bag?"

"They took everything but that."

"No guns or knives allowed inside. Open it."

Manis shook his head. He hadn't worked out this angle. Of course they'd be worried about weapons.

"Let me see inside the bag or you can go back out, freeze your ass off."

Manis shook his head, but less adamantly this time. If he continued to resist, he'd make himself an object of suspicion. But if he let them look, he reasoned on second thought, they wouldn't recognize what he had in the satchel as anything dangerous. Homeless people collected the oddest things. Manis knew that to be true and so would they. He'd seen with his own eyes shopping carts full of baby dolls and knotted wigs and bicycle parts. He'd stuffed his satchel full of rags, and if this man saw the prosthesis under them, so what? Manis would look no different than the other junk collectors.

He unhooked the straps and held open the satchel, but after all that the man hardly looked inside, satisfied just with the gesture. Manis closed it quickly.

"There's a locker at the foot of each bed," the man explained, but don't leave anything valuable in there—keep your money under your pillow. Bathroom's in that direction, showers over there. You got a preference of bunk?"

"Can I see my choices?"

The man walked Manis to a doorway around the corner. Men of all ages were settling all about. Most kept to themselves. A few conducted muted conversations.

In the time it took Manis to work out his entry, Salinowsky had gone into the shelter dormitory and sat down on one of the cots. Manis did a quick calculation. An unmade cot next to Salinowsky was also the last vacant spot on the perimeter.

"I need the outside row," Manis said.

"Twenty six, then. They're numbered."

The man seized an armful of bedding from a rolling shelf and thrust it into Manis's stomach. "You return your bedding to the bins when you leave. You want to stay more than two nights, you got to agree to counseling."

What kind of counseling? Manis wondered, but he didn't ask. As he wandered to his cot, it occurred to him that a place like this held great advantages for a man who wished to remain unseen. For his purposes, the less he talked the better, but such antisocial behavior wouldn't capture anyone's attention. They were all equally damaged. And once Salinowsky lay in pieces on the sidewalk, it wouldn't matter whether the man at the door had glimpsed the prosthetic leg in the satchel. The important thing was that he'd never remember Manis's face.

The dormitory smelled of bleach and human excrement. Manis shed his coat and prepared his bedding, thinking of the inside of an army barracks. He'd served six years and never made it past private first class, but he'd been with the sappers, and that experience had led to a job with an outside contractor in Germany. While there, he had easy if incomplete access to several military bases. Once inside, a shrewd and patient operator could sneak around with a great deal of success. When ready you put your name down on a list, then hopped into a free spot on a transport plane back to the States, no security screening.

Manis lay atop his cot and waited in silence for lights out. In his peripheral vision, he perceived Salinowsky coming and going, shuffling around the room with heavy eyelids. At times he paused and looked as if he'd pass out and fall over, but he managed to stay on his feet until the overhead lights flashed. Then he fell heavily to his cot and undressed, putting his clothes in his footlocker and gently sliding his prosthetic leg under the bed.

At that moment Manis ventured a turn of his head. The leg looked just as he expected it to look, and Manis concluded that this plan had a high probability of success.

Two hours later, with everyone asleep or uncaring, in the dark he used a penlight to study the cuff—where Salinowsky's experience of the replacement leg would be most sensitive. He quietly made a few adjustments to the cushion and used some filth from his own disgusting shoes to get the dirty color as close as possible to the original. Satisfied with this work, he exchanged the real prosthesis for the one with the bomb, knowing that Salinowsky would likely pass the armed forces recruiting station on Beekman Street on his way to or from his post office box. If not today, then tomorrow at the latest. He'd observed Salinowsky for two days now, and the man was a creature of habit.

When the fluorescent lights came up in the morning, Manis slipped from the shelter without stopping for breakfast. He had the real prosthesis in his satchel and he'd left Salinowsky asleep over the bomb.

TICK, TICK, TICK, TICK

11.

DAY SIX: LIGHT

Lewis Salinowsky awoke feeling ill. Nausea stirred in his chest and snot ran from his nose. He had to get off the junk, he thought, just had to. Maybe today would be the day, maybe tomorrow. He'd lost the card for the methadone nun, but he could get another.

Salinowsky strapped on his leg and pulled on his pants and limped in the direction of the kitchen. Father Igor wasn't there, thank God. It was all pretty foggy in Salinowsky's mind, but he felt pretty sure that Father Igor had reamed him out good last night. Not as harshly as a normal person would, but with no hint of his usual kindness. Father Igor, if Salinowsky remembered right, had gone pretty red in the face. He didn't like Salinowsky missing his time in the prep kitchen and he liked even less seeing the shelter volunteer in an altered state. Salinowsky had to empty his pockets just to prove he didn't have any syringes on him, but still Father Igor wouldn't let him into the pantry, where he kept most of his stuff.

The kitchen door was open now, however, the morning crew getting ready to ply their charges with coffee and danish, then drive them out onto the street. You couldn't hang around the shelter during the day and you couldn't goldbrick either. If you woke up too sick to move, they sent for an ambulance and hauled you out on a stretcher. Salinowsky would never let that happen. He couldn't abide ambulances. They reminded him of war.

With nobody paying any mind, he limped through the kitchen to the pantry. His legs felt heavy. Both of them—the one of flesh and the composite one, too. He thought he might get another blister on his stump just when the last blister had callused over.

From the pantry he gathered up a change of clothes, relatively clean ones, Father Igor having allowed him yesterday morning to use the washing machine that was normally reserved for towels. Father Igor had been good to him and in exchange Salinowsky had let down Father Igor for the thousandth time. He knew that and he desperately wished not to have to ask for forgiveness again. There were two ways to accomplish that. The first would be to get clean. The second—maybe easier and maybe harder—would be to move along to another shelter. If his check arrived in today's mail, he thought, maybe the monthly windfall would help him decide which course to take.

When he'd cleaned up and changed, Salinowsky ate his breakfast of cheese danishes and coffee at a cafeteria table full of men like him, men who savored bread as others savored candy. Men who spent their days on survival strategies as intensely as others plotted world conquest. Today they were arguing over what neighborhoods had the best balance of paying foot traffic versus fewest hassling cops. Salinowsky didn't participate. He could think only of his own nausea and the angry redness of Father Igor's face, plus his desperate need for cash and another bundle.

At eight o'clock he made sure one more time that his few possessions were securely stowed in the back of the pantry cabinet. Then he hit the street, limping down Avenue B through Chinatown. On Essex Street they were just pulling into place a cart where you could get cheap eats. Salinowsky sometimes did that for lunch to celebrate on days that his check had come. He might double back later if the mood struck him.

For now, he turned west on East Broadway and waded through the Asian crowds to Bowery, where he crossed to Worth Street and on to Federal Plaza. On days when he picked up his check, he used a check-cashing store on Broadway, then walked down and around the east side of City Hall Park to a spot he liked for panhandling in the Financial District. But he couldn't focus on plans just now. He felt itchy all over.

At exactly three minutes past nine, Lewis Salinowsky walked into the shiny office building that held the post office, went straight to his box, and with trembling hands extracted the envelope that contained his VA check. *Happy Monday.* He stuffed it into his coat pocket and picked up the pace—couldn't help himself in the excitement—limping briskly along Worth Street up to Broadway.

The check-cashing store stood on Broadway near Chambers Street, between a Duane Reade drugstore and a Radio Shack. Blue plywood scaffolding covered the sidewalk and masked the store sign, but Salinowsky knew exactly where he was going. He'd been through this routine many times, had used this store ever since he opened the post office box—three years going on four, he thought, although he couldn't be sure.

He went through the glass door and got into line behind two Hispanic women and a young black guy wearing baggy jeans and a do-rag. The woman at the cashing window was a heavyset Indian. Salinowsky watched over people's shoulders as she counted out the first woman's crisp green bills and turned her attention to the next customer. But something wasn't right. As she lifted her face, some activity behind Salinowsky drew her attention. Her eyes grew wide and her mouth fell open, like she was going to scream. Then she reached over and flicked closed her Plexiglas window.

JOSEPH CAPOBIANCO SETTLED INTO HIS desk chair with a cup of black java and a bag containing two jelly donuts. Generally when he ate donuts, he could hear Jill carping at him in the back of his mind. But today he'd have a guilt-free breakfast. First day back in the office in a week and he'd lost ten pounds to the flu in the meantime. He had room for a lot of donuts.

Before him on the desk, he held a printout of the daily duty roster. If the bird disease progressed for everyone as it had for him, he figured that the squad would finally be restored nearly to full strength next week. Whole damn experience was like a throwback to World War I or something, where disease slaughtered more doughboys than bombs ever could. This being the modern age, of course, he expected all his guys to survive.

Better than survive, he thought. Involuntary weight loss thrown into the bargain.

This morning Capobianco had awakened at home feeling washed out but nearly healthy. He'd dragged his feet through his pre-breakfast routine, but the crisp New York morning invigorated him as he drove along Queens Boulevard with the driver's window of his Ford Taurus half down. The car was a perk of office, and as such it put him in a certain frame of mind. When he reached Manhattan, the honking horns and roaring trucks and rushing pedestrians on the cross streets and on Seventh

Avenue South—they all further acted upon him like a stimulant.

Kahn's and Diaz's names were on the duty sheet this morning and he'd checked in with Kahn on the cell phone, getting back up to speed. With any luck they'd have some material for a mayoral press conference later in the week—though to Gowen that might seem like a lifetime from now. Still, Capobianco felt that the kid, Diaz, had shown good instincts on the veterans case, and while anyone might have arrived eventually at their current strategy, he had to give Diaz credit. Kahn had developed a hard-on about the whole St. Patrick's package thing, and he wasn't wrong to do so, but sometimes after a guy crosses a line like that he does his best work. It's like being shot at, Capobianco thought. The rest of that day you go from disbelief and doubt to exhilaration and back again, but the next morning you wake up with a little more oxygen feeding the brain and a notion that fate put you here to do some good in the world. If getting reprimanded by Kahn wasn't quite a near-death experience for Diaz, maybe it had achieved that effect regardless. Because the kid was sharp on this, you had to admit.

Now Diaz had a plan and Kahn approved. Capobianco didn't doubt his men—not one iota—but the situation itself remained volatile. He picked up the phone and called Gowen.

"You back in the saddle, Lieutenant?"

"Roger that. Desk jockey staring at a pile of paper."

"What do you know about the recruiting office bombings?"

"That's why I'm calling. I think my guys will tie up the big loose end this week. Either they'll stop this guy or they'll make him mad enough to screw up."

"Which guy?"

"That's what we're about to find out. My only concern is that another agency insisted on participating."

"You want me to call off Burbette?"

"He's not the one I'm worried about. If Stoltz of ATF gets wise to what's going down, I wouldn't bet against him stepping on his dick and screwing up the whole thing."

"How did you handle him?"

"I told those guys to steer him to the wrong neighborhood. In addition to that, we'll maintain radio silence until the last possible second. What do you think?"

"I think," Gowen said, "that when the shit's gonna be hitting the fan, a smart guy always positions himself upwind."

"TURN HERE," KAHN SNAPPED.

Diaz tamped down the voice in the back of his head. He expected a long stakeout and this was no time to waste mental energy.

They were riding in an unmarked vehicle, slated to converge on the vicinity of the Federal Plaza post office a few minutes before it opened at nine o'clock, but they were all late. In order to maintain secrecy, Kahn had Burbette on an open cell phone line and Diaz had done the same with O'Shea—no use of the police car's radio. As luck would have it, the two Feds that Burbette planned to bring fell ill with the flu that morning, so he had to scramble for two more, which took time. O'Shea got caught up in some administrative bullshit he said wasn't worth mentioning, but it put him at least fifteen minutes behind. Kahn and Diaz got stuck in the traffic creeping out of the Holland Tunnel. They used their lights and siren, but it still set them back ten minutes.

No one was worried. They figured a guy living out of a post office box was not likely to be an early riser. Diaz pictured them waiting there all week, in fact, doing shifts. Not being accustomed to stakeouts, he wondered how he'd keep himself alert.

Kahn had an egg sandwich in his hand, dripping yolk into the aluminum foil wrapper on his lap. The thing smelled rotten—but maybe that was the melted cheese. He told Diaz to pull to a stop just up the block from the post office and across the street.

Diaz peered through his side window. Everything looked normal. Then, all of a sudden, it didn't.

There was a guy walking with a pronounced limp in the direction of the post office. He fit the sketchy description that O'Shea had provided from army records, tall and exceedingly gaunt. Whether he matched the more youthful picture would require much closer examination.

"Holy crap. I think that's our man Salinowsky." Diaz looked at Kahn, who dropped his sandwich to the floor between his legs.

"So soon? Shit."

They hit their phones.

"No one's in position yet," Kahn said. "Tail him but hold back. I'll get them organized."

Just as Salinowsky reached the entrance to the post office, Diaz opened his door. Kahn grabbed his partner's arm and Diaz twisted around so their eyes met.

"Remember," Kahn said. "Procedure."

Diaz nodded, closed his door, and jogged across the street, putting out his hand to stop traffic. No one hit the horn. Short coat flapping in the cold breeze, black turtle-neck hugging his Adam's apple, hand on his right hip, he had to present as a cop, he thought. But Salinowsky didn't look out through the post office window. Even through all the obstructions, Diaz had a bead on him.

He paused at the glass door. From this perspective he could see the line of post office boxes. Salinowsky confirmed his identity by going to the one they knew was his. A moment later he shoved an envelope into his coat pocket and turned to go.

Diaz would have preferred to approach Salinowsky in the street, but his backup wasn't in place and Kahn had warned him. He put his shoulder against the building and watched Salinowsky exit and limp from the plaza. His pants were too long for anyone to see his ankles, but Diaz figured from the way he walked that the right leg was the prosthetic one.

There were a lot of people on the street going to work. A woman held a closed umbrella in the air and spoke to a crowd in French. Probably a tour of the Financial District. Salinowsky was on course to walk right past them.

Senses on high alert, Diaz reviewed the sources of incipient danger. By the time he arrived home last night, he'd already calculated the chance at eighty percent that Salinowsky was a potential victim—not the bomber. His conversation with Jennifer raised those odds to ninety-eight percent in his mind, which meant that the man in his sights might this very moment be unknowingly carrying a bomb. There was a very small chance Salinowsky wasn't a potential victim at all, and a slightly better than small chance, in Diaz's mind, that he operated as an intentional suicide bomber. The overall uncertainty—in addition to Kahn's warning—kept him from stopping Salinowsky in the street. If the man felt threatened, he might run and plow into a group of civilians, like those French people, before detonating.

Another consideration: Diaz knew that there was an armed forces recruiting office just five blocks south.

Presuming that GPS governed this device, as it likely had the others, Salinowsky could not be permitted to walk in front of that location, either by accident or by design. Notwithstanding Kahn's warning, Diaz intended at all costs to stop him if it came to that.

As luck would have it, he watched as Salinowsky limped in the opposite direction.

Diaz released some air from his lungs and got Kahn on the speed dial. "Subject proceeding on Worth toward Broadway. How we doing on the other guys?"

"Not in place yet. Maintain your distance."

"I don't know," Diaz said.

"I repeat. Maintain your distance."

"Roger that."

Diaz disconnected.

Salinowsky crossed Broadway and limped into the shadow of some scaffolding, which sent a surge into Diaz's chest, thinking he might lose him. He angled his head to cut the glare and watched Salinowsky disappear into a store called E-Z Cash. *Of course.* Guy probably didn't even have a bank account.

Diaz called Kahn again and reported the location.

"We're behind you," Kahn said.

"I'm going in." Diaz reached for his Glock.

He hung up before Kahn could reply, slipped the phone into his pants pocket and jogged across Broadway. As he did so he saw Kahn running toward him down the sidewalk. Their eyes met. Like true partners, they didn't have to exchange a word.

Diaz beat Kahn to the door, but only by a few steps. He didn't hold it for him. He burst through and saw Salinowsky in a line of three or four people. The clerk slammed her window shut as Diaz called out, "Police!"

A black guy in line hit the floor like he'd been shot. Two women grabbed their chests. Kahn watched Salinowsky's spine stiffen. He hesitated for a moment. Then he turned around with excruciating slowness.

Diaz leveled his gun at Salinowsky.

"Police," he repeated. "Get to the floor." But the tall man just stood there.

By the door behind them, Diaz heard Kahn radioing for backup and issuing instructions to evacuate the area. He wasn't using the cell phone any longer.

Salinowsky stood still, his eyes heavy and uncertain. Yelling wasn't likely to move him, so Diaz decided upon a different tack. He opened his free hand. "Lewis, will you let these people leave?"

"Why wouldn't I?" Salinowsky said. "Wha—what's going on?"

"These people need to leave, Lewis. Okay? They may be in danger."

"Danger?"

Diaz gestured to them. "C'mon." He showed Salinowsky the heel of his hand. "You just stay there." He still had his Glock leveled at the tall man's chest. The women started easing toward the door and Diaz saw through a reflection in the Plexiglas that Kahn held it open for them. Surreal. Like a doorman.

"Go to the corner," Kahn told the women. "There should be a perimeter. Stick around."

You never knew who was involved, but Diaz understood that Kahn couldn't take himself away to deal with unlikely accomplices. He could see in the reflection of the teller's window that there were a few blue uniforms outside now, the sidewalk emptying of civilians. But if any other Bomb Squad guys showed up, they wouldn't come for another ten minutes at least.

"You, too," Diaz said to the black guy with the do-rag. "C'mon. Go!"

He watched the man struggle to his feet with his hands raised, clearly afraid of the cop or the gun. Maybe both. He cut Diaz a wide berth as he left.

Diaz didn't look behind him. "We clear, Sandy?"

"Clear."

The teller had disappeared. Maybe she'd ducked under the counter, Diaz thought. For her sake he hoped instead that she'd used a rear exit.

He gestured to Salinowsky with his gun. "I really need you to take off your coat, Lewis."

"My coat?"

"So I can see you better."

"My coat."

"Just drop it to the floor. Do it now."

Salinowsky stood frozen. "I don't know. It's my only one."

"Is your name Lewis Salinowsky?"

"That's what my mother said."

"Take off your coat, Lewis. You'll get it back. You got anything in those pockets?"

"Yes."

"Anything dangerous?"

"I don't know. Some—I don't know."

Diaz studied his eyes. They were milky, puffy. "Drug paraphernalia?" he asked. "Syringes?"

"Maybe a few."

"It's okay."

Finally, Salinowsky shucked the overcoat. It fell quietly to the floor.

"I know guns," he said. "I don't like them."

"Let's put them away, then, okay?"

"Done," Kahn said behind him.

Diaz slipped his gun back into its holster. "Better?"

Salinowsky said, "What do you want with me?"

Diaz pointed. "Do you have an artificial leg, sir?"

"Who wants to know?"

"I told you. NYPD. I'm with the Bomb Squad."

"The Bomb Squad?"

"Would you sit on the floor for me?"

Salinowsky didn't move.

"I'm not gonna ask you again, Lewis."

Salinowsky still stood frozen.

Diaz issued a sigh. He took half a step forward. "Tell you what. Let's both sit."

They heard sirens outside in the background, closing in and then dying to silence.

"It's hard for me," Salinowsky said. "On account of—I'm not like normal people."

"Take your time." Diaz bent at the waist to indicate he was going down.

Salinowsky looked past him at Kahn.

"He'll remain standing," Diaz said. "Guard the door. Make sure no one barges in. As a matter of fact," Diaz said over his shoulder, "you can cover it from the other side, can't you, Sarge?" He thought about who else might be out there, even ten minutes from now. With the flu still ripping through, the squad was fielding skeleton crews, and he suspected the two of them might be the only bomb techs in the vicinity for a good long time. "You got a suit out there, right?"

Kahn hesitated for a second. Diaz knew that, as a sergeant, he was no longer accustomed to donning the bomb suit. But there was no one else. "Okay," Kahn agreed. "Going out. But I'm right here."

Diaz heard the door drift closed. It didn't reassure him.

"We're going to the ground now," Diaz said. "One. Two. Three."

"I didn't do anything," Salinowsky said. But he finally began to move. He lowered himself awkwardly to the floor, first sticking the right leg straight out, then bending the left, finally collapsing to his rear end.

Diaz went to his knees, rested his butt on his heels. "I need to see your prosthetic leg. Can I see it?"

Salinowsky, lips now trembling, lifted his pant leg about six inches.

"Good. That's good. You're cooperating. See, no one's gonna hurt you."

"Oh." Salinowsky looked off. "Is this about the church?"

"What church?"

"St. Euph's."

"Not that I know of. You Ukrainian?"

"Half."

"Used to be a lot of them in that part of town."

"Nowadays not so much."

"Maybe you can give me a tour when this is all over."

Salinowsky looked puzzled. "This? What do you mean by this?"

"Are you carrying a bomb?"

"Why would I do that? I don't even like loud noises anymore."

"That's good. But I have reason to believe you're carrying a bomb."

"I told you I'm not."

"Will you do me a favor, Lewis? Would you take off your prosthesis for me?"

Salinowsky went ramrod straight. "That's my leg."

"I know, but I need to examine it, on account of it may be dangerous."

"I can't walk without it." He paused, lip trembling. "I never hurt anyone. Not even in Iraq. Dove into the road to evade live fire. Got run over by a damn APC."

"I'm sorry. Really. I was there too once."

"What happened to you?"

"Nothing worth mentioning. I was lucky."

"Messed me up plenty good."

"You went to the hospital. There was a nurse there. What was her name?"

"Who wants to know?"

"I think you had an unusual experience in that hospital bed. Someone might be jealous of what she did with you. Do you remember her?"

"Nurse Ritchie, I guess. It's all pretty foggy. We did it standing up. Hurt like hell every time, but felt good too. She mad at me now?"

"Not her. I don't think so. Someone else maybe planted a bomb in the leg. Can you take it off, let me examine it?"

"No."

"I need to look at it, Lewis."

"No, I said. Enough."

A loud sound outside made both of them flinch. Salinowsky reacted worse than Diaz. He spasmed as if electricity had hit him.

"I need a fix. Can you get me a fix?"

"I can't get you drugs, Lewis. I'm a cop. It doesn't work that way."

"But you want something and I have my needs, too."

"I can't get you drugs. I can get you treatment."

"That's nothing. Father Igor can do that. What's your game?"

"I need to see the leg now. It could explode any minute and hurt us both."

"You can't!" He was shivering, more volatile. "I need my fix. The leg is mine!"

Salinowsky reached for his waistband and Diaz had to presume he was going for a detonator. He couldn't outrun a blast but he might outrun Salinowsky's shaking hands. He covered the six feet between them in less than a second and yanked Salinowsky's arms away from his body. He lay spread-eagle over Salinowsky, pinning down all four limbs.

A guy rushed in behind, so much as you could rush wearing a full-body bomb suit. It was Kahn. Muffled, through the visor, he screamed at Diaz to go, but without thinking Diaz had wrenched the leg away from Salinowsky, torn it clean off his stump.

"There's no wire," he said.

"I got it," Kahn said. "Get out! Get him out!"

Diaz grabbed Salinowsky by the back of his shirt and dragged him screaming through the door and out onto the sidewalk, his one remaining shoe scraping along the pavement. Two uniformed cops fell on him and patted him down while Diaz caught his breath.

Kahn sent a uniformed cop with his keys to get the ScanX equipment from the trunk of his car. Three minutes later, he stood over the prosthesis, already sweating in the Kevlar suit and blast-resistant helmet. Detached from its owner, the mechanical leg looked inert and none too clean. If there was a bomb inside, it was well hidden.

It had been a while since Kahn stood over a suspicious item like this. As SDS, he was rarely called anymore to don the suit. *Desperate times call for desperate measures,* he thought, but immediately tried to force the drama of that expression and the novelty of this situation from his mind.

He stood for a moment, assessing the best way to set up the x-ray. With the artificial leg lying so flat, it would be difficult to get a good shot. He contemplated whether to bring in a pulley, attempt to hook the thing and get it partway off the ground. Recalling that the other two bombs in this case had charges directed at the wearer, he slowly walked around so that the thickest section faced away from him. Then he bent to examine it more closely, thinking how calm Diaz looked when he crouched over that bag on the steps of St. Patrick's. *Crazy S.O.B.*

But then Kahn realized that his own breathing had slowed to a uniform pace, almost like meditating. All the training and experience would undergird every move he made from here, but it was composure and concentration that had the best chance to protect him.

Kahn peered through his visor, homing in on the leg. On the edge of the seam, he saw something. He set the x-ray equipment aside and leaned closer as he ran a finger with great care over the seam. Kahn realized he still had on his reading glasses. He'd been staring at his phone as an SOD detective helped him suit up, and he'd never removed them.

The glasses allowed him to see what he otherwise would have missed. It was there clear as day, a serial number stamped into the notch of the seam.

Kahn remembered Diaz's observation that Albert Horn's normal prosthesis had a serial number while none was ever found on the remnants of the one that carried the bomb. No serial number found among the remnants of the prosthesis that killed Gavin Littel either. The bomb maker had overlooked these infinitesimal details.

The discovery now of this serial number gave Kahn the confidence to extract his Leatherman from a pocket of the Kevlar suit. They could summon the robot and tie up much of lower Manhattan for another four hours, but—again thinking of Diaz—Kahn liked his chances to deal with this properly here and now. He flicked open the knife and got down on his knees over the prosthesis. Then he inserted the tip of the knife into the seam and gently pried the two sections apart.

Diaz had Higgins with him in the response truck this time, with Higgins driving and Salinowsky squeezed in between them looking dazed and glum. Higgins always smelled vaguely of curry, and now it combined none too well with the reek coming off of the homeless man. They were in a convoy heading for Allen Street—two cruisers in the lead, followed by the truck Higgins drove and a bomb disposal truck. Also mixed in were a couple of unmarked Suburbans and another response truck with Cam Fowler and his EDC.

St. Euphrosyne, according to the radio, had already been evacuated.

"Tell me again," Diaz told Salinowsky. He had him in handcuffs as a precaution. "The bomb is in the pantry closet?"

"The cabinet." Salinowsky nodded. "I didn't say it was a bomb."

"Excuse me. The other leg, which may contain a bomb."

"You said that, not me."

"But you did switch legs this morning."

Salinowsky nodded. "I rotate them every couple of days. Keeps the blisters down."

Diaz took a notepad from atop the dashboard and opened to a blank page. He handed it to Salinowsky with a pen. "Draw the layout of the kitchen. Mark exactly where the leg is."

"It's hard to write with the cuffs on."

"Do the best you can."

With the motion of the truck and the frequent potholes, all of the lines got laid down wavy. Given Salinowsky's condition, it may have turned out that way in any event, Diaz thought. But he was never planning to assign style points.

They pulled up with sirens blaring, fire trucks already on scene. A familiar face approached as they got out, causing Higgins to break into a broad smile. "Great to see you on your feet, Lieutenant."

"Me, too," Diaz agreed.

Capobianco shook his head. "Thanks for easing me back into it, fellas."

"Never a dull moment in this game," Diaz said, contradicting everything he'd believed until last week.

"Don't I know it," Capobianco said. "Let's get to work. Best approach is around the side door."

Higgins jumped back into the truck and Diaz walked around the corner with Capobianco, gently tugging along Salinowsky, whose leg Kahn had managed to piece back together. It wasn't a good idea for Kahn to go out twice in one day after the stress of the bomb suit, so he'd returned to the station house.

"Nice not to have a crater on this one," Diaz said.

"Yeah." Capobianco strode along. "Well, it's early yet."

They moved a couple of blue sawhorses aside so Higgins could back the truck right up to the sidewalk.

Fowler was patrolling along the side of the building with the Labrador. Cai Yong shadowed them, acting as sweeper.

The man who Salinowsky called Father Igor met Capobianco and Diaz out front, and he confirmed the location of the possible bomb. Father Igor stepped aside with Salinowsky, and the cops opened the truck doors and extended the ramp toward the shelter door.

Diaz and Capobianco watched the screen as Higgins worked the controls to the HD1. It took fifteen minutes to guide the robot in front of the stainless steel cabinet in the pantry, another half hour to carefully empty the contents before they finally saw the prosthetic leg.

When the robot had the leg on the ground, they called it back and rigged it with an x-ray panel. Then Higgins sent it back to shoot the pictures.

"Son of a bitch," Capobianco said a few minutes later, when they had the image up on a laptop computer. They saw wires and a blasting cap and electronic parts. The presumed C4 looked like a solid, misshapen log.

Deciding to execute the RSP on site, they rigged the robot with a PAN and Higgins tried to get it into position with the remote control panel, but for that purpose even their smallest machine proved too bulky for the tight quarters of the pantry.

Higgins looked pie-eyed from staring at the remote screen for so long. "We could just smack it around with the robot and get it to detonate," he suggested.

"What?" said Capobianco. "And blow up half the shelter? Besides, it's a new robot. Take forever to requisition another one."

"I think I can get it from the doorway with the water cannon," Diaz offered.

Capobianco thought about it, nodded, and watched as Higgins helped him suit up.

A few minutes later, beyond the noise of the air pump in his helmet, Diaz sensed the eerie quiet of the abandoned shelter, the bomb just lying there like a coiled snake.

"Manny Diaz," the voiceover in his head declared, "alone with danger."

He positioned himself as far away from the bomb as he could while still taking clean aim.

The beauty of C4 was its stability. Separated from the blasting cap circuit, it would be no more dangerous than a ball of putty. Picturing the x-ray in his mind, he set up the PAN and drew a bead on the spot that he knew would give him the best chance to defeat the device without causing a detonation. Then he took cover and fired.

TICK, TICK, TICK

12.

DAY SIX: DARK

O'SHEA STARED INTO HIS UNTOUCHED SALAD. Outside, in the early evening light, stray trash tripped down the sidewalks of the East Village. He was sitting across from Lewis Salinowsky at Veselka on Second Avenue. Ukrainian soul food, aroma of pig fat and vinegar. He'd watched Salinowsky consume a cup of borscht, six meatballs, several large pierogi, a stuffed cabbage, and a heap of fatty kielbasa without uttering a word. Now the man was poised to dive into some kind of apple turnover buried in whipped cream. He had his fork in the air when O'Shea pulled the plate away from him.

"What the hell."

"Talk first. Then dessert. The taxpayer has to get his money's worth." O'Shea winked.

Salinowsky set down his fork. "Give me the cherry."

O'Shea let him snatch it. He removed the dessert plate to a neighboring table and watched Salinowsky relish the unnaturally red fruit, chewing deliberately. Ten seconds later, a busboy cleared the plate, and a couple sat down.

O'Shea looked contrite. "We'll get you another. Start talking."

The meal had sobered up Salinowsky. He was still gaunt and pale, and he didn't smell too hot, but his eyes no longer looked like those of a waste product.

"Got nothing to tell besides what I told that Spanish cop."

"Who? Diaz?"

Salinowsky shrugged. "I guess."

"The guy who saved your life, we're talking about. Just another spic to you."

"Naw, I'm not that way."

"What way are you?"

Salinowsky looked into his hands.

"You're a brilliant conversationalist, you know that, Lewis?"

"I don't get much practice lately."

"Tell me about this nurse, Sallye Ritchie."

He looked into his hands again. "That her name? I never knew the first name."

"This her?" O'Shea showed him a picture.

Salinowsky pursed his lips. "Yeah, I suppose it is. I'd know for sure if you showed me her ass."

"I don't have any photos of that. What'd she do for you?"

"Man, I was in pain and half high on morphine. Far as I remember, she gave me a few rides is all." His mind was working. Several thoughts seemed to play across his gaunt face. "Probably more fun for her than it was for me, but she marched around like it qualified her for sainthood. I remember that part."

"You think she has the potential to be violent?"

"How the hell would I know? I saw her when she came in the room. That was it."

"Did she mention anyone else in her life—father, brother, boyfriend?"

"Not that I recall."

"What a help."

"She wasn't there to shoot the breeze. Why don't you ask the other nurses?"

"We're working on that. Did you know these other GIs, Littel and Horn?"

"Were they in my unit?"

"No."

"So why should I know them?"

"She ever reach out to you after you left the hospital?"

"Not at all," he answered quickly.

"You to her?"

He hesitated. "I sent her a letter in Germany once, okay? Never heard back. After that it didn't even cross my mind again."

"Did the letter have a return address?"

"I guess so. Sent if from the post office where I keep my box."

Idiot, O'Shea thought. "That's how they tracked you. Must be. Did you know that your situation wasn't unique?"

"Not until you told me."

"And the bomb? Any idea who planted it?"

"If I did I would've shared by now. Had to be one of the guys who slept in the shelter last night or one of the guys who works there. Maybe they even did it after I left, for all I know. Wouldn't let me into the cabinet last night."

"You said the leg you put on this morning came from the cabinet. That means the leg you got out of the cabinet was not the bomb."

O'Shea knew the logic of his own statement was impeccable. The bomb hadn't been placed in the cabinet by the perp. It was the other one—Salinowsky having inadvertently switched. But the vagrant seemed to have trouble following. "Whatever," he said.

"Were there any new visitors to the shelter that you saw?"

"There are always new visitors. You'd have to ask Father Igor who was who. I wasn't in condition to observe much."

"After stopping at your dealer?"

Salinowsky smiled. "Man I was high as an effing kite last night, wouldn't have recognized my own grandmother."

"And this morning?"

"I don't have a good life like you, Detective. I do everything I can to dull the feeling."

O'Shea waved over the waitress. "Another piece of that apple thing for my friend. And a check."

She dropped the items in another minute. O'Shea put two twenties on the table and tore the receipt off the bottom of the check. He handed Salinowsky his business card.

"Anything comes to you, don't hesitate. I wrote down Diaz's number on the back, if you'd prefer to talk to him. The guy who's doing these bombings is still out there. You may save a life."

Salinowsky nodded and lifted his fork off the table, ready to dig in again. But O'Shea coveted the cherry. Before Salinowsky could react, he plucked it from the whipped cream and popped it into his mouth. It tasted more of sugar than fruit, but it hit the spot. He was still chewing when he pushed back his chair, nodded to the waitress, and left the drug addict to the remainder of his dessert.

He may not see this guy alive again, but the NYPD would. They had a tail on him.

* * *

Salinowsky lingered over the apple strudel. His stomach felt like a brick but he was determined not to leave any for the dish washer.

When he thought back over events of the past few hours, he decided that the whole day had been a gift. He hadn't once hit the junk and he felt better than he had in weeks. Not that he expected his body to quit cold turkey, but the whole incident had instilled a strange kind of hope. Maybe, he thought, he'd even go back to his sister's house. But then he remembered that some monster was trying to kill him—to blow him up of all things. He recalled hearing some of the guys in the shelter talking about those two explosions last week, seeing some headlines on the street. He had no way of connecting that to himself until the cops had mentioned the nurse, Sallye Ritchie.

Limping back to the shelter, he tried but couldn't even picture her face. The photo that the cop had showed him brought recognition, but he couldn't conjure her in his mind now. He could still see her hands, though, translucent skin and bony fingers. The tendons worked up and down as she caressed him. He wondered whether he'd ever have another woman again.

Salinowsky got to the shelter just before doors closed. They had a free bed for him and he couldn't help noticing that the staff looked at him with a higher degree of compassion than before. But he was tired of being a pathetic creature. He would get his life together now, he told himself as he undressed.

That night, alert for danger, Lewis Salinowsky slept with his artificial leg cradled in his arms.

TICK, TICK

13.

DAY SEVEN: LIGHT

WHEN DIAZ GOT TO THE STATION house he found Kahn and O'Shea meeting in Capobianco's office. The lieutenant waved him in and instructed him to close the door. There was no chair for him so he leaned against a filing cabinet, suddenly feeling very much like the junior man again.

O'Shea began speaking. "Why I thought we should meet in person, rather than giving the lieutenant a fill over the phone, is that my lieutenant didn't want yesterday's excitement to overwhelm the fact that we still haven't solved this case."

"Yeah," Capobianco said, "I had a call from Inspector Brennan, too. Still, you guys did a helluva a job all around. I'm proud of you." He leaned back in his chair. "But Brian's right. All yesterday amounted to was a render safe on a lone device. It got us a step closer but it didn't conclude anything."

Diaz folded his arms across his chest.

O'Shea nodded to Kahn. "Have fun dressing up yesterday?"

"Yeah, just like Halloween but without the shaving cream. It's a real joy wearing that thing indoors, too. Multiplies the claustrophobia about thirty times."

"No natural light in that store," Diaz added. "Scaffolding over the windows didn't help either." It had been worse for him in the basement shelter, where there were no windows at all, but Diaz chose not to mention that.

"You wanna play hero, you gotta deal with these little discomforts," Capobianco said.

"I'm not arguing otherwise," said Kahn. "Brian asked is all."

O'Shea cleared his throat. "So while you guys were making the streets safe in Gotham and recovering from the trauma, I had a sit-down with our favorite still-living vagabond."

"Go on."

"He doesn't know shit. Spent more time eating the dinner I put on my T and E than giving up the goods on anyone or anything. He barely even remembers the nurse, if he's telling the truth. And I have no reason to think otherwise. He was drugged up then and he's drugged up now."

"The guy has PTSD," Diaz said. "When he heard a bang outside yesterday he nearly jumped out of his skin."

"Self-medicating." O'Shea nodded. "So when I was done with him, I gave the nurse a call. No disrespect to your prior interview, Diaz."

"None taken. Did you think she was nuts?"

"I didn't experience that."

"Maybe you gotta meet her in person."

"I'll look forward to that day. She came across on an even keel and, like she did with you, she admitted to an affair with all three men. Beyond that she wouldn't cop to having a clue about who's doing this."

"She tell you about the battery?" Diaz asked.

"Not voluntarily, but I asked who was beating her up. She gave me the same song and dance she gave you. Fell down the stairs."

Capobianco adjusted in his chair. "So what did you come here to tell us, Detective?"

"Just to emphasize, like I said, that despite the heat you all experienced yesterday this case is cooling off quick."

"It's the woman," Kahn said. "She has to be the key to all this. Did we finally get someone up there to follow her?"

"Not clear yet," Capobianco said. "As of this morning the Mass state troopers and the FBI were still arguing over jurisdiction. Now that the targets don't seem to be the recruiting stations, federal interest has cooled off. Meanwhile, the crimes are all local, so Mass-a-two-shits is reluctant to act against one of its own citizens without an arrest warrant, which of course we can't get, since we have nothing to hold her on. Par for the course."

Kahn shook his head, equally unsurprised.

"I do think we'll get a search warrant soon," Capobianco added. "DA's talking to the judge this morning. So that's where we're at. But I don't trust anyone in New England to do our work for us. Who here volunteers to pound on the nurse? I'm speaking figuratively, of course."

No one laughed. Diaz rocked to the balls of his feet. "I think I should go up there again. We were establishing some rapport, me and her."

"Take O'Shea with you. It's a two-man job and I don't want Fisco on my ass for leaving A and E out of it." Capobianco turned to O'Shea. "Deal?"

"You got it, Lieutenant." O'Shea smiled. "Who doesn't relish a road trip? And I'd like to see some of that rapport in action first hand."

Still no one cracked a smile.

"I'll call ahead and see if the Mass State Police are ready to back us up when the search warrant comes through. What about the homeless guy? We think he's still a target?"

O'Shea shrugged. "Depends on how determined the bomber is—or whether he even knows that we intercepted his latest device. With no explosion, I imagine it won't get prominent play in the press. Usually it only makes the front page when you guys screw up. But you never know."

"Someone gonna protect Salinowsky?"

"He's not cooperating on that front, but I got a tail on him anyway, a detective from the Fifth. On the bright side, the guy's not such an easy target now that he's alerted. Not unless the bomber decides to change his MO."

"Worse than that, maybe the bomber will just move onto the next victim. And we're in the dark on who that would be."

"The nurse only admits to these three, Lieutenant. You think there's another?"

"Seems like there's always another, doesn't it, guys?"

THE RIDE TO MASSACHUSETTS IN an unmarked Crown Victoria was uneventful. O'Shea drove the whole way and they stopped twice, once to pee and again for lunch, which was thin-crust pizza at a place that O'Shea knew in New Haven. They were in touch through Capobianco with the Massachusetts state troopers, who would meet them at the house with the warrant.

"Let's go to the hospital first," Diaz suggested when they closed in on Bedford. "Maybe catch her off guard."

It pleased him very much to give O'Shea turn-by-turn directions the rest of the way—just like Kahn was always doing to him—and when they arrived at the VA hospital he instructed him on where to park, too.

At the information desk this time they asked for admission to the ward, which necessitated a stop at the administrative offices. After a few phone calls for everyone to cover their asses, the detectives were in. Wearing hospital-issue IDs on lanyards around their necks, they took the stairs and strolled down the hall to the nurses' station. Sallye Ritchie, they learned, was not scheduled today or the next. Diaz hated the sound of that. So far as he knew, an agreement to the tail hadn't yet come through.

"Who's her boss?" O'Shea asked the middle-aged black woman who stood before them. She wore a name tag that said, "V. Burnes."

"That's me," she said, studying O'Shea's badge.

"Can we ask some questions?"

"Of course." She nodded. Her head sported close-cropped, jet-black hair with dyed orange highlights. It reminded Diaz of a Cincinnati Bengals helmet. Amazing the things people found attractive.

"Is there a more private place?" O'Shea asked.

"I don't have a separate office. We can go to the lounge."

She led them in silence. When the door closed, she said, "What's this about? What's Sallye done?"

"What makes you sure she did anything, Nurse Burnes?"

She hesitated.

"Ma'am," Diaz said, "we're here to investigate a series of murders by bombing. I met with Nurse Ritchie last week and, to be honest, she seemed kind of odd. Nothing you say is likely to surprise us."

Burnes blinked. "I'm sorry. I jumped to the wrong conclusion. I can't imagine her bombing anyone."

"What can you imagine?"

"You met with her in person last week?"

"Yeah, a few days ago."

"Then you know what she looked like."

"You mean the bruises. How common is that?"

"Every few months it seems, and getting worse. I've tried referring her for counseling but she wouldn't hear of it. I thought, when you mentioned—well, I thought maybe she'd had enough."

"Done violence to whoever's beating her?"

"Yes."

"Do you know who that is?"

"It's a little embarrassing. I've eavesdropped some on her. Out of concern, you understand. I've heard the name Warren now and then."

"That's a last name?"

She shook her head. "First."

"You think he's the boyfriend?"

"I'm sure he is."

"She told us she fell down the subway stairs in New York."

"Anything's possible, I suppose. If so, she's quite prone to accidents. A few months before it was a fender bender and she blamed the steering wheel. Before that, I think she claimed to have fallen off her bicycle."

"Have you known her to behave inappropriately with any of the patients?"

"How do you mean?"

"Sexually."

"Not at all. Why would you ask that?"

"Has she spoken to you at all about this man, Warren?"

"Not really. She's a bit of a loner, doesn't socialize much with any of us. Just does her job—quite well, I should add—and goes home."

"Is that where we'd find her now, do you think?"

"Oh, no. She's off to New York."

O'Shea perked up. "New York? Wasn't she just there? How often does she go?"

"Every month or so, usually. But she told me this time that she had to run back for something. That's another reason...when you said...I suspected—"

"You said she kept to herself. Why'd she tell you now?"

"I require all my staff to let me know if they're leaving town, just in case we have a national emergency. Since nine-eleven. You know, procedure."

"Procedure," Diaz echoed without irony.

But Burnes took it as something of an accusation. "We're dealing with people's lives here, Detective."

"So are we," said O'Shea with a polite smile. "When did she leave town?"

"I don't know. I haven't seen her since yesterday afternoon."

Manis bought the local newspapers from a deli in downtown Brooklyn and leafed through them on the F Train. He never used the Internet to search for evidence of his handiwork. It left footprints that he knew he couldn't erase.

Two of three papers contained small stories about the removal of a bomb from a homeless shelter in St. Euphrosyne Church. Neither article mentioned Lewis Salinowsky by name or that the bomb was a prosthetic leg. Both said police would not speculate on any connection to the veteran bombings. There were no casualties, which meant for sure that Salinowsky had escaped.

By the time Manis entered the apartment his blood was boiling. He walked in on Sallye watching *Glee* on television. She was sitting on the couch with her back to him, quietly singing along. He dropped the papers on the table and went over and boxed her ears. She collapsed into a defensive posture, covering her head, and he went around and punched her hard in the face. It felt good—the first time he'd ever hit her unconnected to a sexual act. He took it as a sign of his own recovery, but now he had more than that to deal with.

"Why?" she said, crying on the floor.

"Lover boy Lewis got away. What happened? You tipped him off?"

She was bleeding heavily, all over the couch as she tried to pull herself up. "Not on the furniture, bitch!" He punched her in the side of the head and she fell to the floor, crying for him to stop. It was also the first time he'd hit her when she didn't rebound with a shit-eating grin. He liked that. She didn't control this situation. For the first time since Germany, he thought, she wasn't leading him around by his dick. Now he saw it all in a new light. She'd never lose her attachment to those men. And Manis, for his part, suddenly no longer felt the same attraction to her. Now he only had to take care of business.

He walked to the bathroom and returned with a bath towel, threw it at her, said, "Get up and quit your whining. Isn't this what you always wanted, taking pain for others?" Yes, he understood. Finally, he understood everything. She was punishing herself for that first time with the man he'd once been. It settled in his mind with great clarity.

She didn't answer him, just sat on the floor with her head tilted back over the cushions, pressing the towel into her mouth and nose.

"Tell me how long you've been in touch with Lewis," he said.

She lifted the bloody towel from her face long enough to say to the ceiling, "I don't know what you're talking about."

"Lewis Salinowsky? The one you always said was your best lay ever? You saved his life for another day."

"Saved it how?"

He rushed her, fist in the air. "Don't play stupid with me! You know what's going on!"

She covered up but he didn't hit her, reminding himself that he had total control now.

"You better start talking. You going to claim you didn't know?"

"What I've always wanted is to be with you."

"You got a funny way of showing it. Why'd you pay me the surprise visit last night?"

"I told you, I wanted to see you."

"Bullshit!" He raised a fist and she cowered again. "Wanted to see what I was doing, more like."

"No."

"Let me get a look at the nose."

Before she could react he closed his fingers on her jaw like a vise and lifted her head further. "Oh," he said, "it's broken real good this time. Smashed. You want more?"

She shook her head. "No. Please."

"That's better. More respectful. Tell me what you know and what you did."

She raised herself shakily from the floor and sat on the couch, away from the bloody side. "The police came to me and told me someone had killed those others."

"You thought it was me?"

"I suspected."

"Turns out I'm good for something after all."

"I always knew that you were, Lew—" She caught herself. Freudian slip.

Manis slapped her on the cheek with an open hand. It stung his palm and she looked so shocked, so broken, so divorced from her prior character that all of a sudden he wanted to cry. A picture had sprung to his mind of Sallye as a young teenager. He sank to a chair while attempting to blink it away and recapture his composure.

"What did you tell the cops?"

"I didn't—" she began.

"Shut up! No ate-ee-ists in da fox-oles." She didn't reprimand him for the accent this time. He snarled at her. "What's a matter, fox got your tongue?"

She shook her head. Blood dripped from her nose onto the floor, but most of the flow had stopped.

"So you told him," Manis said.

"I don't know him. He's just, like, an idea, a distant memory that I used to turn you on. To please you, Warren."

"You're lying. I saw the letter."

"I never replied to it."

"But you carried it around. You love him. Love what you did with him, anyway. And you know what? It's funny because he's already ruined, a shadow of himself. If you visited him, you'd see."

"I don't even know where he is, never have."

"That's easy. He's at St. Euphrosyne."

"What's that?"

"You really don't know? It's a church in downtown Manhattan. The loser lives sometimes in the shelter there."

The curiosity. He saw it in her bruised black eyes. He'd chosen correctly. He said from a long distance, "I won't kill him now, you know. It's over between you and me."

"Over?" Resistance flashed in her. "So you killed those others for nothing?"

"Not for nothing." He stared into the middle space. "I had my reasons."

"And now it doesn't matter anymore? What a waste." She flicked her wrist. "And what a cowardly thing to do, ambushing them from afar."

"That's not how it went down. You think it was easy, what I did? I looked right into their eyes, both of them, even if they didn't know who I was. Like this."

He seized her by the shoulders and locked their watery gaze. Then he kissed her. She opened her mouth to receive his tongue. He thought about biting her but didn't. There was already salty blood in his mouth. Her blood. He ran it over his teeth.

There was a better way for this to end, he thought. He couldn't leave witnesses behind.

When he let go of her she said, "You still want me."

"Yes," he pretended to admit, though he almost choked on the word. She was done for, but he needed her still. "Clean yourself up. I'm going out for the rest of the day. I'll be back tomorrow afternoon. Can I trust you here alone?"

"You think I'd steal from you, asshole?"

"Not what I meant. Stay out of the locked room. You might get hurt."

"Where are you off to?"

Her face asked the rest of the question. It asked whether he was going this very moment to kill her precious Lewis. She'd try to stop him, if she could. He just knew it. He had a card that the shelter workers had given him the other night. As he put his coat back on, he pretended to drop that card by mistake and not notice. It fluttered to the floor behind him as he hit the door. Bait.

She had to see but she said nothing. That's how he knew the trap was set.

DIAZ AND O'SHEA TRIED CALLING Sallye Ritchie's cell phone number, which the head nurse had provided with some reluctance, but they couldn't get an answer.

"We could hightail it back to New York," Diaz said, "be there by three."

"But we have nothing to go on. How far's her house from here?"

"Not far."

"I'll call Burbette while you drive."

They climbed in and O'Shea soon reached the Fed. It wasn't a long conversation. He turned to Diaz.

"Says it would take days to get a trace on that phone, even if we had the warrant in hand, which of course we don't."

"We still got the warrant for the house. We may as well search that."

"Boffo, Diaz. But I'm getting a bad feeling."

They pulled up a few minutes later. Everything looked as Diaz had left it, except that Ritchie's car was gone and a state trooper greeted them. He was young but he had the paperwork. He helped them pry the door open with a crowbar and removed his hat when he entered.

"Don't mess it up too bad," he said.

O'Shea looked at him. "What are we, the friggin' mafia?"

The kid was smart enough not to answer. He stood in the corner of each room as they went through.

"This place is spotless," O'Shea said, digging through drawers.

They found no personal phone book and few personal records, but Diaz did come upon an old photo album in the back of a closet.

"Bag it?" O'Shea asked.

"Sure," said Diaz. "We can look through it in the car."

"You remove anything," the trooper said, "you got to fill out an evidence form." He was showing off, not worth arguing with.

"Roger that," O'Shea said. "Diaz, mind filling out the form while I take a last look around?"

Diaz appreciated hearing these orders as suggestions, rather than how Kahn would've put them. O'Shea was first grade, making him senior, but Diaz didn't report to him, so the relationship felt different.

When he was finished with the paperwork, he climbed into the passenger seat of the Crown Vic to wait for O'Shea and began flipping through the photos. It was a white album with padded covers and gold trim. Pretty old-looking and smelled sour—cellophane. Some of the photos seeming like they went back to the Seventies. They showed Sallye as a small child, as a teenager, as an enlisted woman in uniform, frolicking on the beach in a one-piece bathing suit, posed on some steps in what looked like a prom dress. Could this be her whole life in a twenty-page album? If so, did this boyfriend, Warren, rate a picture?

"Manuel Diaz," said the voice in Diaz's head, "not wasting a moment, from afar seeks a mind meld with his primary suspect."

You in there, Warren? Oh, Warren? Come out, come out, wherever you are.

He was so absorbed that he didn't see O'Shea cross the driveway until the door opened. It startled him and he snapped shut the album. "Find anything else inside?"

"Nah," O'Shea said. "I was just taking a dump. You?"

"I used the trunk."

"Ha ha. I meant, did you find anything?"

A thought crossed Diaz's mind. "You know, that MP of mine's been fast with some stuff, but it's taking him awhile to get together the list of people with access to C4. I asked him twice already. Maybe, now that we got a partial name, I should call and nudge him."

O'Shea looked at his watch. "Gotta be—what—pretty late German time. He's still working?"

"It ain't a clock-punch situation, Brian. It's the fucking army. If he's awake, he'll answer."

"They let you sleep in the army these days?"

"Just when no one's shooting at you."

It took eight rings but Nunez did pick up. "I'm kind of, um, in the middle of something." He sounded more than a little groggy.

"We got a hot situation here," Diaz said, undeterred. "Whatever happened to that list of the C4 people?"

"C4 people?"

"The people with access to high explosives?"

"Oh, that. Yeah, I'm working on that. Got a partial list."

"We'll take it."

"Can it wait for the morning?"

"Negative."

The MP hesitated. "You ain't the boss of me."

"Cut it out, Nunez. Can you get to it?"

"Okay. I'm off base but I can go back."

"Terrific. If you find anyone with the first name of Warren on that list and he's our man, you'll get a key to the city."

"For real? New York City?"

Lewis Salinowsky's morning fix was wearing off already. Cheap stuff, cut thin. He sat on the bench in Columbus Park. Cardboard sign. Coffee cup with jangling change. Heavy eyelids. Same as it ever was.

Get the name of that nun again, he thought. The methadone. Couldn't hurt. He tried to picture it, saw in his mind a window like at the check cashing store, pills in crushable paper cups pushed across the counter to him. *Thank you, sister.*

When his eyes regained focus, someone stood three feet in front of him. Red canvas sneakers on uneven pavement, traction sand dusting the toes. He ran his eyes up the tight jeans to a patent-leather belt, square buckle, wide-wale turtleneck clinging to tiny breasts. She was petite all around. Her coat hung open. Narrow neck. The face, while swollen, was small-boned. It looked like someone had taken a mallet to her nose, but she smiled.

"Lewis?"

Just hearing his name from the mouth of a woman... "Who wants to know?" His lower lip trembled. Was he hallucinating?

"That *is* you, I'm sure. I've thought a lot about you all these years."

He grabbed the sign and folded it closed across his lap. This was too much for twenty-four hours. "How did you find me?"

"The shelter. They gave me five spots where they thought you might be. This was the second."

"So you're real?"

"Of course I'm real."

"You've changed."

"We both have. Would you come with me?"

"Where?"

She bit her lip. "I have a safe place. Just for the night. We need to talk."

"Oh, I couldn't. Look at me."

"We'll clean you up. Just like old times. Get you out of harm's way."

He considered those old times, almost forgotten memories now reawakened. Something was coming alive in his pants, a part of him that he thought might never rise again.

She saw, too. She squirmed in her coat. "Oh, Lewis."

"Not you. Let me clean up myself. I'll meet you. Where?" He held out his Sharpie. What an instrument. The giver of life.

"If that's how it has to be." She wrote the address on the back of his cardboard. Crisp and clear, but not taking up too much space. She tore it off. "Don't talk to any strangers before then and keep an eye on your leg. Can you get there in an hour? You'll need the Five Train."

Salinowsky nodded. She was a vision. It all flooded back to him at once, that hospital bed with the smooth brushed aluminum rails, exactly what he'd done with the pillow to protect his injured leg while she guided him behind her, how his good knee had given way and he'd nearly tumbled to the floor in ecstasy. All of it. He'd lied to O'Shea. He remembered every glorious second.

And here she was again, offering her protection, maybe her bed.

It was too good to be true. He'd bring the rest of his bundle of heroine, in case he couldn't face what she offered him, in case it was too much, in case he needed to escape again.

Diaz and O'Shea were halfway home when Nunez called back, sounding a good deal more alert.

"Sorry about that, Diaz. You caught me off guard."

"Pants down?"

"I wish. Just sleeping off a drunk. But enough with the small talk. The list I got is partial, remember, but it's fairly long. And on that whole thing there's only two guys first name of Warren. One I know to be KIA about thirty-six months ago. Other is last name of Manis."

He spelled it and Diaz wrote it down. "You got anything on him?"

"Not much off hand. He was combat engineers until about six years ago. Must've been an honorable discharge. It looks like he kept his clearance for another couple of years."

"You don't get to keep your clearance when you're discharged."

"Probably hung around to work with an outside contractor. That'd explain it."

Diaz reflected. "And that would make it a lot easier to sneak stuff off the base, wouldn't it?"

"Well, no shit, Diaz. You gonna catch this bastard already?"

"Sure gonna try, Captain." He gave O'Shea the thumbs-up as he disengaged. "One guy so far. Name's Warren Manis."

O'Shea took out his phone and dialed the AES office. Diaz listened as he read the name to one of his associates, waited and waited with eyes darting along the road ahead. He groaned as he hung up.

"What the hell is it?" Diaz said.

"Whole lot of nothing. There's nothing obvious coming up. No priors or anything like that. He's not in the phone book. The shoe leather brigade will have to dig a whole lot deeper."

O'Shea steered the Crown Vic aggressively around a pair of slow-moving tractor-trailers. He reached over and flicked on the flashers, floored the accelerator, and entered the left lane doing ninety-five miles per hour. He didn't slow down.

"What's the rush?" Diaz asked. "We don't know our next move yet."

"If this guy's findable, my boys will find him," O'Shea said. "And when they do, we'll wanna be in the neighborhood to claim our bite of the apple."

Diaz leaned back against the headrest. "I guess I was wrong about you."

"How so?"

"You seem so easygoing. I didn't figure you for a guy who cared about medals."

"Easygoing and stupid are two different traits, Manny. I might not be keeping score, but others are."

Diaz looked out at the median rushing by. The ground appeared to be frozen solid. "I'd like a piece of this prick myself when we do find him," he said.

"After all your hard work, that goes without saying." O'Shea chuckled, twisted in his seat. "I gotta hand it to you, Diaz. You were a terrier on this case. You showed good instincts. I bet Fisco would take you any time if you ever wanna cross town." He shook his head, looking inward. "Took me too long to see this thing as you did. Maybe Fisco shouldn't stop there. Maybe he should give you my job."

"I don't want it, Brian. And you didn't do so bad. No one could've known."

"You did." O'Shea laughed again. A hearty devil-may-care laugh. Nothing seemed to bother him.

Looking over at his big red face and blond eyebrows, Diaz couldn't help smiling, too. Where, he wondered, did a man get a personality like that? If you could buy it off the shelf, Diaz would readily go into the store and empty his wallet tomorrow.

From the roof of a low-slung industrial building across the street from his place, Manis had watched Sallye leave. She'd have no reason to suspect that he'd double back—he'd never done so before, ever—but this was a day of firsts and there were more to come.

For all her prior haughtiness, Sallye fell prey to her desires as easily as he ever had. He saw how Lewis's name worked on her, and he knew what she would do, given the opportunity.

She'd left without her overnight bag, which meant she'd be back, didn't plan to flee or call the cops just yet. Thinking he'd be gone for the night, she'd take her time planning how to save Salinowsky while pleasing herself—the pleasing part never too low on her agenda.

If she was coming straight back, Manis figured he had at least an hour. He descended the stairs and crossed back to his apartment.

He looked around. The bitch had made an effort to clean up, covering the couch in a cotton sheet. There was evidence that she'd showered, too, before changing. The only blood was on an icepack that she'd carelessly discarded in the sink. Something compelled him to wash it off and return it to the freezer.

Then he went into the bathroom and used a pair of large scissors to cut his beard close. He shaved twice with a razor, clean for the first time in a decade. He looked ten years younger at least.

Proceeding to his workshop, he packed a knapsack with four pounds of C4 and several blasting caps. He left the rest of the hardware, which he could more easily duplicate. He rushed to the dresser and stuffed some underwear, a few shirts, and a few pairs of socks inside the pack. Lastly he took his laptop computer and his small Dopp kit. He set the whole thing inside the workshop door and checked his watch. Forty-five minutes remaining.

From the workshop Manis grabbed the last, most important item. He had wrapped four blocks of C4 together in electrical tape and placed them in a wooden cigar box atop a spring-loaded switch, the nub of which protruded out a hole he'd cut in the bottom. Rigged also as a relay switch, the device included a pair of 9-volt batteries, which would decay in about six hours time. Guaranteed explosion.

Even if everyone managed to flee, he thought, at least he'd send a message to the cops about fucking with Warren Manis.

Between mattress and box spring, he slipped a one-by-six wooden board to provide the switch with firm resistance. He'd tested the spring a thousand times. It would take more than the weight of the mattress to set the switch, but not much more.

In a few minutes longer, everything lay hidden under the mattress except for a pair of protruding wires, waiting to be joined.

When he'd satisfied himself that all was in order, Manis retrieved his M9 pistol from under the kitchen sink and returned to his workshop. He burned the pictures from the wall in a metal trash bin, stuffed into his pockets a few of his favorite pieces of hardware, and said goodbye to his treasured machines. They were his friends, these machines, a friendship made more intimate by their secrecy and the countless hours he'd spent alone with them.

Because this had once been the foreman's office to the factory floor, there was a side door that he could use if he had to escape quickly—if she brought the cops. He had two grenades in his pockets and the pistol. With his escape plan and the element of surprise, that should be enough to extricate himself if it came to that. But for now he contented himself with turning on the closed-circuit television and monitoring the cameras that covered his apartment entrance and the street.

Kahn waited alone in a response truck at a pull-off by the Henry Hudson Parkway. O'Shea gave a wave, but he took off as soon as Diaz got out of the Crown Vic.

"Where's he going?" Kahn asked.

"Wants to be at the office if and when the break comes in." Diaz followed the disappearing car with his eyes. Almost wistfully, Kahn thought.

"We need gas," he said.

"I'll drive," Diaz volunteered.

They stopped at a service station on Hancock Place and 124th Street. Kahn, having gotten a complete update from Diaz over the phone, knew exactly what the photo album resting on the dashboard was all about. Curious to see what this nurse had that got everyone so hot and bothered, he grabbed the album and leaned up against the hood of the response vehicle while Diaz went inside for snacks. Kahn had been in and out of the truck all day, and his back throbbed. He hoped he wasn't getting sciatica again. He'd struggled with it a few years ago, could barely bend over, and began to fear he'd have to apply for disability. What was the point of disability if you couldn't swing a golf club? Then, like a miracle, the pain had gone away on its own.

He set the album on the hood and stretched as he turned the pages. There was nothing of use in there and he half wondered why Diaz and O'Shea had bothered to take it. They were rushing about like headless chickens, chasing bombs, cleaning up the aftermath. No wonder they got on each other's nerves sometimes. This work could test the patience of the Dalai Lama.

The pump clicked and Kahn topped off the tank and took a receipt. Diaz came out of the store chewing a candy bar, and Kahn climbed back into the truck, this time on the driver's side, taking care to swing his legs around like the physical therapist had taught him.

Diaz lifted an eyebrow and waved a fresh Snickers bar. "Got this for you."

"Not a good idea at my age." Kahn patted his belly.

"Suit yourself."

They rode in silence over to the West Side Drive and down. Then Diaz swallowed the last bite of his candy bar and said, "You think this is our guy?"

"Yes, I do."

"Me, too. The combat engineer angle is dispositive."

Kahn laughed. "Dispositive? You learn that when you looked up 'procedure' in the dictionary?"

"Maybe."

"You're right, though."

"Part I wonder about is whether the nurse is an accomplice."

"Or an accomplice after the fact."

"You think she knows?"

"She suspects. She went to New York again so soon because you rattled her. Either she's come here to confirm her suspicions or to confront him. Possibly both."

"So you're saying I done good?"

"You want a pat on the head, go to the lieutenant. He's into that sort of thing. You ask me, a job well done should be its own reward, okay? I have a dog to worship me. You can get one, too. They give them to anyone these days."

Diaz grinned. It had taken some time, but they were finally growing on each other.

"What about your wife and kids?"

"What about them?"

"They don't worship you?"

Kahn rolled his eyes. "Ever have a wife, Diaz?"

"No."

"If you had you wouldn't ask that question."

"That's what I thought you'd say. Just wanted to make sure I had you figured right."

"Yeah, I'm a real enigma."

"What is that?"

"Forget it. You ever come across the sappers while you were in combat?"

"All the time. They're like us. They got a lot of respect for gadgets. Spend a lot of time with their equipment."

"Suppose I would've guess that."

"But they're more rigid than we are."

Kahn nodded, thinking, *Procedure.*

"One thing I'll say," Diaz continued. "If they tell you they're gonna drop a bridge, then they're gonna drop a bridge. They won't have to do it twice. They won't skimp on the plastic."

"Well, Manis already proved that he can put enough gum together to drop a person. Let's hope he doesn't have greater ambition."

"Or the ordnance to see it through."

They were passing the Lincoln Tunnel entrance. Neither of them associated the conversation about the bridge with blowing up this tunnel, another piece of critical infrastructure. You couldn't live life while seeing everything around you as a potential target.

Kahn's phone rang. *Finally!* O'Shea had the suspect's address.

"I'm driving. Hold on." Kahn passed the phone to Diaz and told him to write it down. As he listened to Diaz reading it back, he formulated a route. He'd shoot across Houston Street and take the FDR Drive to the Brooklyn Bridge, cut through Brooklyn Heights to Red Hook. He thought about what Diaz said about combat engineers and overkill. Maybe, he thought, against all odds they could close this thing down without any more casualties. He checked his rearview mirror before swinging into another lane and nearly missed crashing into a beat-up Korean church van.

Missed being the operative word. It gave the man hope.

MANIS SAT ALERT AT THE monitor for longer than he'd expected. Finally, he saw her coming from the street. *Alone.* That surprised him. Maybe he'd already beaten the horniness out of her. Or maybe Salinowsky was too freaked out to come.

He stuffed the M9 into his waistband and loosened his shirt over it. Just as Sallye walked through the front door he emerged from the workshop, leaving the door unlocked. Secrets didn't matter anymore.

Upon seeing him she went pale.

"Surprise," he said.

"Change of plans?"

It took her a moment to recognize him without the beard. Her eyes went to his mutilated hand, which gave it away. The clean shave was a profound change, but he could see that she didn't want to indicate how much it unsettled her. She shirked her coat onto a chair and tried to play nonchalant but couldn't manage to camouflage her nerves from him. If she hadn't been hiding anything before, she surely was now. He'd have to remain alert.

She startled him by walking up and slapping him across the face. "That's for earlier."

He had to control himself so as not to reach for the gun. He stepped forward, his right hip to her left, as if they were going to tango, and pinched her between the legs.

"Ow!"

"Where were you?"

"I went out for a walk."

"Seeking something?"

"Yeah. Peace and quiet. This has gone too far, Warren."

He laughed derisively at that, went to the refrigerator and poured a glass of orange juice. "The nurse gets a taste of her own medicine. You can't hurt me anymore, Sallye."

"I never laid a hand on you. You're the one who hits me all the time."

"You insisted upon it. I'm not talking about physical hurt. I'm talking about the heart."

"Poor baby."

"You want me to hit you again, don't you?"

"No." She met his stare, but her voice grew tremulous. "You really hurt me, Warren, these last days. We have what they call a codependent relationship. It's not healthy."

"We're way past that."

She looked away. "You never should've killed those men."

As she distracted herself, he stirred a fine powder into the juice. "You never should've teased me with them."

"You could have asked me to stop."

"I *begged* you to stop." He stepped around the counter and back toward her. She flinched, but he only ran the fingers of his bad hand through her hair. The strands tickled his erogenous zone. He ran his tongue across her cut lips, which were rough with scabbing, then kissed her long and hard, harvesting a last taste to remember her by. She didn't resist.

He said, "How many times did I tell you I didn't want it this way? You kept pushing and pushing. Those men… their blood is on your hands."

"I'm sorry. Is that what you want to hear? I thought, deep down, you enjoyed it as much as I did."

"When Salinowsky dies, *his* blood, too, will be on your hands, Sallye. Unless…" He left it hanging.

"What do you want from me, Warren?"

"I want to make love to you the old-fashioned way, like we once did. Like people in the suburbs. Regular people. Missionary-style. No screaming or hitting or telling stories."

The thought of it made her tremble. "But we were never regular people. I was a girl and you were a man."

"But we loved each other, didn't we? All the way from Germany I followed you. Before that, all the way from Texas. And you encouraged me."

"I was looking for something lost. But you'd become someone else." She shook her head sadly, the deep truth now as exposed as his face was with the beard gone. "I thought I was the one who'd become a different person—who was all grown up. But that car accident…it really changed you, didn't it?"

"I flew through the windshield. You ever fly through a windshield, Sallye?"

She shook her head again.

He touched the scar across his brow, ran a hand over his own jaw. "It's hell on the visage, especially when you land on pavement."

"I always wished you hadn't lost that accent."

"That education they sent me for while I recovered—becoming an engineer. They educated the Bronx out of me."

"Say it. No atheists."

"No ate-ee-ists in da fox-oles."

"You sound just like him."

"I never wanted to go back that far—revisit the man I was."

"But I was trying to find him—or a replica—and all this while…" Now she fully accepted. Her jaw went slack. "Statutory rape means I never really chose it for myself. Ever since we got reacquainted in Germany you've been trying to make up for it. And ever since then, too, I've been determined to get that control back, though I never understood why."

"I wanted to be kind to you, but you wouldn't have it."

"I'm addicted to the hurt."

"And the hurting."

"I see that now. Can we start again?"

He shook his head slowly. "I'm done now with my suffering. I earned my forgiveness a long time ago. Drink this, Sallye." He handed her the orange juice concoction. "Drink it all up."

"Why?"

"Because I said so. I own you."

"I was a girl when we met, Warren. You always owned me. I can't change that, can I?" She went to take a sip and he grabbed her hair from behind, his good hand over her hand on the glass, tilting her open like a spout. She slobbered, but he got most of it down.

It changed her almost immediately. She was so small and the dose was large. In addition, the midazolam was fast-acting. The glass slipped from her hand and splintered on the floor.

"Take off your clothes, Sallye. You've been a bad girl."

She was nearly limp. Through the broken glass she shuffled to the bed, but he stopped her.

"Not there. Not yet. Over here." He pulled her toward his chest, lifted her turtleneck over her head. She was wearing no bra.

He laid her down on the floor, in the broken glass. It didn't matter anymore. Her eyes were closed. It would all soon be over.

Quickly he pulled off her red sneakers and her socks. He undid her jeans and removed her underpants. She lay there unmoving. A wisp of flesh and bone. To lift her off the floor was nothing. He placed her with care on her back in the center of the bed, made a trip into the workshop, and emerged with four iron rings on plates, some thick nails and a hammer.

Using quick, short, expert strokes he nailed the plates to the wooden floor near each corner of the bed, tied her hands and ankles to each cotton rope so that she lay there spread-eagle. He could have his way with her like that for days, but all desire had left him. If only she'd loved him for who he'd become. He was better, after all. Better than the man he'd once been, the man who'd taken her innocence all those years ago.

He fetched a syringe from behind the toilet seat in the bathroom. It contained flumazenil, an antidote to the date-rape drug that he'd forced her to swallow. The veins in the fold of her arm were prominent. He made the injection and watched her eyelids shoot open. A moment later she was struggling against the restraints, arching her back.

"What the hell are you doing?" she said.

"Shh." He laid a hand on her flat stomach. There was some blood on the blanket where she'd ground the broken glass into her skin.

"This isn't funny, Warren."

"It's not meant to be. Be quiet and arch your back again, just as you did. Arch it and slowly rest it back down. Listen with care."

Sallye did it. *Click*.

"Hear that sound?"

She nodded, panic setting into her eyes.

"You're lying atop a powerful bomb. Four pounds of very prejudiced C4, enough to obliterate everything in this room. A woman's body is no match for it. As you treated me these past years, so I now treat you. Slow-drip torture, followed by an explosion."

She looked around, her mind working.

"You're wondering," Manis said, "why it hasn't gone off. It has a dead man's switch, armed when you compressed it. That was the click."

She lay stone-still now, frozen in fear. She wanted to live and so did he, but only one of them would have that wish fulfilled. He reached down and attached the wires, then gently coaxed them under the mattress.

"There. It's done. The terrorists invented this method—clever guys. With a dead man's switch there's no backing out. Someone cuts the wire—boom. Lifting your weight up releases the spring. Boom." He laughed, then remembered something. "Oh, and one more thing. There's a battery decay, too. Six hours or so and it all goes ka-boom no matter what you do."

"What a shit you are."

He gritted his teeth. "You'd think after all we've been through, that you'd learn to watch your mouth."

"I hate you," she said. "I've always hated you."

He bristled. "But you never even knew me, Sallye."

They were the last words he would ever speak to her.

LEWIS SALINOWSKY CHOSE TO STAND on the Five Train, his arm draped across the overhead rail. He wore a new shirt that Father Igor had given him last Christmas and his cleanest pair of pants. He had no coat—didn't own a coat that he could wear in the presence of the nurse. Way back when, she'd seen his most private excretions, his blood and his pus and what he'd left in the bedpan, but he could not subject her to the accumulated stench of the street. It would be a deal killer, and Salinowsky yearned not to kill this deal, his salvation.

On the way back from the park he'd stopped into a CVS and spent six precious dollars on Mennan Speed Stick and a new pair of tube socks, one of which he donned on his good foot and the other of which he'd pulled over the end of his prosthesis. At the shelter he begged admittance from the day watchman and dragged a disposable razor across his craggy face, nicking his chin. The water heater only ran in the morning, so he showered in cold water.

Once he'd dressed, he walked upstairs and through the baptistery to the main church, which was accessed through a cloister hidden from the street. He found the door open and went in, sitting in the third pew, facing the elaborately decorated altar. Father Igor never insisted that any of the homeless men attend services, and Salinowsky rarely had. He wasn't much for prayer—until this moment had felt nearest to God when he had a needle in his arm. He bowed his head, but he didn't know what to say, what to think.

He felt for his back pocket, which bulged with half a bundle of heroine and a single syringe. Aching for it, he rolled up his left sleeve and sought a vein on his scarred and mottled skin, then patted his clothing looking for a rubber band, but there was none. He hurriedly removed his belt and wrapped it around his arm. He was about to draw it taut when he stopped.

Salinowsky thought of his dinner with the cop last night, how sweet the strudel had tasted when he finally got hold of it, eating it in solitude. *Good things come to those who wait.* Hadn't his grandfather imparted that wisdom to him? Lewis had waited a long time. He'd waited so long that he forgot what he'd been waiting for, but now he knew. He had lied to the cop when he said he only wrote one letter to Nurse Ritchie. He'd written many letters but he didn't know whether any of them ever got through to her. Now he looked up to the carvings in the choir, the smooth foreheads and full cheeks of the saints, and he thought of Nurse Ritchie. Sallye. Smashed face and all, she was an angel come to him.

Then Lewis Salinowsky did something he never thought he'd do. All those times when he pictured himself at the methadone window had been preceded by a different image, a vision of his last high. Now he stood and wrapped his belt back around his waist. He removed the small bag of powder and the syringe from his pocket and walked to the font by the sacristy door and placed the items in the dry basin. As he left the church by a little-used back door, he rolled back down his sleeve, his hands shaking.

Outwardly he seemed weak, but inner strength had settled upon him. He had a goal now and he wouldn't run from anything anymore. He saw with clarity that the man in the suit who'd been following him was gone, probably still waiting for him to emerge from the main shelter door. He considered whether to go back and confront his shadow, but instead he chose a crowded subway train and melded into and out of the chaos. A few more evasive maneuvers and for sure he'd lost the tail, whoever it was.

Minutes later he watched the lights on the board go black with each stop the train passed, until he arrived at Carroll Street Station. On the sidewalk he looked at the piece of cardboard upon which she'd written the address. He walked in the direction of the river until he found it, rang the buzzer and waited.

No one came but he heard a faint voice inside, calling. Her voice. The little angel voice. He tried the doorknob and found it open. He stepped inside.

THE APARTMENT HAD EXPOSED BRICK, a kitchen counter to the left and a couch and shelves of books to the right. Near the middle, off center, a queen-size bed rested in an alcove, and on that bed lay Sallye Ritchie, naked. But something was wrong.

She stared straight up. As the door closed behind him, she said to the ceiling, "Warren?"

"No."

"Who?"

"Lewis."

"Thank God. Come this way. Be careful."

She was beautiful to him—it had been so long. But even in all the complexity of this strange life this was too strange. She called for help but as he approached her she started moaning for him to stop.

"Don't touch the bed. There's a bomb!"

She was hysterical. He would sit beside her, gently untie her, minister to her as she once had ministered to him.

"Stop!" she screamed. "Just stand there. Stand there and listen, Lewis."

She explained about the bomb and how the bomb worked, that she couldn't shift her weight on the bed, couldn't get up.

"Get help," she said. "Call the police."

He shook his head. It was all too much. He suddenly wished he hadn't thrown away his bundle.

The floor crunched underneath him. *What was that?*

She said, "There's a phone by the kitchen sink. Please. Call nine-one-one and get out. Save yourself."

Save himself? Isn't that what he'd been trying to do all along?

She was crying. "Please, Lewis. Please. You were always so kind, Lewis. So gentle. Be kind again."

He picked up the telephone and looked at her lying there as he followed her instructions. She was pink in a lot of places, exposed, raw. It had been so long. He wished he could touch her.

But he needed a bundle most of all—the bundle he'd left in the church.

He stepped to the bed and reached out a hand toward her privates.

"Don't," she said.

It was all too strange. He needed a bundle, really needed it with every cell of his being. He crunched across the floor and left.

* * *

Diaz, working the radio as Kahn drove, responded to the dispatch call as the setting sun lit the Brooklyn piers aglow. A 9-1-1 call from their very target. According to the dispatcher, there had been no one on the other end of the line. But the message rang clear to Diaz. It was all coming to a head.

Then his phone buzzed. Capobianco. "The guy from the Fifth lost the tail on Salinowsky."

"No way."

"Couldn't follow a goddamn cripple. Now he could be anywhere—with Manis, near Manis, dead at the hands of Manis..."

"Any reports of an explosion?"

"Negative. But the night is young."

Diaz watched as Kahn went apoplectic at the news. He'd never seen him this way. It might have amused him if the stakes weren't now so high.

Ten minutes later, they pulled to a stop in front of a warehouse in Red Hook. First responders had already blocked off the corners, where fire engines idled, and a pair of blue-and-whites had parked in the middle of the street.

Kahn pulled the truck up alongside the curb. One of the uniformed cops approached as they got out. "You ain't gonna believe what's inside."

He gave them a fill on the sidewalk but stopped at the door to the brick building. "I'm not going back in there."

"That'd be advisable," Kahn agreed.

They fetched limited body armor from the truck bay—vests and helmets. Diaz entered first, Kahn close behind him. Given the brief he'd just heard, even with the armor he felt as naked as the woman he saw across the room on the bed. "Hello. What makes you think there's a bomb here?"

She told them. Sallye Ritchie. She couldn't remember exactly how Manis had described the device, but her story was convincing. Then she added something about battery decay.

"Holy fuck," Kahn mouthed silently.

"We're going to withdraw from the room," Diaz told Ritchie.

"Don't leave me," she said, her neck stiff, her eyes wide. She'd made no effort to look at them, afraid to lift her head.

"We have to get our equipment, ma'am. So we can disable the device. We'll return in a minute, I swear."

He was thinking hand entry, no body armor. If he showed up in the bomb suit, she'd panic and no amount of Kevlar would save him. Not from four pounds of C4 at close proximity.

The detectives stepped back outside. Kahn took one look at the uniformed cops and started yelling at them to get back, form a larger perimeter.

"Should we take our cars?" one of them asked.

Kahn told them to move the cruisers behind the fire trucks on the corner. He and Diaz did the same with the response truck.

Capobianco had now arrived in a Suburban. Burbette was there, too, and before anyone said three words, Andy Stoltz, the ATF guy, screeched up in a black Dodge.

He jumped out, a short man with black hair and a putrid tie. "What's up?"

"There's a bomb," Burbette deadpanned.

"What are we doing about it?"

"This is New York. We're letting the NYPD handle it."

When Burbette escorted Stoltz away, Kahn turned to Capobianco. "This is bad, Lieutenant. Is there anyone in the warehouse?"

"They're evacuating that as we speak. The whole block."

"We can't use the robot," Diaz said. "It's hand-entry RSP all the way."

He and Kahn related what they'd observed.

Capobianco looked at Diaz. "Is the device at all visible?"

"Negative. We'll set up the ScanX system using all the panels."

"Any sign of a timer?"

"She mentioned a battery decay. Regardless, she won't stay still forever."

"All right." Capobianco pursed his lips. "Who wants to go? Only one of you."

"I'm volunteering," Diaz said, "if the sergeant here can maintain the staging area."

"Fine with me," Kahn agreed almost too readily.

While they spoke, Higgins had pulled up in another of the Bomb Squad response trucks. He threw open the back doors, and Diaz shed his body armor and grabbed the x-ray panels.

A FEW MINUTES LATER, Diaz stood by Manis's kitchen counter with the ScanX panels under his arms. "Don't be alarmed," he called across the room.

She didn't reply. Stress could exhaust a person. He wondered whether she'd fallen asleep. If so, that would be very bad. She might wake up and reflexively lift her weight from the bed.

He approached at a measured pace, carrying the panels in front of him as lightly as he could. If the bomb detonated, they'd become shrapnel that would cut him to ribbons, but he consoled himself with the notion that he'd be dead before he felt a thing. His plan was to analyze whatever image he could get of the bomb and then formulate a disarming strategy from there. The disrupter out in the truck could render the device safe if he got a good look, but the disrupter was a remote tool that you could only use in a non-life-threatening situation. This would be hand-entry all the way.

A few steps later he was close enough to place the panels. As he leaned them against the side of the bed, Ritchie opened her eyes. The sight hit Diaz like a jolt.

"Don't move," he said.

"I wasn't planning on it."

Diaz became aware that he was already sweating profusely. He closed his eyes and inhaled deeply. He opened them again, calmer now. Her face had been smashed and she was naked as a jaybird and presumably lying atop a bomb in an alcove with her arms and legs strapped down in the shape of an X. If he didn't know better, he'd think it was a sadomasochistic set-up. Then again, in a manner of speaking, maybe it was. Regardless, for all that he'd seen at home and at war, Diaz didn't think he'd ever witnessed anyone in so compromising a position. It was a hell of a price to pay for your sexual perversions.

"Who called the cops?"

"Lewis."

"He still around?"

"I don't think so, but he's not my problem anymore."

Diaz let some air out of his lungs. It sounded like the dropped tail didn't matter. Salinowsky and Manis hadn't crossed paths today. Sallye and the Bomb Squad would find themselves in this situation either way.

"Everything's gonna be okay," he said, as much to himself as to the nurse. "I'm just assessing the situation.

We'll x-ray what's under the mattress. Could be things aren't as bad as you presume."

"If you believe that, you guys don't know Warren at all. He's a freak, but a clever one. Especially when provoked." She huffed ironically. "In fact, you get the best out of him when he's provoked. Everyone saw what he did to those others and I saw the look in his eyes when he left here. He's devious as hell. I'd watch my step if I were you."

"I intend to," Diaz said gamely, looking around for trip wires. "And we'll get you out of this."

He heard her try to clear her dry throat without moving, without coughing. *Jesus Christ,* he thought. *If she sneezes we're both done for.*

She said, "Who am I talking to, anyway. Is that you, Manny?"

"Yeah," he replied, surprised she didn't already know. But she had her eyes fixed to the ceiling. She was wise not to try looking at him. If she lifted her head, her back might follow.

"I'm gonna do everything I can to save you."

"Good luck with that. We're both going to die here."

"No. I've seen worse. We just need to remain calm."

"You should've screwed me when you had the chance, Detective."

He thought of Jennifer, their quietly intense lovemaking. She'd orgasmed like crazy while he maintained his record of more than three years without an erection.

"What would sex have accomplished? We'd still be here."

"Who knows, maybe not. The flap of a butterfly's wings..." She gave the slightest shrug. It worried him.

"Try not to talk, okay? I need to concentrate."

"My pussy isn't distracting you?"

He didn't answer. There were few things more unsettling than the idea of a crazy person with her ass on the trigger. It would almost be a bad joke if it weren't so serious. But if she wanted to die, he thought, she easily could've killed herself already. All she had to do was roll over.

Diaz paused, searching further for trip wires as he closed in. The voiceover in his head said, "Detective Third Grade Manuel Diaz approaches the target with caution, knowing that one false step could mean the end."

Not seeing any wires or loose floorboards, he finished placing the panels.

"I'm stepping back now. I'm going to fetch something that I left on the counter. It's just an x-ray device, a smaller version of what you see at the dentist's office. I'm gonna set it up and look at the images on this laptop over here. Okay?"

"I wish you wouldn't leave me."

"I'm still in the room, just out of your peripheral vision. We're both walking out of here alive, Sallye. But you have to trust me."

She didn't answer. He went and shot the plates for the first time. "There. You see? Nothing to it." She remained silent as he shifted the panels. He'd need multiple shots. There was nothing more important than understanding exactly what was under that mattress, exactly where every part of the device rested.

As he worked, he asked, "You say you heard it click?"

"Yes," she said. "He told me it was armed."

It could all be a bluff, but Diaz knew he'd be a fool to assume that a guy who'd already built three real bombs would turn to bluffing. He wished he could climb under the bed and make an assessment from that angle, but the box spring was too low to the ground.

"I'm just going over here into the kitchen to study these pictures."

"Don't leave the apartment. If you do I'll start squirming. I can't stand it."

"You're okay. You're okay."

"I hate you," she said. "You're enjoying this."

"Believe me. I'm not."

"Can I get a blanket, at least? I'm cold."

Diaz thought for a second. "That isn't advisable. Just sit tight."

"Can you turn up the heat?"

"Okay." As he went to the thermostat, his mind worked. He needed to reach Kahn in the staging area, but he'd left his radio and cell phone behind, not wanting anything to distract him. All communications he must initiate himself.

"I'm gonna use the apartment phone and call outside to my partner." She didn't say anything.

Kahn picked up on one ring. "What do you got, Diaz?"

"Looks like a flat shoebox—or a small cigar box. Two wires coming out, but I can't risk cutting them. The charges are densely packed and I can see the switch and the blasting cap, but the way it's wired—" He shook his head, although no one could see. "Could be a magnet in there or something. I do see a spring and a detonation plate."

His mind ran through his options. He thought again of the PAN, but he couldn't use it on a hand-entry situation, even if he could line up a clean shot, which was doubtful.

"What're you gonna do, Detective?"

Diaz perceived that Kahn struggled to keep his voice on an even keel. He found himself wondering whether an accidental detonation would also kill Kahn in the staging area. No point in them all dying.

"Why don't you back off, Sandy?"

"Back off?"

"Abandon the staging area."

"What are you talking about, Diaz?"

"All this C4... It ain't safe there, that's what."

"Nonsense. I'm not going anywhere. This is how we do it. Procedure. And you're not going to take any action that endangers me, are you, Detective?"

"Tell you the truth, I—I don't know what I'm gonna do."

Crap, he thought. *Shouldn't have let the civilian hear that.* He lifted his gaze from the x-ray images, suppressed a sigh of frustration, put his hands on his hips, and looked around. His eyes settled on the bookcase. A new thought drifted in.

"Hey, Sallye. What do you weigh?"

"A hundred pounds soaking wet. And I may've lost five pounds lying here being gawked at by you and your comrades."

"Remember, I'm not the one who took your clothes off. I got an idea, though."

"Anything. Just get me the hell out of here. I've had enough."

"By the way, did Manis say where he was going?"

"Sure. He forwarded his travel documents to me so you could catch him."

"Okay. Settle down. Is there a scale in the bathroom?"

"A scale?"

"I'm wondering how much Manis's books weigh."

"What time do you think he strapped you to that bed?" Diaz asked, eyeing the bookcases further.

"I have no idea."

He looked at his watch. A few minutes past five. Early February darkness out the window.

"Do you remember the nature of the light outside when you came here and saw him? It was a sunny day today. Do you recall where the sun was?"

She thought about it. "It was well past noon, I think. The sun was low in the sky, but it hadn't disappeared behind the building across the street yet."

He didn't find that information very helpful, but he kept silent about it. He'd been on the scene nearly two hours himself. If her description of the battery decay had been accurate—and if Manis hadn't lied to her about it—they might have another three hours or they might have much less. If it was much less, they were doomed anyway, so he'd presume two hours to go. He picked up the phone and called Kahn again.

"I have a plan, Sandy. I need some kind of board five or six feet long, thin as possible, not too wide."

"Like finish plywood?"

"No. It has to be much smoother than that. I'm going to displace the weight."

A pause. Diaz didn't want to get too specific. He didn't want the nurse to anticipate too soon. It might make her restless.

"Like a surfboard maybe," Kahn said. "Without the fin, of course."

"Roger. And several gallons of baby oil. You think you can find those things on short notice?"

"We'll get on the horn immediately, Diaz. It's New York, thank God, the place that has everything. You want me to call you back?"

He thought of a ringing phone breaking the silence and Sallye flinching. "Negative. I'll call you."

"How much time do you think we have?"

"Two hours tops, but I'll need an hour, I figure, just to be safe. I'll make what preparations I can."

As soon as he hung up, he went and stood by the side of the bed. "They're getting me some supplies. It will take awhile."

She swallowed. Her breathing was shallow, which might indicate that she'd begun to panic.

"Would you like some water?"

"Yes."

"Try to lengthen your breathing and relax."

"Oh, sure."

He went to the pantry closet and found a water bottle. "I'm going to drip some of this into your mouth, room temperature. Ready?"

"Yes."

He crouched beside the bed and reached out his arm with the open bottle until it was extended completely. Careful not to shift his weight, he tilted the bottle gently. She relished the first few swallows, then turned her head away and some spilled on her cheek. She flinched, but not dramatically. Still, it was enough to make Diaz freeze.

The explosion, if it came, would not be something heard or felt. It would happen faster than the speed of sound. He wondered, as he had many times, whether he would perceive a bright flash or blackness before the end.

He took a sip of the water himself and rolled away from the bed, not wanting even to rise from his crouch in its proximity, lest he fall forward by accident. As he stood up near the wall, he thought of his walk on the shoulder of the parkway, of how the vacuum created by a passing car might suck you into the path of the next one. He felt the same now. Life meant not giving in to the gravitational pull, resisting the force that drew you.

Jennifer's face flashed in his mind, her beautiful smooth skin and her smile, arms folded, leaning against the doorjamb. He didn't think of her in relation to the woman lying here on the bed. This woman was just a job, the mechanism of his possible undoing or the means by which he would defeat a criminal. He saw her flesh only as something that needed to be saved in order to accomplish the mission. And his own flesh—that was only a limitation that nature had imposed on him.

"A hundred pounds?" he asked Sallye. "That's what you said you weigh?"

"That's what I said."

"You're sure? It's important for me to know as precisely as possible."

"I weigh myself every week in the hospital. Last time maybe it was one-oh-one with my clothes on."

"Okay."

He went into the bathroom and took out the scale, placing it on the floor in the center of the living room. He weighed himself—212—then began to gather books, weighing each armful and doing the subtraction. When he had a hundred pounds of books in a stack near the bed, he went to the kitchen phone and called Kahn. It was 5:38.

"We found a skateboard manufacturer," Kahn said, "not two miles from here in the Navy Yard complex. They use waxed polyurethane, and they got a big sheet of it that they're cutting special for us."

Diaz pictured what he had to do. "Have them bevel and polish the edges if they can."

"Step ahead of you."

"And the oil?"

"Got it here in the staging area. We wiped out three drugstores."

"How long for the board?"

"I'd say another half hour tops. We got two guys waiting there already, and the people doing the work are on site."

Diaz walked to the alcove and sat on the floor by the bed with his back against the wall. He thought about whether it would help to sedate the woman, but you never knew how a person would react to drugs. If they made her squirm for a brief moment before she went out, nothing else would matter.

"IF I LIVE," SALLYE ASKED, "am I going to jail for this?"

"Well, what'd you do?" Diaz said.

"Made some bad choices."

"Did you participate in the killing of those men?"

"Not at all."

He picked at a floorboard splinter. "How long have you known it was Manis?"

"Only for sure since this morning."

"Then I doubt it. Were you telling me the truth when we first met, that the bombings were news to you?"

"Yes, I was. I swear."

He almost laughed to himself at that. In her current position, he couldn't see her lying. She was practically strapped to a cross.

"An abused woman," he said seriously, "and accessory after the fact at worst. The court will have sympathy for you. You may get probation, nothing more."

"If it's any consolation, I regret what I did with those men in the hospital. I was damaged early on, you know."

If it's any consolation? Diaz didn't think he was the one who needed consoling, not unless he got his head blown off. He wasn't going to ask what the rest was about, for fear of stirring her up with memories. "You want more water?"

"No."

"You warm enough now?"

"Yes, I am."

He took a deep breath. Her calmness was beginning to scare him. In his experience, when a crazy person becomes calm, it could be a sign that they were about to crack. He'd known three suicides in his life, and two of them he'd seen on the day of their final act. Both had been calm and cheerful, all of their burdens lifted by their fatal decision.

Sallye Ritchie's chest went up and down on the bed above him. She seemed almost in a trance.

Diaz stood up, using the wall, and his knees nearly buckled, wanting to propel him into a run. He almost had to restrain himself physically, knowing his job remained unfinished. And, besides, he couldn't outrun the detonation of high explosives.

He walked as slowly as he could to the kitchen phone, wondering for the first time in a month what might have possessed him to long for this kind of danger, what might have possessed him to tempt the gods of destruction. But then it occurred to him that he already knew. Like the interlocking stresses that caused Sallye and Warren to drive each other crazy, Diaz was doing something similar to himself. He'd become addicted to a negative feedback loop, and—like these two maniacs—it would drive him to self-immolation if he allowed that to happen, if he allowed himself to be drawn further into the vacuum, into the absence of love.

The apartment was dead quiet, just Sallye's breathing.

"You awake?" he called.

"Absolutely."

"Don't fall asleep. I'm phoning my partner now."

He picked up the receiver.

"We're ready for you," Kahn said.

"Pass the stuff through the door. Don't come in."

He warned the nurse, so the sound of the door opening wouldn't startle her. A draft came through. He met Kahn's eyes and shivered.

"Everything all right?" Kahn asked.

"You got a procedure for this, Sandy?"

Kahn lifted one eyebrow and one corner of his mouth and shrugged, as if to apologize for being such a hard-ass all this while.

"No matter," Diaz promised him. "We're all leaving here alive."

But he couldn't be sure he believed that himself.

What lay before him was uncharted territory, but he didn't intend to tell Ritchie that. He explained to her what he planned to do. "It'll be very important," he said, "for you not to try to help me by shifting your weight."

"Okay," she said.

He wondered whether he should ask first if she really wanted to live, but events would soon force that decision upon her without further reflection. If the answer was no, it remained his job in any case to go down trying to save her. Just like the other three dozen guys in the squad, all of whom always ran toward the bomb when called upon, damn the consequences.

The board that Kahn had passed through the door was smooth and shiny, painted in a sparkly russet color with a subtle waviness to the design. The dimensions were five feet long and two-and-a-half feet wide, Diaz estimated.

It looked to be about a quarter-inch thick, and the edges were beveled and polished all around, as he'd requested.

Diaz opened the first two bottles of baby oil and began slathering it on, using his hands.

"I'm greasing the board now," he said, "to minimize resistance."

She remained silent.

When he was done, he lifted it up for her to see. He explained that a certain degree of added pressure wouldn't set the bomb off, since it would only keep the switch depressed. But they must at all costs avoid the release of pressure. That was a nice theory, anyway. In truth, for all the x-rays he couldn't know for sure what Manis had in store for them.

"You'll feel the poke of the edge of the board," he explained. "Try not to react. Just keep breathing."

She nodded ever so slightly as he used both hands to suspend the board within an inch of the mattress. He tilted the tip and felt the resistance of her ribs. She reacted only with her breath, which caught for a second, but then she forced herself to exhale.

It took Diaz twenty-five minutes to get the board under her, progressing by fractions of an inch, telling her how good she was doing with each sliver of progress. When, at long last, she was straddling the center of it with her back, he went and got the books. He piled them evenly on each end, until he had them arrayed in neat stacks.

He was sweating profusely, feeling almost dizzy with dehydration, but raging adrenaline lent him steady hands. "I'm going to cut you free now, Sallye. Arms first, then feet. The arms I want you to bring to your sides as slowly as possible. When you're ready, place your hands on your hips, palms up, so I can take them in a minute."

"A minute? Does it have to be that long?"

"We've come this far. Let's not screw it up. Your legs—" he thought about it—"keep them spread."

"You pig." She laughed. She was becoming giddy. He hoped she could control herself.

He washed his hands with soap in the kitchen sink to get the remains of the oil off. Then he extracted his Leatherman knife from the scabbard on his leg, released the blade, and cut the ropes with as little motion as possible.

She moved her arms with such caution that Diaz had to bite his lip to keep from urging her on. He used the kitchen towel to wipe the sweat from his forehead, and stood at the foot of the bed, where he reached forward and took her hands.

In one motion she came up off the mattress and into his arms.

Then Diaz ran like he'd never run before. He knew he couldn't outrun whatever an explosion sent flying, but he thought he had a chance against a stack of teetering books.

He was through the door in a matter of seconds. Kahn, still in the staging area, saw him burst out and took off running next him, both of them heading behind the response truck and around the corner of the building at a dead sprint.

A moment later, Diaz collapsed to his knees as an EMT seized Sallye Ritchie from his arms. Crouched on the ground, he swallowed a deep gulp of cold night air and closed his eyes in ecstasy. He couldn't recall the last time he'd taken so sweet a breath.

TOCK

14.

DAY SEVEN: DARK

THE FIRST REAL MEAL THAT Joseph Capobianco ate in eight days consisted of chicken with the skin roasted crispy, rosemary potatoes, broccoli casserole, and half a loaf of Italian bread. He topped it off with two pieces of store-bought banana cream pie.

"Making up for lost time?" Jill asked.

"Don't start." He paused with the last bite an inch from his mouth. "When's Samantha coming home?"

"Tomorrow."

"She never called?"

"Once or twice while you were sleeping."

"She missed all the excitement."

"Watching you sleep or watching you puke?"

"C'mon. I meant the veteran bombings."

"Thank God she missed that. You said when we finished dinner you were going to tell me how the bomb went off."

"We don't know."

"You don't know?"

"We may never know. Not much left of that bomb or anything else in the room. It was either the battery decay or the switch popped up. For my money, it's the batteries. I don't think Diaz could've outrun the switch."

"It happened right after?"

Capobianco nodded. "Three minutes later. Fortunately, while Diaz was working, the guys had covered the windows with ballistic blankets. They'd just gotten the woman into the ambulance when the damn thing detonated."

"Did the building go down?"

"No. That structure was built to industrial standards. But I'll tell you, Jill, a few of us nearly jumped out of our shoes."

"You didn't expect it?"

"We did, in a manner of speaking, and we didn't. Anyway, on Gowen's advice, I told Diaz to take off the next few days."

"You needed Gowen to tell you that?"

"No, but it gave me cover. Besides, I thought it was wise for the mayor to know I was back on the job."

"The mayor called you?"

"Negative. Gowen spoke to him. I guess I don't rate."

"You do with me."

"Thank you, sweetheart."

"Now do the dishes."

He smiled. "My pleasure." It felt good to have this case over. And it felt good to be holding down his dinner.

Manis didn't bother to check the newspapers. He took the train to Kennedy Airport, where he had an old Toyota Camry in long-term parking under an assumed name. He left Queens and began driving northwest, listening to WINS-AM radio as he went. The signal faded out by the time he hit northern Westchester, but he was able to pick up more news on CBS-AM, which dropped about halfway through Putnam County. All that way, the drama continued. But he left New York City radio range before he heard the conclusion.

Past Millerton, in the northeast corner of Dutchess County, Manis found a dirt road and pulled off near dense woods. Using the side-view mirror, he shaved his head bald. Then he fetched a shovel from the trunk and walked until he could see his car no more. He scraped aside three inches of frozen matted leaves and dug a hole in the ground, burying the pack with his explosives and his pistol, identifying the site for future reference by triangulating marks on the bark of a nearby oak and two beech trees.

About halfway back to his car, he burned his real passport and driver's license on a large boulder and ground the ashes down with the sole of his shoe.

He drove all night to the vicinity of Cleveland Hopkins International Airport. In a nearby Target store he purchased a suitcase full of clothes. Using a false passport, he flew to Dulles International in Washington with plans for a connecting flight to Munich, Germany. So as not to call attention to himself, he used a round-trip ticket, purchased with a phony credit card.

On the layover in Dulles he used an Internet connection in the terminal to learn that Sallye Ritchie had survived his surefire trap and that detectives of the NYPD Bomb Squad had saved her. It made him angry to be denied that closure. He went into the airport bathroom and puked a pint of bile.

In mid-air on the way to Munich he more calmly contemplated what he'd accomplished in New York and what he'd failed to do. He ran his damaged hand over his face, thinking of the man he'd once been and the man he was today. A bomb was the disordering of matter, but it soon found new equilibrium, albeit in heaps of fragments and dust. If the NYPD Bomb Squad had defeated the device he'd so carefully built for Sallye, that didn't mean he couldn't build another one. And better.

He closed his eyes for the long flight and let his mind drift to devices yet unmade. Before he awoke, a new day would dawn over the Atlantic.

DIAZ HAD SPENT FOUR HOURS and thirty-seven minutes in a room with a naked woman and a powerful bomb. Once he'd lifted the nurse off of the poly board and carried her out, he was finished for the day. Kahn offered to drive him home, and Diaz was too tired even to enjoy giving his partner turn-by-turn directions.

The door to his apartment opened before he got the key in, as if Jennifer had been waiting at the peephole.

She embraced him and said, "Oh, Manny. I've been watching the news."

He smiled to see her, gave her back a weak squeeze, and poured himself into his bed.

When he awoke it was past midnight and she was sleeping next to him in her clothes. She sat up when he left the bed. He was starving and they agreed to go to an all-night Mexican joint on Amsterdam. They shared a plate of nachos and a chicken quesadilla, drank Modelo beer and took turns daring one another to eat jalapeño peppers.

Along the way he told her everything she wanted to know about the past forty-eight hours, making her laugh and making her cry, as if he were still in danger. When he was done, she asked, "Did the experience change you?"

He looked into her blue eyes and grinned. "I'm not gonna walk on the parkway no more."

"What about the other thing?" she wondered.

"That I haven't tested," he said. "But don't get your hopes going."

"That's all right." In disappointment, she looked more beautiful than ever.

Diaz wanted to reassure her. He smiled, wiggling his fingers in the air. "Still got all ten digits."

They went home and made love in their special way on Jennifer's bed until they collapsed in exhaustion, Diaz as satisfied as a man in his condition could be. Lying together awake for a long time afterward, they stared at the stains on the ceiling until their eyes grew heavy in the warm apartment air. The clanging heat pipes of morning sang a familiar lullaby.

The End

GLOSSARY

A and E—Colloquialism for AES

AES—Arson and Explosion Squad, an NYPD investigative unit also known as A&E

ATF—The Bureau of Alcohol, Tobacco and Firearms

CSU—Crime Scene Unit, the NYPD's name for the CSI department

DARPA—Defense Advance Research Projects Agency, the main research arm of the US Department of Defense

EDC—Explosive Detection Canine, a dog especially trained to sniff out bombs and the ingredients of explosives

EOD—Explosive Ordnance Disposal, the US military's equivalent of a Bomb Squad

ESU—Emergency Services Unit

ETK—Explosive Test Kit, used for detecting explosive residue in the field

FBI—The Federal Bureau of Investigation

F6A—A model of robot popular with local police force Bomb Squads, used for remotely observing and mitigating dangerous conditions. Smaller than the Wolverine

HD1—The smallest robot used by the NYPD Bomb Squad

HDS—Hazardous Devices School, conducted by the FBI out of Huntsville, Alabama, where all bomb techs in the nation train

IABTI—International Association of Bomb Technicians and Investigators

IED—Improvised Explosive Device

IMEI—A type of cell phone "fingerprint"

JTTF—Joint Terrorism Task Force, consists of designated federal and local agencies and police forces

ME—Medical Examiner

MOS—Military Occupational Specialty

MP—Military Police

NSN Number—A type of cell phone "fingerprint"

NYPD—New York Police Department

PAN—Percussion-Actuated Non-Electric Disrupter

PO—Police Officer

PSA—Police Service Area

RDX—Research Department Explosive, also known as cyclonite, more powerful than TNT

RPG—Rocket-Propelled Grenade

RSP—Render-Safe Procedure

RUC—Royal Ulster Constabulary

SABT—Special Agent Bomb Technician, a designation in the FBI's Bomb Squad

ScanX—The brand of portable x-ray devices used by the NYPD Bomb Squad

SCR—Silicon Control Rectifier, a solid-state switching device, similar to a relay switch

SDS—Sergeant Supervisor Detective Squad

SOD—Special Operations Division, highly trained squad formerly known as the SWAT team

TCV—Total Containment Vehicle

USSS—United States Secret Service

VIN—Vehicle Identification Number

Wolverine—A model of robot popular with local police force Bomb Squads, used for remotely observing and mitigating dangerous conditions. Larger than the HD1 and F6A

ACKNOWLEDGMENTS

I AM THE BENEFICIARY OF MUCH generosity in life and specifically with regard to this project.

First and foremost, my heartfelt thanks to Lieutenant Mark Torre, commander of the NYPD Bomb Squad, for his guidance, patience, and insights. Mark was introduced to me by Kevin Miles, who retired in 2013 as the FBI's longest-serving and most experienced bomb tech. Kevin cheerfully gave me an education in the subject before Mark became available, and he later reviewed the manuscript and made invaluable suggestions. Both of these men demonstrated with every interaction what it means to be a stand-up guy, and I am honored and grateful for the seriousness and thoroughness with which they provided their assistance.

Also, many thanks to all of the NYPD Bomb Squad detectives whom I've met, both inside headquarters with official permission and out on the street with the garage doors open when I stopped by as a citizen. The example of bravery and humanity that you folks set every day serves as an inspiration to us all.

We live in an age when hype and overuse have diluted the meaning of words like courage, heroism, and selflessness. But these words come to me in full force when I think of the man who introduced me to Kevin and Mark, my dear friend Paul Bucha. In his capacity as a recipient of the Congressional Medal of Honor, Paul spends a great deal of time giving speeches and making public appearances. As it happened, he had made a presentation to a group of bomb techs shortly before I mentioned my ambition to write a fictional series about the exploits of the NYPD Bomb Squad. By his introduction to Kevin and Mark, Paul has enabled me to make this a better book. By his example, Paul has enabled me to be a better person.

Patrick LoBrutto edited this book and, as always, improved it by lending his keen eye for story. My agents Jane Dystel and Miriam Goderich believed in it and backed up that belief through action. Thanks also to Sharon Pelletier at Dystel & Goderich for seeing it through.

By the time anyone set eyes on this novel, my wife, Pam, and my daughter, Macklin, had already been living with the concept for years. They have never let me lose sight of what is truly important in life: to create, to respect, and to love. They are my lodestar and my ballast.

BOMB SQUAD NYC

Incident 1: *A Danger to Himself and Others*
Incident 2: *The Long Black Hand*
Incident 3: *Death March*
Incident 4: *Bottle Rocket*
And more...